From Here
to Forever

From Here to Forever

Monica McKayhan

sepia™

FROM HERE TO FOREVER

A Sepia Novel

ISBN 1-58314-606-7

© 2006 by Monica McKayhan

This book is a work of fiction. The names, characters, incidents and places
are the products of the author's imagination, and are not to be construed as
real. While the author was inspired in part by actual events, none of the
characters in the book is based on an actual person. Any resemblance to
persons living or dead is entirely coincidental and unintentional.

® and TM are trademarks. Trademarks indicated with ® are registered in the
United States Patent and Trademark Office, the Canadian Trade Marks Office
and/or other countries.

www.kimanipress.com

Printed in U.S.A.

From Here to Forever

1

Maxie

Miles. He's staring; those big, beautiful, light brown eyes won't leave me. They follow me as I move around the room. He's begging for attention. Wants me to hold him; to offer my breast to him. He wants to drain the few minutes I've reserved for myself, wants them back as if he owns them. Selfish. Won't allow me just one moment to gather my thoughts. One moment to myself. Not one moment.

He began. Like the sound of an engine starting up, slow and vague at first, then once it was revved, it got louder and louder. Then it was fully started, that engine. And I wanted to cry too, but instead I picked Miles up out of his crib.

"Oh baby, what's the matter?" I asked him as if he understood, as if I didn't already know. His face held no moisture; he was just screaming at the top of his lungs as if he'd lost his mind.

I sat down in the rocker that was located next to the bay window in his nursery and held him, pulling out my golden breast and placing the nipple into Miles's wanting mouth. My breasts were sore from the breast-feeding, and from the milk weighing them down like a ton of lead. Don't know why I didn't just grab a couple of cans of Enfamil or Similac from the corner store and get it over with. But I'd decided to breast-feed because it was supposed to be healthier for the baby, not to mention Rico had talked me into it.

"It's better for the baby," he'd said, as if he'd be offering his own breasts as a sacrifice to our infant son.

Our infant son. The sound of it seemed so foreign to me. But I knew he was mine, because I had the scars and stitches from my vaginal delivery to prove it. I couldn't prove it by looking at Miles, because he hadn't inherited anything from me, only Rico's skin color, brown eyes, and lips. He was definitely Rico's child, his spitting image. And Rico was proud, chest all stuck out as if he'd done something more than help me breathe. Wouldn't leave my house. He'd been there since we brought Miles home from Daniel Freeman Memorial three weeks before. Although he had his own place in Inglewood, he preferred my place, as if there was some magic my house held that his didn't.

This motherhood thing was new to me. Everything in my life was new: new city, new home, new son. All in less than a year, I'd been uprooted from life as I knew it, migrated from Atlanta to Los Angeles like a gypsy, pregnant, wanting to be closer to my man. And there I was, in my new split-level, three-bedroom abode in Baldwin Hills, rocking Miles and praying that he'd pass out the minute he tired from sucking on my sore breast.

"He's eating again?"

I looked up and offered Rico a smile. "Yep. Greedy little man. Got my breasts all sore."

Rico laughed, and stared at us with that goofy look on his face, the one he gets when he's feeling sentimental.

"Let me go get my camera."

"No, Rico." I rolled my eyes. "Not that thing again, please."

He'd been getting footage of Miles and me since the day of delivery. He'd taped the entire event, and then was there, camera in hand, capturing the wheelchair ride to the car. He'd taped Miles's first feeding at home, Miles's first bath, Miles sleeping, and Miles screaming at the top of his lungs. He was getting on my nerves with the camcorder, and I'd decided that the moment I found it lying somewhere unused, I would stomp on it, and put it out of its misery.

"Will only take a second." He disappeared and then came back into the nursery with his camcorder. "Gotta capture this moment, baby. Y'all look so sweet."

"I'm breaking that camera when you turn your head."

"Girl, don't you touch my camera," he said, moving around us as if he were doing a Victoria's Secret shoot in Tahiti. "There will be consequences if you mess with the camera."

I stuck my tongue out and that only encouraged him more.

"That's it, baby. Gimme some more of that right there," he said. His smile was so beautiful.

"Rico!" I was done feeding and he knew I didn't want him filming me when I shook the excess milk from my limp breast and whipped it back into my nightgown. He paused filming, but only for a moment. After that, he was right back at it. "You are sick."

"I've got to have something for the authorities to

identify you, just in case you try and leave the country with my son."

"Get out of here."

Miles had fallen asleep in my arms and I crept slowly over to his crib, laid him down in there, and kissed him gently on his forehead. He was definitely my greatest accomplishment, I thought, as I watched him snoring lightly, his tiny stomach moving up and down beneath his one-piece pajamas. I had been so afraid of becoming his mother, so afraid that I wouldn't be any good at it. My own mother committed suicide when I was twelve, and the very thought of having a child of my own petrified me.

I'd even considered abortion. I had gone to the clinic and everything, only later coming to the realization that I really could do this; that if I could muster up just that little bit of motherhood that was hidden inside of me, I'd be okay. And after he was here, I had so much love in my heart for him, I couldn't even imagine my world without him in it.

"Coming?" Rico whispered as he waited for me at the door.

"I'm coming." I pulled a small blanket over Miles, and turned the light off.

Rico grabbed me around my waist and led me down the hall to my guest bedroom, where we peeked in at Brianna. She was asleep with Barbie upside down on the pillow next to her. Blue's Clues and SpongeBob had both been thrown on the floor. They were obviously not as important as Barbie, who got to sleep in the bed. Brianna looked like an angel with her freshly done cornrows that I'd touched up that afternoon. She was Rico's child all right, had his and Miles's light brown eyes, although her chocolate-brown skin belonged to Dana, her mother. Rico and Miles were both a smooth vanilla.

We closed the door, leaving it a little cracked open so she could find her way to the bathroom if necessary. Rico led me down the hall to my bedroom. My mahogany sleigh bed was a gift from Reggi and Fred, Rico's parents, who own one of the oldest furniture stores in Inglewood. The bed I had in Atlanta was old and wasn't even worth loading onto the U-Haul, so I left it. When I got to California, this one was sitting pretty in the middle of my bedroom floor with a big red bow tied around it; an identical red bow was tied around the dresser. Reggi and Fred were cheesing as proud parents do when their children are opening gifts from Santa on Christmas morning, anticipating my reaction to their gift. They were nice parents, although I didn't have anything to compare them with. After Mama had committed suicide, all I knew were a few foster parents who were far from what I'd considered nice. I never knew my father.

Reggi and Fred were as close to parents as I could get. They treated me with respect and they loved their new grandbaby to death. I hadn't even had the opportunity to buy my child a new outfit, because since the day he'd come home, they'd kept his dresser drawers stocked with onesies, two-piece outfits, undershirts, booties, little miniature sneakers, and Pampers out the yin-yang.

I found my place on top of my goose-down comforter. I lost myself in the plushness of it, the softness massaging my body, my behind finally healing from the hemorrhoids from Miles's birth. If I never got hemorrhoids another day in my life, I wouldn't complain.

* * *

"You forgot about Ben & Jerry's," I reminded Rico.

"I didn't forget. We're out," he said. "You finished off the last of the butter pecan last night. Remember?"

"Guess that means you have to go to the store."

"Maybe you didn't hear me correctly." He smiled. "*You* finished off the last of it, hence it's your turn to go to the store."

"You wouldn't really send me to the store in my condition, would you?"

"Do I have to sleep on the sofa tonight?"

"Of course."

"Then the keys are in the pocket of my sweats."

"Rico, you know we can't sleep together, especially with Brianna in the house. What if she gets up in the middle of the night? It's just not a good thing for a nine-year-old girl to see her father laid up with some woman."

"Maxie, you're not some woman. Brianna knows how we feel about each other. Besides, we already have a baby together."

"I can't do anything for three more weeks anyway."

"Who said we had to do anything? I just want to be close to you." He began to caress my spine and nibble on my ear. He smelled so good and the nipples of my breasts began to harden from his touch.

"It's not a good idea until we're married."

"Which will be?"

"Which will be when it is."

"How many times do I have to ask before you say yes?" His tongue began to probe the inside of my mouth. "We have a son together. The four of us are already a family. It's you who's holding us up."

"You promised me no pressure," I whispered, trying desperately not to fall into his sensuous trap.

He had promised. Before he moved me to L.A., we both agreed that we weren't ready for marriage. That all we knew at that moment was that we were in love and wanted to be together. I had my place, he had his. And that's all I was ready for. One step at a time. The baby was enough for right now. I knew I wanted Rico, wanted only him; wanted to give him a dozen more little beautiful babies just like Miles. But I could only think about today, and maybe tomorrow, not an hour past that. I was afraid of moving too fast. Wanted what we had to last forever.

"I'm not pressuring." He held his hands in the air as if he were surrendering. "No pressure."

"Okay, then."

"Okay, then."

"You going to get Ben & Jerry's?"

"Nope, you are." He got up, dug his hand into the pocket of his sweats, and threw the keys to his Explorer on the bed. "And grab some whip cream and fresh strawberries too, while you're out."

He headed for the sofa sleeper, pillow and blanket in hand.

I dragged myself into the bathroom to wash my face. I pulled on a pair of oversized sweats and my Bob Marley T-shirt. Just as I was pulling my golden locks into a ponytail, I heard the garage door going up. He'd had a change of heart. I rushed to the garage door as he was pulling out.

"Thank you, baby!" I yelled to him.

He blew me a kiss, and I realized that I was a blessed woman. Because in less than thirty minutes, I'd have all four of my favorite men all in one place: Miles, Rico, Ben *and* Jerry.

2

Rico

With precision, I carefully maneuvered my Explorer into a tight spot at the A.M./P.M. gas station and deli mart, Usher's "Yeah" pumped up so loud I could hear the bass throbbing in my chest. That's the way I liked it, loud enough to hear every instrument in a song—every horn, every drum. It's something about hearing the instruments coming together like a symphony. I was always testing my speakers out, just to be certain that they still worked. And when I pulled up next to a couple of brothers in a green lowrider Chevy and they began to bounce to my sounds, I knew that my speakers were working just fine.

"Like them sounds, my man," the brother on the passenger side, with cornrows down his neck, said as I jumped out of my truck. "Are those JVC's?"

"Nope," I said. "Four ten-inch Bose with an eight-hundred-watt amp."

"Yeah?" he asked, taking a puff of his Newport and blowing circles of smoke into the air. "I like that."

"Yeah, me too."

My alarm squeaked as I pressed the lock button and threw my keys into the pocket of my sweats.

I searched the freezer for a pint of butter pecan ice cream, and another pint of chocolate. I grabbed Brianna a package of Skittles, her favorite candy, and threw them all on the counter for the Arab dude to ring up. He was busy on the phone with someone, and I cleared my throat to let him know that I was waiting, and didn't have all night.

"Will this be all, sir?" he said in his accent, and when I nodded a "yes," he gave me my total. I handed him a ten.

I hit the lock on my key ring and jumped back into my truck. When I pumped Usher back up again, the brother with the cornrows threw up the peace sign and I nodded.

"Be easy, my man," I said.

"No doubt."

I looked into my rearview mirror, waited for the sister in the silver convertible Mercedes to pass, and then proceeded to back up. It was too late to swerve to avoid hitting her when she immediately decided to throw her car into reverse. My bumper hit her passenger door. She placed her hand over her mouth as if she'd made a boo-boo. I pulled back into the spot where I had parked, then jumped out to assess the damage. My bumper had a little paint across the rear. Her passenger door held a ding from my bumper.

"I'm so sorry." She jumped out and headed my way.

"What were you doing?" I asked, irritated, because I never could understand women drivers. "What did you back up for? Didn't you see my taillights?"

"I'm sorry," she said. "But you looked like somebody I...know."

"I looked like somebody you know?" I yelled, in disbelief at what she'd just said.

"Rico, it's me," she said, and when she got closer, I realized it was Dana.

"Dana?"

"Yeah," she said. "I thought that was you. Long time no see."

"Yeah, it has been a while. Like three years." I asked, "What you doing in L.A.?"

"Your mother didn't tell you?" She smiled, and I remembered those beautiful dimples and the curve of those pretty lips all too well. Her beautiful brown skin was identical to Brianna's. "I moved back a few months ago. I stopped by to see Reggi the other day."

"She didn't tell me," I said.

"I wondered if you still lived in the same place. Wanted to call, but didn't have the number. Reggi didn't wanna give it to me without checking with you first. Said she'd let you know I was in town."

She was wearing a black leather outfit. The pants hugged her hips nicely and underneath the jacket, she wore a silk, low-cut top that gave me and every brother in the parking lot a nice glance at the roundness of her breasts. I forced myself not to stare.

"Well, now I know," I said, and pulled my cell phone out to call the police. "Nice ride you got there. Hope you got insurance on it."

"I do," she said, coming closer and her perfume began to hypnotize me. She handed me her business card. "But we don't need the cops for this. We can settle this ourselves, can't we? We'll just exchange information. I'll go have the damage assessed and you can settle up with me later."

"Settle up with you? I wouldn't have hit your car in the first place if you hadn't backed up like that!" She was pissing me off. Still the same old Dana, not owning up to her responsibilities.

I remembered why I hated her so much. My mind went back to the way things had ended up.

It was a rainy day in the City of Lost Angels. I had gotten off early that day, because it's next to impossible to finish a construction job in the rain. Headed home, but stopped by the florist on the way to pick up a dozen roses for my woman. We'd argued the night before, and I couldn't get her off my mind all day. We were arguing more and more, and over dumb stuff. I knew in my heart that she was seeing some other dude, but I couldn't go out like some sucker. I had to fight for what was mine. We had history, Dana and me, and she was my wife, not his. I pulled into the garage, dropped my wet, muddy boots at the door, and stepped inside through the kitchen, roses in hand. I grabbed a brew from the fridge and started looking for her.

"Dana." I called her name all through the house.

She wasn't home and the phone was ringing off the hook. I grabbed the cordless from its base. It was Brianna's school. Brianna had never gotten picked up, and the woman on the other end of the phone was frantic. She'd been trying Dana's cell phone, our home phone, and my cell phone all evening, and had been unable to reach us at any of the numbers.

"I'm sorry," I told the woman on the other end of the

phone. "I thought my wife had already picked her up. I'll be there in a minute."

I rushed to pick up Brianna and returned home to find that Dana still wasn't there. I was worried, and after trying her cell phone again, I began to call all her girlfriends. They swore they hadn't seen or heard from her. I called Alice, Dana's mother, who claimed she hadn't heard from her in months. I checked every hospital in the metro area before finally calling the cops. I reported Dana missing, but knew they wouldn't do anything until she'd been gone at least twenty-four hours.

After driving around looking for her, Brianna asleep in her pajamas in the backseat, my nerves on edge, the windshield wipers making a swishing noise as they wiped away the raindrops from my windshield, I finally decided to go home. I tried to get some rest, but knew I'd be awake all night, sitting next to the picture window in our living room, jumping each time a pair of headlights passed to see if they belonged to Dana's red Saturn.

One solid week I sat in that window, missing work, wondering, hoping, even praying for her return. But she never returned. Finally she called one night to say that she would not be coming back any time soon. That this was all too much for her to handle right now, and she needed some time to think things through. What did she have to think through? She had a husband and a child at home who needed her there. What was more important than that? I wanted to reach my hand through the phone and yank some sense into her. Now that I knew she wasn't dead or somewhere in a gutter, I wanted to strangle her and tell her that I had been worried sick. And what's worse, she was messin' with my money. I hadn't been to work all week, and we had too many bills to pay for me not to show up at work. But I played it cool. I calmed down, and decided to approach her in a different way. I didn't want her to hang up the phone and I'd spend another week worrying.

"Come home, Dana, and let's talk this out," I'd pleaded with her. "Where are you? I'll come get you."

"I'm in Seattle." Her words rang in my head so many nights after that. My mind went back to the phone bill I'd found once. I'd stood there flipping through the pages of it, wondering why there were twenty-eight calls to Seattle on there. It all started to make sense, and when I'd asked her about it, she swore it was a mistake on the phone company's part and that she'd call them first thing the next morning to get it straight.

"In Seattle? Who you know in Seattle?"

"Tony," she said, and hung up.

I'd known he existed, but never knew his name until then. Part of me wanted to go get her: find her, fight for her. But I didn't. She'd made her choice.

I looked at Brianna, who was standing there, looking at me, her thumb stuck in her mouth, her ponytails flying in different directions on her head. I'd tried my best to comb her hair that day and at least make it look decent. I looked into her big brown eyes, but didn't have the heart to tell her that her mother wasn't coming home.

"Go get your pajamas so Daddy can help you put 'em on."

That was all I could say.

"Rico, you're the one who hit me. If you call the cops, they'll say the same thing."

"You did hit her car, bro. I saw the whole thing." The

brother with the cornrows was one of many bystanders who'd gathered at the scene. "But if I was you, I'd just get her number and see what she talking about. Sound like she wanna do more than just assess the damage to her car."

He and his boy started laughing and checking Dana out from head to toe.

"Stay out of this, my man," I said. "Look, Dana. I only hit your car because you started backing up unexpectedly. The damage to my truck is minor. We can just squash this, right here, right now. I'm not paying you a dime. You go your way, I go mine. That's what you're good at anyway."

"Call the cops then. I'm sure they'll see things differently."

"Fine. I'll call the cops." I dialed the number, told the woman on the other end of the phone which convenience store we were at, and to send someone over to take a report.

"You always were stubborn," she said once I'd hung up.

"Call me what you will." I pulled my phone out once again and dialed Maxie, turning my back to Dana for a little privacy.

"Hello," she answered on the second ring.

"Hey, baby. I'm still at the A.M./P.M. Just ran into someone's car."

"Really? You okay?"

"I'm fine," I told her. "Waiting for the cops to come and take a report. I'll be there shortly."

"Okay, baby," she said. "Call me if you need me to come down there."

"All right."

When I hung up, my eyes found Dana, who'd been hanging on my every word.

"Girlfriend?"

"Fiancée," I said, although Maxie wasn't really my fiancée yet. Not officially. I'd asked her at least three times since she'd moved to L.A., but her response was that she wasn't quite ready. Wanted to wait until she was settled in. Then once she was settled in, she wanted to wait until after the baby was born. As soon as Miles was born, I got down on one knee right there in the labor and delivery room.

"Well?" I'd asked, holding a beautiful engagement ring between my fingers.

"Well, what? Rico, get up off of that floor, you're embarrassing me," she'd said.

"You said after the baby was born."

"I know, but I didn't say *right* after the baby was born. Do you have any idea what I've just gone through?"

"I uh—"

"I can't think about that right now, Rico." She began to whisper because the nurses had gathered to see the event for themselves. "We'll talk about it when we get home. Okay?"

I'd agreed. I was pressuring her, even after we'd both agreed that we wouldn't pressure each other about the subject. That we'd let nature do its thing, and if it was meant to be, it would be. But the thing was, my heart had changed after seeing Maxie carrying my child and all that she went through to bring him into the world. I fell in love with her all the more.

It was never like that with Dana. I did my part as her husband, played the role because it was the right thing to do. Even when she was pregnant with Brianna, I was excited about being a father, but the love that I felt for Maxie, I'd never felt for anyone before. And I was too chicken to go into the delivery room when Brianna was born. I went in only minutes after she was born, so I never witnessed a birth like I had with Miles. I had never realized what a woman went through during childbirth. It was nothing short of amazing. And from that point on, I knew I had to make Maxie my wife. There was just no getting around it. But I had to give her the time and the space that she needed. She was adjusting to so many new things in her life, and although I didn't like being put off, I understood. I would wait, but I didn't know how long I could.

"That's sweet, a fiancée. I heard about her," Dana said, leaning against her car in a sexy trying-to-get-my-attention sort of pose. She pulled a small compact out of her purse and began to freshen her lipstick. "Heard you're a new daddy too."

"Yeah, I am."

People began to walk away, seeing there was no real drama. They left the two of us in the parking lot, as we waited for the LAPD to arrive.

"Is that where my daughter is? At home with your fiancée?"

"Matter of fact, she is."

"I wanna see her, Rico."

"She's not ready for that."

"What do you mean, 'She's not ready for that'? I'm her mother."

"Nope, you're not her mother. You gave up that title when you walked out of her life."

"I was wrong to leave like that, yes. But I'm back now and I wanna try and salvage what I can with my daughter. Want to build a relationship with her before she forgets who I am."

"Do you really think that she knows who you are?"

"Yes, I do. I haven't missed one birthday or Christmas. I've sent her cards and gifts for every occasion. Didn't you give them to her?"

"Yeah, I gave them to her. But cards and gifts don't take the place of being a mother!"

"I know that." She tried to get the crocodile tears that were forming in her eyes to fall. But they wouldn't. "But you can't keep her from me."

"I can, and I will. We're doing just fine without you in our lives. She's happy, and I don't need you confusing her right now."

"You can't just say no."

"I just did."

"We'll see about that. I'll take your behind to court."

"Take me to court, Dana!"

"I will." She threw her purse on her shoulder and sashayed around to the driver's side of her car.

"Not gonna wait around for the cops?"

"Go to hell, Rico!"

I smiled.

"Still the same old Dana, huh? Always running away."

She jumped in the car, slammed the door, and burned rubber out of the parking lot. I shook my head and took a look at the business card she'd handed me. It read: DANA ELKINS, ACTRESS/ CHOREOGRAPHER. She was still carrying my last name, although we'd been divorced for two years. Still chasing after her dream of becoming an actress. I stuffed the card into my pocket.

I finally grew tired from waiting for the LAPD to show up, jumped in my truck, pumped Usher back up again, and drove home.

"You'll never believe who I just ran into."

"Who?" Maxie was on my heels as I carried the brown paper bag to the kitchen.

"Dana."

"Dana, as in Brianna's mother, Dana?" She was busy making sure the ice cream hadn't melted.

"I hit her car."

"That's who you hit? Did you do much damage?"

"Just a little ding," I said, grabbing two bowls from the shelf. "Had the nerve to tell me she wants to see Brianna."

"What did you say?"

"I told her to take me to court."

"And?"

"She said that she will," I said. "Ma didn't even tell me she came by there."

"She went by Reggi's? They were just here this morning. Didn't say a word about it. I wonder why."

"I don't know, but I'm calling over there first thing in the morning to find out," I said, filling two bowls with ice cream. I carried them both into the bedroom.

"Did she look the same?" Women were always sizing each other up.

"Yeah. She looked the same. Gained a little weight." In all the right places, I thought to myself and wanted to say, but knew better.

"Still attractive...to you?"

"Dana has always been an attractive woman, Maxie. I won't deny that. But she's also very irresponsible. Always running away from her responsibilities. Just like

24

tonight, after the accident. She gets pissed because I won't let her see Brianna, and she jumps in her car and drives off. We never even got around to making a police report."

"Maybe you should let her."

"Let her what?"

"See Brianna," Maxie said, leaning her back against a pillow and stuffing a spoonful of ice cream into her mouth. "Why don't you let Brianna decide?"

"Are you kidding me?"

"I'm serious. I know what it's like to grow up without a mother. You always feel as if a part of you is missing. And you're constantly trying to fill the void with other things. But you never can."

I listened quietly, my eyes affixed to the television set as the announcer on *Sportscenter* gave me the results of the game that I'd missed earlier.

"I'm not saying you should give her custody of Brianna. All I'm saying is that a little girl should know who her mother is. Even if she's a bad mother, Rico, she's still her mother."

"Maybe I will," I said, kissing Maxie's butter-pecan-flavored lips.

"Let her see Brianna?"

"No. Let Brianna decide," I said. "I'll ask her what she wants."

"That's a step," she said. "And what if she does want to see her?"

"Then I'll let her."

"And you'll be okay with that?"

"Yeah. If it's what Brianna wants."

"It's the right thing to do, baby."

"You think so?"

"I know so."

If it was so right, then why was I so afraid? Afraid that my daughter might love her mother more than me? Afraid that I might lose her?

3

Dana

After placing books on my bookshelf and pictures on my mantel, I lit a few candles. Then I emptied boxes full of my black artifacts and placed them around the room in an attempt to make my new little apartment feel more like home. I put on a Jill Scott CD and set the tone for my evening. I'd planned on decorating my space with a contemporary feel, reds and blacks in the living room, golds in the kitchen, and purples and greens in my bedroom. I'd already hit up Pier One for knickknacks and candles to set it all off.

I hadn't expected to run into Rico so soon, though. I'd wanted to plan our meeting a little better, and I certainly didn't mean to piss him off. I wanted to see my daughter and the chances of that now were thin. Reggi had promised to talk to him for me, to break the ice. Said she'd convince him that Brianna needed me in her life. So I tried to be patient and let her do her thing. He listened to her, always had. And she knew her son better than anyone did. But she was taking too long at getting around to it, and I was growing impatient. I had planned on making a surprise visit to his house; the house we once shared together. He still lived there. But I'd decided it was best to go through Reggi, instead.

Rico was a creature of habit. Safe, secure. Those were the things that I'd loved most about him in the beginning, but were also the very things that drove me away. We were different. I was more of a free spirit, a gypsy in my own sense, a dreamer. And the thought of spending the rest of my life as someone's wife and mother frightened me. I felt trapped in a life that I hadn't chosen. Rico and I got married because I was pregnant, and though I grew to love him, it still wasn't enough.

I wanted adventure and excitement, and found just that in Tony. He was unpredictable and offered me everything that Rico wasn't. I met him at an audition. He was auditioning for a role in the same television sitcom that I was, although neither one of us ended up with a part. When he invited me to have lunch with him at the Vietnamese restaurant around the corner from the studio, I figured it was harmless. We sat there for hours talking and laughing like old friends, and before long, I was at his place rolling around on his water bed. Our affair went on for months, until he finally landed a job in Seattle. When he moved away, I thought my life had come to an end. I missed him and couldn't focus on much else, particularly my husband and child, who needed me at home. They had taken second place in my life, and my sole desire was to be where Tony was. I ran our phone bill through the roof, calling him every chance I got. Even when Rico was home, which was rare, because he spent so much time working, I'd call Tony and pretend I was chatting with one of my girlfriends. Most of the time, Rico was always working at some construction site. Always talking about starting his own construction company, but never doing it. Instead, he worked his fingers to the bone for someone else. In the beginning, I would complain about his long hours and he'd always promise to spend more time at home with Brianna and me. I'd complain again, and he'd go into his spiel about how he needed to work in order to provide a nice home for us, put food on the table, and allow me the niceties that I often enjoyed.

"How else do you think we can live like this?" he'd ask.

"All this means nothing, Rico, if you're never here to enjoy it with us."

"You're right." He'd kiss my lips. "And I'm going to make time for us this weekend. I promise."

Sometimes he would make good on his promises, and the three of us would drive down to La Jolla, a beach community in the heart of San Diego, and spend the weekend. Those were the times I remembered most about my life with Rico. Those times made me feel as if nothing was better than being his wife and Brianna's mother. I basked in those times.

But the long working hours continued. And once I met Tony, I started to care less and less whether Rico was home or not. I wanted him to work. His long hours gave me the opportunity to steal precious moments with my newfound lover. I'd drop Brianna off at Reggi's or convince one of my girlfriends to look after her from time to time. Nothing else mattered except spending time with Tony. Not to mention that every week I was being turned down for parts that I knew I should've gotten. The acting business was a different animal, and often less talented people got roles you knew should've been yours.

But because they knew somebody, who knew somebody, they often became the star. Not being able to find work was weighing heavy on me, and sent me into a world of boredom and despair. When Tony asked me to move to Seattle with him, I jumped at the chance.

"Just come here for a while. If you don't like it, then I'll send you home."

"What about my daughter?"

"We'll send for her later," he'd said. "I don't really have room for a kid in my little apartment. But once we get a bigger place, we'll send for her."

"I can't just leave her here."

"That's her father, right? Your husband?"

"Yeah."

"She'll be okay with him, won't she? Besides, it's just temporary."

He was right. Rico loved Brianna and I knew she'd be okay with him. And although he was just as much a novice at this parenthood thing as I was, I knew he'd figure it out. He was a survivor. Besides, if I left her, I wouldn't have to worry about child care once I started pounding the pavement looking for work. As an aspiring actress, I found that auditions could be draining physically and mentally. I didn't need the extra weight.

I felt like a thief in the night as I drove away with a laundry basket full of clothes, and a few of my favorite CDs. I drove the eleven hundred miles to Seattle to be with a man who I thought could save me from my safe and dull life. It took me a year to realize that he was going nowhere in life, and another year to figure out what to do about it. And in between figuring it out and the fistfights, I often planned my escape, but never followed through. That is until the night he threatened to put a bullet through my head, the gun pointed right at my temple, the coldness of it causing me to shiver. I don't know what caused him to change his mind, possibly the prayer that I'd said in my head as I stood there, frightened. He lowered the gun, cursed me for driving him to that point, and stormed his drunken behind out the door.

I knew I had to go.

Once in L.A., I stayed with Alice, my absentee mother, for a few months until I could save up enough money to cover first and last month's rent on my own apartment. It took a while because the pay as a sales clerk at Mervyn's could only stretch so far. But it was steady, and although I hadn't given up on my acting career, my big break wasn't coming as quickly as I'd hoped.

Alice was starting to work my nerves with her nagging. The house was never clean enough. She was used to living alone, and she'd made it more than clear that she was ready for me to leave. Even when I was a child, she never wanted me around, claiming that my father was a better parent. So I moved in with him after they were divorced, visiting Alice every other weekend or whenever she found the time.

"I don't mind you staying here, child, but can you please pick up after yourself? This ain't no hotel I'm running here," she'd said, and I was glad that I would be moving soon. "Don't leave one glass in the sink, Dana. It takes every bit of one minute to wash the glass, dry it, and put on the shelf!"

I sat there, looking up from my script. I'd finally landed a part in a new television series that would be aired in the fall. I'd saved up for my deposit on my apartment, and I was feeling pretty good about life. The only thing missing was having my daughter in it. And I had plans under way for even that.

"Sorry. Won't happen again," I said. "I got the part in the television show I was telling you about."

"Doggone right, it won't happen again!" she said, ignoring the part about the television show. "And I need you to get lost for a while, I'm expecting company."

"Did you hear what I just said?" I asked her.

"Yeah, yeah. I heard you." She lit a Salem Light, took a puff.

"Well, aren't you going to congratulate me?"

"All I can say is you better not quit that job at the department store, running around here chasing after some pipe dream. You ain't a child no more, Dana. It's time you grew up and found yourself a real career. And ain't no TV show gonna pay the bills around here." She took another puff from her Salem. "And don't forget you still owe me fifty bucks for last month's rent."

"I'll have your fifty bucks," I told her. "At the end of the week."

"Good."

"And I'm moving at the end of the month."

"Going where?" She laughed as if I'd told a joke.

"I found a place. An apartment over in Culver City."

"And how you intend on paying the rent?"

"I have this acting job now, and I still have my sales job at Mervyn's."

She laughed harder this time.

"I guess you met some man that's going to take care of you, huh?" she said, and coughed from the cigarette. "To make sure the bills get paid?"

"I don't need a man to take care of me, Alice. I'm doing this on my own."

"Right," she said. "You ain't never done nothin' on your own, child. Always had somebody taking care of you. First it was that husband of yours, Rico. You had it made with him, and didn't even know it. Then you ran off with that foolish man from Seattle. Always looking for someone to take care of you."

"Just like Daddy took care of you?" I asked. "He was good to you."

"Your daddy wasn't no saint, honey," she said, always on the defense when I mentioned my father.

"Why do you hate him so much, Alice?" I never called her "Mother," because to me she never had a maternal bone in her body.

"Let's just say, I had my reasons," she said. "Now back to this thing about you moving out. What brought all this on?"

"I need my own place if I'm ever going to be able to build a relationship with my daughter."

"Your daughter? That child don't know you. You abandoned her, remember? Or did you forget? What makes you think you can walk back into her life again after all this time?"

"Like you abandoned me?"

"I didn't abandon you! You chose to go live with your good-for-nothin' daddy and his wife, Sophie. So don't you ever say that I abandoned you."

"You didn't come back for me. You never offered me the chance to come and stay with you."

"You made your choice, child."

"Why did you let me move in with Daddy? Why didn't you stop me from leaving?"

"Because you had your mind already made up."

"You wanted me to go, didn't you?" Tears were forming in my eyes. "You wanted me to go then, and you want me to go now! Don't you?"

"Don't raise your voice to me, Dana. This is still my house!"

"I hate you, Alice," I said, with so much hurt and anger in my voice. "I don't know why I came here in the first place."

"Because nobody else would take you in. That's why!" she said. "Where's your good-for-nothin' daddy now? Why didn't he take you in when you moved back to California?"

"He's in a nursing home with Parkinson's disease. How dare you speak about him like that?"

"What about that big old house of his? Why didn't you move in there?"

"Not enough room. Sophie and her daughters live there."

"Her grown daughters who aren't any relation to Henry and should have places of their own. Yet his only daughter moves back to L.A. and she can't even find a place to lay her head," she said. "You think you're so smart, don't you? You think the world revolves around Henry. Well, I'm here to tell you, it don't. He got everything he deserved! I don't wish nothing bad on nobody, but your daddy ain't no saint." She put her cigarette out in an ashtray. "Now get this kitchen cleaned, girl. I got company coming."

I rejoiced on moving day. I left without saying another word to Alice. She was right about one thing: I came to her because I had nowhere else to go. And I was grateful for the place to stay. But another day in the same house with her would have been the death of me...or *her*.

I sat in the middle of my living room floor, a shoe box filled with photos in between my legs, as I placed them into photo albums. I picked up one, stared at it, and smiled. It was a picture of Brianna when she was three. She was sucking on a cherry Popsicle with the juices from it dripping down her face and all over the white T-shirt she was wearing. She was so cute with her long ponytails hanging down on each side of her head, her stomach so fat that the T-shirt barely covered it. I laughed at the sight of it.

I knew I had to see my daughter. Reggi had sent me photographs over the years, but I wanted to see her for myself—live and in living color. I would never end up like Alice, old and miserable, and never having a real relationship with my child. I wanted something different for me, and for Brianna.

4

Maxie

Both my sisters pulled up at the same time. Button drove her husband Earl's baby-blue, sixty-seven Chevy. She stepped out of the dropped top, her honey-colored skin, which matched mine, glowing under the sunlight. Her jet-black hair fell onto her shoulders. Tattered, sexy, low-cut jeans hugged her perfect figure. She wore a multicolored halter top cropped just enough to give a full view of her diamond belly button ring. She didn't look as if she'd given birth to a child only five months before me. She tossed her hair to one side as she talked to someone on her cellular phone.

She leaned up against the car, smiling when she saw me standing at the door.

"Hey, sweetie. I'll be in there in a minute," she said, and then went back to her phone conversation.

Alex pulled her black Escalade into my driveway, the windows tinted so dark I could hardly see inside. She stepped out, with her tall slender frame and bronze skin, wearing a pink Nike sweat suit, and matching Nike sneakers. She opened the back door for her two little rug rats, who jumped out and ran toward me as if they already knew who I was. But the truth was, they didn't know me. And neither did Alex for that matter. She was my sister, but we were strangers. Had been for most of our lives.

Our mother had committed suicide when we were children. The three of us—Button, six, Alex, ten, and I, twelve at the time—found our mother dead in the bathroom of our little Section Eight subsidized home, her wrists slit. The memory of the bloody water in the bathtub still causes me to awaken with chills in the middle of the night. After the funeral, we stayed with our Uncle Walter, Mama's brother, for a while. That is, until he was arrested and thrown in jail. It wasn't long before we ended up in foster care. My sisters were immediately adopted by a family, but unfortunately I was too old to be included in the package. It's no secret that potential adoptive parents are petrified of teenagers; in their minds, a twelve-year-old is just on the brink of becoming the bitterness that leaves a terrible taste in people's mouths. They feared juvenile delinquency, truancy, sassy attitudes, the whole nine. And honestly, since the day menstruation had found me, I'd become moody, standoffish, and had a tongue that could be considered a lethal weapon. It was my defense, my protection from a cruel world that had stripped me of my childhood.

People always fell in love with Button immediately, because, just as her nickname suggested, she was "cute as a button." And although Alex was the inquisitive one, asking a million questions all the time, she seemed innocent enough, and didn't pose a threat. As for me, I was that strong, violent wind that could shake any calm sea. I guess that was more than Sarah and William Weaver, the sweet little conservative couple who adopted my sisters, wanted to deal with.

I was sent away. I went from home to home, being abused at just about every one of them, until finally running away at sixteen. Needless to say, I lost contact with my sisters, although my desire to find them never ceased. And now that I'd found them, I was determined not to ever let them go.

I stood there, with my front door open, a cool California breeze sneaking past me and into the house.

"Well now, you must be Nicolas Jr." I smiled at my nephew, who'd made his way up to my doorstep, and then shot right past me without even saying hello.

"He is too full of energy," Alex said, making her way up onto the porch, Ashley behind her.

"Yes, he is." I smiled at my niece, who returned the smile, looking like a miniature version of her mother with the same bronze skin. "And you must be Ashley."

"Yes," she said, her hair in a style much too grown-up for a ten-year-old. "You'll have to excuse my little brother. He's so stupid."

I glanced over my shoulder at Nicholas Jr., who sat in the middle of the living room floor. He had found my remote control and was undoubtedly searching the channels for the Cartoon Network.

"Ashley, that's not a nice thing to say about your brother," Alex said.

"Mommy, it's true." She rolled her eyes at her mother.

"It's not true. What did I tell you about that word—'stupid'?"

"Sorry," Ashley said.

"Hi, Maxie," Alex said. "I guess I don't have to introduce you to Ashley and Nicholas Jr."

"I guess you don't." I laughed, hugged Ashley, and then my sister.

They both went inside, Alex making her way to my spacious kitchen, an open and inviting space just steps away from the living room. The high ceilings in my living room gave a feeling of greatness, and the warm colors I'd chosen for the walls made you feel right at home.

When Button finished her call, she headed my way as I stood in the entryway, the sweet smell of morning dew still lingering on the flowers just outside my door.

"How's it going, Maxie?" she said, smelling like the Estee Lauder counter at the mall as she hugged me.

"Where's the baby?" I asked. Her son, Tyler, was about five months older than Miles.

"He's at home with Earl," she said, moving past me. "Somethin' smells good up in here."

"I cooked breakfast," I said. "Hash browns, scrambled eggs, and turkey bacon. I hope you like turkey bacon, because I don't eat pork."

"Cool with me," Button said and headed straight for my kitchen as if she were at home.

"Have anything lighter?" Alex asked, as she plopped down in an easy chair in my living room, and started flipping through an *Essence* magazine. "I gotta watch these hips, you know."

"Oh please," I said with my hands on my hips. "If you plan on hanging with me, you gotta eat! Now come on, let's get these kids fed."

Button had already made herself at home, and was

piling food onto a plate as I walked into the kitchen, Alex and Ashley behind me.

"I can see you're no stranger to my kitchen," I teased.

"Not at all, girl. Did you see how I just made myself right at home?" She laughed.

"I saw."

"The girl has no shame," Alex said.

"It's okay. I want her to feel at home," I said. "And you too."

"Have I told you how glad I am that you're in L.A.?" Button asked me.

"No."

"Well, I am." She poured herself a glass of orange juice. "And you need to let me do something with those locks when you get a chance."

"What's wrong with my locks?"

"They could just use a touching up, that's all." She stuffed a piece of turkey bacon into her mouth. "And where are my niece and nephew?"

"Miles is asleep, thank the Lord. He kept me up half the night," I said. "And I need to go check on Brianna. She's getting dressed."

Before I could finish my sentence, Brianna walked into the kitchen wearing the outfit I'd laid out for her.

"Maxie, I wanna wear my white sandals instead of these," she said, holding her brown sandals in the air. "Can I?"

"Sure, baby. Whichever ones you want to wear," I said. "You remember Alex and Button, don't you?"

She'd met my sisters at the hospital when Miles was born and at the baby shower Rico's mother, Reggi, had thrown for me.

"Hi, Brianna," Button said, in between bites.

"Hi." Brianna waved at my sisters.

"And you remember Ashley, don't you?" I asked, remembering how we'd had a hard time prying the two girls apart after they'd run themselves silly in Reggi's backyard, picking flowers, playing hopscotch, and jumping rope all afternoon.

"Hi, Ashley." Brianna smiled.

"Hello, Brianna," Ashley said in her grown-up voice.

"Maybe you can show Ashley your Barbie dolls later on," I suggested.

"Okay," Brianna said sweetly.

"My Barbie dolls are in the car," Ashley said, with her hands on her hips. "I have five of them, and they each have their own wardrobes."

"Can I see them?" Brianna asked.

"Okay," Ashley said.

"Run on up to your room and put your other shoes on," I told Brianna. "And hurry up so you can eat some breakfast before we go to the mall."

"Yes, ma'am."

"And did you brush your teeth?"

"Yes. And I washed my face and up under my arms like you told me to," she said, smiling, and then ran to her room to change shoes.

"If I didn't know any better, I'd think you were that child's mother," Button said. "You're so good with her."

"I have grown quite attached to her," I said, and fixed Brianna's plate.

"And where's her fine daddy at, anyway?"

"He's at his mama's. Giving us some girl time."

"That's sweet," Alex said, as she fixed Ashley's plate. "When are the two of you getting married, Maxie?"

"We haven't really set a date."

41

"And from the looks of your ring finger, you're not even engaged yet," Button chimed in. "What are you waiting for? You love him, right?"

"Very much." I tried to make my sisters understand. "But a lot has gone on in my life. I'm just trying to figure it all out."

"But wouldn't it be easier to figure it all out together? You and him?"

"Noooo," I sang and smiled. "I need to figure it all out on my own first. Don't wanna lay all my baggage on him. He has enough to worry about with trying to raise his daughter. And now that Brianna's mother is back in L.A...."

"Her mother is back in L.A.?" Button asked. I had shared with her how Dana had run off and left Rico and Brianna for another man. "How do you know?"

"Rico ran into her at a convenience store the other night." I poured Brianna a small glass of orange juice. "She wants to see Brianna."

"What?"

"And I think she should," I explained to my sisters.

"You think she should? She ran out on them. How does that give her any rights as a parent?"

"She might've been a bad wife and mother. But I'm thinking about Brianna. She deserves to know her."

"You're more of a mother than she could ever be, Maxie," Alex said, placing bacon and eggs on Nicholas Jr.'s plate, and calling him into the kitchen to eat.

"True. But I'm not her mother. And she deserves a relationship with Dana, if that's what she wants."

"What if she decides to run off again? Wouldn't that be more harmful to Brianna?"

"Probably. But she still deserves the chance."

We were all quiet for a moment, but their looks told me that they didn't agree.

"Look, I grew up without a mother. The two of you didn't. It's just not a good thing for a young girl to be without one."

"She has one. You," Button said.

"But I'm not her real mother."

"Neither was our mother. The one who adopted us. But she did a pretty good job."

"I wouldn't know."

"Maxie, I wish I could've changed what happened to you. Wish we could've all grown up together," Alex said.

"That's a sweet thing to say, but things happened the way they were supposed to," I assured her. "Besides we're all together now. And that's all that matters. Right?"

"I'll drink to that." Button raised her glass of orange juice, and then took a swallow.

"Now let's hurry up and eat so we can get to the mall and get our shop on!" I said, not wanting the conversation to ruin my upbeat mood.

"Now I'll drink to that," Alex said. "I have Nicholas's American Express and it's burning a hole in my pocket. And he gave me a pretty big allowance this week."

"Girl, he gives you an allowance?" I had to ask.

"Well, let's just say he suggested a spending limit."

"Please, I wish Earl would give me a spending limit. I would look at him like he's crazy. I work a nine-to-five just like him, and I have my own money," Button said.

"Well, I don't work. My husband takes care of all the finances in our home. And he knows how carried away I can get at the mall sometimes," Alex said. "I remember once he took all my credit cards away and wouldn't let me buy anything for two months!"

"He put you on restriction?" I asked.

"I guess you could say that," she admitted.

"And what about the time he wouldn't let you leave the house for two weeks, because you'd stayed out too late the night of my birthday party?" Button asked, mouth full of scrambled eggs. "Never mind that you were at your sister's house."

"It wasn't like that, Button."

"What was it like then?" Button asked.

"Never mind."

"And what about the time he made you quit your job because there were too many men working there? He thought they might be checking you out."

"Button!" she snapped. "That is not why I quit my job."

"Well, why?"

"I quit my job so that I could stay at home and take care of my children."

"And to help with Nicholas's campaign?"

"Yes. To help with his political campaign. What is wrong with a woman standing by her man?"

"Nothing, as long as he returns the favor."

"What's that supposed to mean?"

"After you finished college, Alex, you were so excited about the offer you received from that engineering firm. You were gonna be an engineer just like Dad. But Nicholas never supported you at all when you first started there. In fact, he made you resign after just three months."

Alex was silent. She poured herself a glass of orange juice and found her place at my kitchen table.

"And when you wanted to start your own catering business," Button said, "did he support that?"

Alex was still silent.

"And what about the art?"

"The art?" I had to ask.

"She's an artist," Button explained to me. "And a good one too."

"I'm okay," Alex admitted. "But art is just a hobby for me."

"A hobby, Alex?" Button asked. "When did it become just a hobby? I remember a time when it was all you cared about. You talked about having your own art gallery."

"Those days are long gone. That was before I was a wife and mother."

"Can I see your work sometime, Al?" I asked.

"It's really not that great, Maxie."

"She's being modest," Button said. "It's really good. And she has to steal moments in her day just to work on it."

"I work on it while Nicholas is at work, and while the children are at school. Painting relaxes me," she said. "What about you, Button? Why didn't you finish your degree? Because Earl came along and swept you off your feet?"

"I never wanted to go to college anyway."

"It's almost like he was going nowhere in life, and wanted you along for the ride."

"No, you didn't go there, Alex!" Button said. "I love Earl. Always have. He didn't have anything to do with me dropping out of college. I made that choice all by myself. And for your information, I'm doing exactly what I want to do with my life. I'm the best beautician in the entire San Diego metro area, and I own my own business. A very lucrative business, I might add, without a college degree. And my husband supports everything I ever think I wanna do. And I support him. So let's not go there, okay?"

"You support him while he works on cars in your backyard?"

"He restores old cars. What?" Button was standing now. "His line of work not good enough for you, Alex?"

"I never said that."

"Is that why you asked Nicholas to talk one of his colleagues into offering Earl a job?"

"I have no idea what you're talking about."

"You have no idea what I'm talking about, huh? Well, maybe this will refresh your memory. Some white dude calls our house out of the blue, and offers Earl a position at his law firm in their mailroom. Earl had never even set foot in his law firm, never even filled out an application, but the man says that the job is his just for the taking."

"Okay. So I pulled a few strings," Alex said. "But I did it for you. And for the baby. I knew you were pregnant, and that you and Earl could use the money."

"We don't need your handouts, Al. Earl makes a decent living restoring old cars. And we are very content with our lives." Button hopped back onto the bar stool in front of the island in the middle of my kitchen and finished off what was left of her breakfast. "At least we're happy."

"What's that supposed to mean?"

"Can you say the same?" Button made her way over to the sink and rinsed her plate off. She bent over, placing it in the dishwasher, and revealing the tattoo that was plastered across her lower back. "Are you happy, Alex?"

"I'm done talking about this, Beatrice! I'll be in the car." She pulled her keys out of her Burberry purse. "Ashley and Nicholas Jr., let's go!"

FROM HERE TO FOREVER

I knew when she called Button by her real name, Beatrice, and slammed my door behind her, that this was going to be an interesting day.

5

Rico

Ma's old kitchen was the same as it was during my childhood: table filled with newspapers scattered about, coffee brewing in the same old percolator on the stove, the back door opened to let in smells from the garden where fresh squash, okra, and tomatoes were growing. The open door also gave a full view of the six-foot-deep pool where I'd swum at least a million laps, and hosted several pool parties during high school. The linoleum on the kitchen floor had been changed at least a dozen times in my lifetime. But Pop had finally sprung for some beautiful tile about a year ago, and I'd helped him lay it in the kitchen and the bathroom. The kitchen table had changed every two years, or whenever Ma thought she wanted some new furniture, which was often since they'd owned Reggi and Fred's Furniture Mart since I was at least three years old. Now it was a mahogany country table where I sat enjoying a veggie omelet and a cup of decaf with my mother.

"I would've gotten around to telling you that Dana

was back in town, she just didn't give me a chance," Ma said, livening her decaf with a shot of Kahlua. "I will never understand that child. How someone can just walk away from her own child and husband like that, I just can't see. I'm in no hurry for her to rush back into Brianna's life. Or yours for that matter."

"Maxie thinks I should let her see Brianna."

"I don't know about that," Ma said. "But I guess she is the child's mother. But if you let her back in, don't let her upset your life in the process. You be very careful about how you go about it, son. Let it be on your terms and your time."

"I've already thought it through, Ma. And I will lay some ground rules, when the time comes."

"She's irresponsible, and needs to prove herself to you all over again."

"Don't I know it?"

"And when are you and Maxie planning on tying the knot and giving my grandchildren a real home, instead of running back and forth between two homes like that? It just don't make any sense, Rico."

"Soon, Ma, soon. Maxie just needs a little more time. She's been through a lot."

"What is it with these young women thinking that they've actually done something by giving birth to one baby? I raised five children with my bare hands. You see these hands?" she asked, raising her eyebrows and holding her vanilla-colored hands in the air; the hands that matched her flawless vanilla-colored face and mine. I was the only one who shared my mother's complexion and looks. My sisters and brothers were all a chocolate brown and looked like Pop. "These are the hands that used to beat your butt."

49

I laughed.

"Don't laugh. Y'all were a handful. Gave me a hard time. Y'all were bad."

"Not me, Ma, I was a good kid."

"I don't know who told you that lie. You were rotten. Especially after Kenny and Elise were born. You had been the baby for a while, but when they came along, you acted a plum fool. Started cutting up in school, all kinds of stuff."

"But I eventually got it together."

"Yeah. After I beat your behind one good time, you were just fine."

My mother and I shared a laugh, as her fingers stroked her light brown shoulder-length hair. She had aged gracefully, the only indication of her fifty-seven years being the subtle wrinkles around her eyes. Her tall thin frame was toned because she spent at least an hour each morning in their home gymnasium in the basement, pumping free weights, and an hour each night walking through their Ladera Heights subdivision. She played tennis every Tuesday, golf on Friday, and bid whist on Saturday nights with her middle-aged female homies.

"Playing cards tonight?"

"Yes. I've got to win my money back from that Evelyn, with her cheatin' behind."

"Miss Evelyn cheats?"

"As long as I've known her."

"I can't even imagine. I thought she was a holy woman."

"Rico, what's that got to do with cheatin' in cards?"

"I'm just saying."

"Some of the biggest liars and cheaters, you find them right there in the church." Ma laughed.

My older brother, Duane, walked through the door, carrying his daughter, Coral.

"Hey, Ma." He kissed my mother's cheek.

"Hey, baby." Ma grabbed Coral from Duane and kissed her plump cheeks. "And how's Grandmama's sweetheart?"

Coral held on to Ma's neck. All the grandchildren loved her just as much as she loved them.

"Here's the mail. The cute little mail lady handed it to me." Duane placed the stack of envelopes on the kitchen table. "Never seen her before, is she new?"

"Yes, Lord. Always getting our mail mixed up with the neighbors' mail," Ma said. "She's not too bright, either. They need to get Ralph back on this route. He was old, and couldn't see very well, but at least you got the right mail. I hated to see him retire from the post office."

"That's because he used to flirt with you."

"Hey, an old woman got to get it where she can." Ma laughed, sat Coral on her lap, and started flipping through the mail.

"What's up, little bro?" Duane asked, and we shared a handshake.

"Not much. What's going on with you?" I asked my older brother.

"Not a whole lot." He grabbed a coffee cup from the shelf. "Something sure smells good in here. What is that?"

"I made Rico an omelet earlier. You want me to make you one?" Ma asked.

"Naw. Bridgette's got me on this diet. One egg and two strips of bacon for breakfast, and grapefruit juice for dinner."

"Lord." Ma shook her head. "And what's that supposed to do, Duane?"

"Probably help him lose that big gut of his." I patted my brother on the stomach and held my cup out for him to refresh my coffee while he was pouring his.

"You got a lot of nerve, my brother. You're not too far behind me on the stomach."

"Man, this is baby fat." I laughed.

"Okay, baby fat. You'd need to join me at the gym, before Maxie runs off with some dude with a much better physique." He laughed, and looked just like Pop with his tall, almost two-hundred-pound frame. He shaved his head bald to hide the fact that his hair was beginning to recede like Pop's. "How's my future sister-in-law anyway?"

"She's fine."

"And Miles?"

"Greedy. Eats all day, and stays up all night."

"Like his daddy, huh?"

We all laughed and I took Coral from Ma and bounced her in the air.

"Who's your favorite uncle, girl?" I asked my two-year-old niece as she giggled.

"Be careful with that baby, Rico," Ma said.

"I got her, Ma." I threw her in the air again.

"She don't even know her life is in danger." Duane laughed. "Where's Bri?"

"She's with Maxie. They're having a girls' day out. Going shopping and stuff."

"Bridgette told me to invite the two of you over for dinner whenever Maxie is feeling up to it."

"That'll be cool. I'll let her know."

Ma had started opening a piece of mail, and Duane dropped a little of her Kaluhua into his coffee. She began to intently read a handwritten letter, and the look on her face had me concerned.

"What's that, Ma?"

"It's another one of those letters from Vietnam. Addressed to your father. The first one I just handed over to Freddie and didn't ask any questions, although I wanted to. It was from some Vietnamese woman. When the second one came, I asked Freddie about it, and he just brushed me off, saying it was nothing but junk mail," Ma said. "I promised myself that the next piece of mail that came to this house from Vietnam, I was opening it myself!"

"What's it say?" I asked.

She looked at me blankly for a moment, as if she'd heard me say something, but wasn't sure what. She continued to read.

"Who's Bao Hoang?" Duane asked, picking up the envelope.

"How old is your sister Rachel?" Ma asked, not hearing either of our questions.

"She's thirty-eight," Duane said. "Two years older than me. Why?"

"And you were born in what year? Nineteen-sixty-eight, right?"

"Yes, ma'am. And Rachel was born in '66."

"Ma, what's up?" I was beginning to worry.

"Your father's a cheatin' bastard! That's what's up," she said and threw the letter my way. "Read that."

I began to read the letter from Bao Hoang aloud:

Dear Fred Elkins:

My name is Bao Hoang. My mother is Louella Hoang. She told me that you are my father, and told me that there would come a time when I would need to find you. But only when I was ready. You met my mother in Vietnam during your time in the U.S. military in 1967. I was born in December of that same year, a Christmas baby. Mother told me that you promised to come back for us and bring us to the States so that we could be a family, but you never returned. And once the checks stopped coming, she lost contact with you. Mother died two months ago. Don't worry, she lived a very happy life, and so have I. But I would like to meet you, if you don't have a problem with it, just to close this chapter in my life. I'm in Vietnam right now, finalizing Mother's affairs. But I will return to the States soon. I live in Arizona with my wife and child and will be in Los Angeles on business. I will try and contact you while I'm there.

Best,
Bao

Duane's mouth dropped open, and I struggled to understand what I'd just read.

"Pop has a Vietnamese son?" Duane asked my mother.

"Sounds like it." She was pissed, and I looked for something to say that would save my father from her wrath, but I couldn't think of a thing to say.

"Your father and I were married in 1965," my mother began. "Rachel was born in '66 and he was drafted almost immediately. He went away to Vietnam and came back to the States in November of '67. That would mean that this child was born right about the time you were conceived, Duane."

"That's if this is all true," I said, still in denial. "You don't know this dude, Ma. He just writes a letter out of nowhere, claiming to be Pop's son. Where's he been all this time? And why didn't this Louella Hoang ever try and contact Pop before now? Or you for that matter?"

"She did contact him. I saw the letters; I just never read them," Ma said. "And why would the child lie, Rico? And why would he send a letter to your father all the way from Vietnam, and after all these years, if he didn't have something to say?"

"Why don't you just ask Pop?" Duane said.

"Ask Pop what?" My father walked into the kitchen, wearing khaki shorts and a Hawaiian-style shirt. He lifted his baseball cap to scratch his head, as his eyes lit up at the sight of Coral. "Is that my sugar lump over there?" he asked, and Coral ran into his arms.

"Pa Pa," she said, and they were the first real words she'd ever said. She'd learned how to say "Pa Pa" before she'd learned how to say "Daddy." Duane was jealous at first, but we all had come to the realization that the relationship between our parents and their grandchildren was one that we would never understand. It didn't include us. It was an exclusive club, and we, the parents of these little rug rats, were not allowed to join.

"How's Pa Pa's sugar lump?" He picked her up and nibbled on her chubby cheeks.

"Freddie, put the child down. I need to talk to you."

Pop continued to try to understand the sentences that Coral was putting together in baby talk.

"Freddie, I said I need to talk to you!" Ma said again. "Read this letter."

"What is this, Reggi?" Annoyed, he took the letter, put Coral down, took his reading glasses out of his shirt pocket, and placed them on his face.

He read the letter silently. Once he was finished, he set it on the table, took his glasses off, and placed them back into his shirt pocket. Ma stared at him, waiting for an answer, waiting for him to deny or explain. She waited for him to tell her that it was a lie; that this Bao Hoang had the wrong Fred Elkins; that there was no way he could've fathered this thirty-seven-year old, half-Vietnamese man, who was claiming to be his son, because he'd been faithful to Ma since the day they'd exchanged vows almost forty years ago. Pop cleared his throat.

"It just happened, Reggi."

My mother was hurt. I saw the pain in her eyes, the pain of a woman who'd been betrayed. And even though it had happened all those years ago, I could tell that it still stung as if it were just yesterday.

" 'It just happened'?" Ma repeated his words. "That's all you got to say? It just happened?"

"It was a mistake." He was almost whispering, embarrassed because Duane and I were hanging on his every word as if we'd been betrayed as well. My father stood six feet tall, chocolate-brown skin, gray, receding hairline underneath his Yankees cap. "What else do you want me to say? I made a mistake. I thought it would just go away. And it did until now."

"I can't believe what I'm hearing, Freddie. You mean to tell me, you had an affair with some Vietnamese woman while you were supposed to be over there fighting for your freakin' country...and now you have this... this...love child...and he's out there somewhere... a half-Vietnamese, half-black love child!" She was raising her voice, and I knew she was way past the shock point and was now at the thoroughly-pissed-off point. "And all you got to say is it was a mistake? And one that was never supposed to surface! And if he hadn't written this letter, I would've gone to my grave not knowing?"

"Baby, listen." My father finally realized the depth of his troubles.

"Don't 'baby' me, Freddie! This woman said you were coming back for her and her child, so y'all could be a family! When exactly were you going back for them, huh?"

"Reggi, we been married for thirty-nine years. I was never going back for her. If I was, I would be married to her right now. But I'm right here with you."

"And what is this about you sending her money? You sent money to Vietnam from our bank account? You took money out of this household"—her finger thumped the table with every syllable—"from my children to send to her?"

"She was dirt poor, Reggi. She lived in a little one-bedroom shack with her mother and five other sisters. And she had my child. What was I supposed to do?"

"Get out!"

"What?"

"Get out of my house, Fred Elkins!"

"What are you talking about, woman? This is my house too."

"We'll just see whose house it is." She grabbed a butcher knife from the drawer and waved it in my father's face. He backed up as she lunged toward him. "You get out of my house right now, and don't you ever come back!"

"Reggi, you don't mean that. We can work through this now."

"If you don't think that I mean it, you keep standing there, you lying, cheating, good for nothin' son of a—"

"Ma!" Duane cut her off. "Not in front of the baby."

Duane grabbed Coral and headed for the living room.

I grabbed Ma from behind and pried the butcher knife from her tight fist.

"This is crazy, Reggi. We're too old for this foolishness," Pop said. "Rico, tell your mother how crazy this is. You gon' stab me with a butcher knife over something that happened thirty-some-odd years ago?"

"Pop, I think you should just go. Grab some clothes. You can stay at my place until she calms down."

"Reggi, listen to me," he continued to plead.

Ma was struggling to get to him, and I was struggling to hold her back.

"Pop, go!" I yelled at my father. "Go get some clothes, and go to my place and wait for me."

"I can't believe this mess. Getting put out of my own house." He started mumbling, and shaking his head as he left the kitchen.

"Ma, Pop's going home with me while you figure this out. Okay?"

"I can't believe this, Rico. All these years, I've been a fool. And he's just so smug about it. Like he don't even care! Because it happened so many years ago, it's not supposed to matter anymore," she said. "Well, it does matter! You hear me, it does!"

"I know, Ma. I know."

"Ma, I'ma take Coral on to the house. I'll come back and check on you later on, okay?" Duane said.

"Yeah. You take that baby on home. I don't want her to see me act ugly with her grandfather."

"I'll be back in a little bit." He kissed Ma's cheek. "Everything will be okay."

"Bye-bye, Grandmama's sweetheart." She kissed Coral, and her voice was sweet for a moment. But then it changed just as quickly. "You get out of my house, Fred

Elkins, and I mean it!" she yelled to Pop, who'd gone upstairs to pack an overnight bag.

After Pop had packed a bag, he came back into the kitchen to plead his case to Ma. It took all I had to keep her from grabbing the butcher knife again.

"Pop, please just go."

"Reggi, this don't make any sense at all." He started toward the garage.

"You don't talk to me!" she yelled.

Since she couldn't get to the knife, she grabbed her half-filled coffee cup and flung it at Pop's head as he ducked out the door. It just missed him. Coffee splattered all over the wall as the shattered pieces of the ceramic cup fell to the floor.

I held on to her from behind as she began to cry. My heart went out to her. She was hurt, and because of it, I was hurt too. Pop had betrayed all of us. Here we were thinking that we had a father who was near perfect, always preaching to me, Duane, and Kenny about being faithful to our women, having integrity, and being honest, and here he was about to get stabbed with a butcher knife for cheating on our mother.

I was disappointed; in myself mostly, for holding him in such high regard. I suddenly felt as if my entire life had been a lie. I'd always taken such pride in being a good man, and boasted that I was just like my father. But now I was ashamed to even think I was like him.

6

Maxie

As I watched my sisters try on clothing that transformed them into supermodels, I prayed for the day I could fit into my size 7s again. I couldn't do much walking, because my body was still healing from Miles's birth, so I sat on a bench outside the Charlotte Russe's Boutique with the children. I wished we'd taken Alex's advice and opted for the mall in Beverly Hills, instead of the Foxhills Mall, where the music was so loud the walls vibrated, youngsters sported saggy pants, and you could purchase your very own grill of gold teeth.

Nicholas Jr. was running wild, and Ashley struggled to keep him under control. He was bad, and if I'd been in better physical condition, I probably would've beaten his behind myself. Miles was screaming because he was hungry, and I pulled my breast out right there at the mall and began breast-feeding him. Brianna pulled a Pamper and a container of wipes out of the diaper bag, anticipating that after Miles's feeding he would need to be changed.

She was so mature and helpful that I had grown to not only love her, but appreciate her help with Miles.

"Thank you, sweetie. We'll find a restroom in just a minute so we can change Miles."

"Oh I forgot the stuff for his rash," she said, digging into the diaper bag again for the prescription ointment the doctor had given me for Miles's diaper rash.

Button and Alex came out of Charlotte Russe's, each carrying a bag of loot they'd purchased.

"You should see the dress Alex bought up in there," Button said. "She just wasted her money, because we all know that Nicholas is not letting her out of the house in it."

"Let me see," I said.

"I usually don't buy stuff like this," she said, pulling the dress out. "But this was so cute on, I had to have it."

She held the short, black, formfitting dress up against her body.

"It's cute," I said. "But where's the rest of it? And where you planning on wearing it?"

"I don't know," she said. "I don't go anywhere, so it will probably just hang in my closet and collect dust."

"We'll just have to change that," Button said. "Let's go out tonight, y'all."

"Out where?" I asked.

"To the club. Get our party on!" Button said, doing some new dance that I wasn't at all familiar with.

"I don't go out to clubs," Alex said.

"And I don't have a babysitter," I said, realizing that my days of coming and going as I pleased were over. "And besides, I shouldn't even be out at the mall this soon. I must be crazy having my child out here around all these germs. But I was just so tired of sitting at home, the walls were caving in. The doctor put me on bed rest in my seventh month, and I haven't been anywhere since. So I'm grateful for the fresh air. But after I change Miles, I think I should head on home."

"Okay, since y'all are party poopers, let's just grab a bottle of wine and hang out at your place, Maxie," Button suggested. "You *can* hang out at Maxie's, can't you, Alex?"

"Sure. Nicholas is out of town until tomorrow afternoon. I'm free for the rest of the day."

"Why don't you and the kids just spend the night then?" I suggested to Alex. "And you too, Button, if Earl is okay with it."

"I'll stop by the house and grab us some clothes," Alex said.

"I'll call Earl and see if he needs me to pick up Tyler." She flipped open her cell phone. "This will be fun, just like a slumber party!"

"We can grab some DVD's from Blockbuster," I suggested.

"And let's make tacos for dinner," Button said. "I love me some homemade tacos."

"You love to eat," Alex said.

"That, I do." Button pressed the keys on her phone.

The kids were busy watching *Lilo and Stitch* on the DVD player in the guest bedroom. Alex browned ground turkey for the tacos, while Button cut up tomatoes, lettuce, and onions. I poured us each a glass of wine, and put in one of Rico's Frankie Beverly CD's. When the phone rang, I picked it up on the first ring.

"Hello."

"Baby, it's me." I'd missed hearing Rico's voice all

day, and it was soothing to my ear. "How's your day going with your sisters?"

"Fine. Alex and Button are spending the night. We're having sort of a slumber party."

"Sounds like fun."

"I miss you," I said, realizing that since my sisters were spending the night, I wouldn't see my sweetheart until tomorrow.

"I miss you too." He sighed, as if he had something on his mind.

"What's wrong, baby?"

"Ma and Pop had some drama today. She received a letter in the mail from some Vietnamese dude claiming to be Pop's son."

"Really?"

"Come to find out, Pop had an affair with a woman while he was stationed in Vietnam. The guy is a year older than Duane, and a year younger than Rachel. Ma's pissed! She tried to stab Pop with a butcher knife!"

"For real?" I laughed at the thought of my future mother-in-law taking a butcher knife to her loving husband. "I'm sorry, baby. I know it's not funny."

"No, it is kinda funny, now that I sit back and think about it," he said. "She threw him out too."

"Really? Where did he go?"

"Guess."

"Your place." I smiled. Rico was the middle child—Rachel and Duane were older, and Elise and Kenny were younger. He was always right in the middle of every-thing. Always the neutral one, the one to keep down confusion, and the one to keep the family together. He was always the calm in the middle of the storm.

"I'm trying to get a hold of Elise or Rachel to go over

and sit with Ma," he said. "She doesn't need to be alone."

"You want me to go over there?"

"No, baby, you enjoy your time with your sisters," he said.

"You sure, Rico? Because Button and Alex will understand."

"I'm sure. The time with your sisters is important, and I don't want anything to interfere with that. You having fun?"

"Yes," I said, taking a sip of my zinfandel. "I am."

"Brianna okay?"

"She's fine."

"Miles?"

"He's fine too," I said.

"Well, you enjoy. I'm gonna go home and have a chat with my father. I'll call you in the morning."

"Call me before you go to sleep tonight."

"I will."

I hung up and already missed him.

"Where's the taco seasoning, Maxie?" Button yelled from the kitchen.

"Check the shelf over the stove," I told her, and then helped Alex cut up lettuce.

After the children were put to bed, Alex, Button, and I camped out in my family room in our pajamas, sipping glasses of zinfandel and listening to Mary J. Blige's "No More Drama."

"See, that's what I'm talking about, no more drama." Button finished off the last swallow of her wine and immediately refilled her glass. She wore hot-pink Victoria's Secret pajamas with the word PINK plastered across the front of her chest. With a raised glass, she said, "Mary J. was going through something when she wrote that song."

"She was overcoming something," I interjected.

"Whatever the case, it was her best album yet," Button said.

"True that," I said, sporting an old T-shirt and Rico's checkered boxers, my legs folded underneath my bottom on the sofa. I held my glass in the air. "I've adopted 'No More Drama' as my theme song."

"Me too! No more drama from the haters who said that my beauty shop wouldn't make it past the first year." Button stood, and placed her glass on the coffee table. With one hand on her hip and the other making a two-snaps-up motion, she said, "I'll have you know that it has now been three years since I first opened the doors."

"See, that's what I'm talking about," I said.

"Why is it your theme song, Maxie?" Alex asked.

"No more drama from a painful childhood," I said.

"I can't even imagine what it was like for you, Maxie," Alex said. Her bronze-colored silk pajamas matched her skin.

"Me either," Button said. "Going from home to home like that."

"Were the foster parents at least nice to you?" Alex asked.

The mood in the room suddenly went from upbeat to somber.

"I wasn't at the first foster home two months before my foster father raped me. I was removed from that home, and sent to another one because his wife was convinced that if it had indeed happened, that I'd done something to provoke him," I said. "Ain't that a trip?"

My sisters were silent. But I was suddenly twelve years old again, and my mind drifted back to a house of faded wallpaper and plaid furniture. My bedroom had been a storage area with a twin bed squeezed in amongst all the junk. I vividly remembered fighting and trying to push Mr. Robinson's heavy body off of me, but he was much too heavy and much stronger. And when he pinned my arms to the bed, I lost the fight.

"At my second home, I was abused by my foster mother, Miss Fisher. She would hit me with a broomstick across my back if I looked at her wrong. Or if I mouthed off to her, which I often did. I would mumble things under my breath, because I hated her so much. She was a witch. Her ugly wig was always twisted on her head."

I wanted to lighten the mood a little, so I laughed at my own comment. But my sisters didn't share my laughter. They just stared at me, traumatized by my words. I continued.

"I was a very rebellious teenager and I had a lot of anger. The abuse continued at every home I ended up in. If it wasn't physical, it was sexual abuse. For years I thought it was normal to be abused by adults. Because it happened so often."

"Maxie, I'm so sorry." Alex's eyes held tears that were threatening to fall. Button's face was soaked from the tears that were pouring out of her. I was reminded of the night our Uncle Walter, who had cared for us after our mother was dead, was arrested, leaving us alone on that dark road. Orphans.

The way Button was staring at me told me she was six years old again. I wanted to hold her and tell her that everything would be all right and wanted to protect her. But I couldn't move from that spot on the sofa. I was paralyzed. I shook from the pain of reliving my childhood, but it was somewhat therapeutic talking about it.

"I got a gun when I was sixteen," I said, and laughed sarcastically. "I knew some guys in a gang who got it for me, and taught me how to use it."

"Did you ever have to use it?" Alex asked.

"When I moved into my fifth home. The Jacksons were churchgoers. Mrs. Jackson sang in the choir. Mr. Jackson was a minister. The social worker, with her messed-up blond hair and dull pastel-colored suit, tried convincing me that the Jacksons were nice, God-fearing people. 'Pillars in the community,' she'd said. I didn't even know what pillars in the community meant. But I figured it couldn't be a bad thing." I took a sip from my wineglass. "I wasn't there a week before Mr. Jackson tried sneaking into my room, with his stomach hanging over his belt and receding hairline."

"Oh my God," Alex said softly, and gently placed her hand over her mouth.

"One day when I stayed home from school…I had a bad cold—it was my own fault for running around with no shoes on in the rain, but we were right in the middle of a game of dodge ball, and—Anyway, Mrs. Jackson insisted that I stay in bed. I told her I was fine, and that I wanted to go to school. Begged her to please let me go to school, but she insisted. It wasn't long before my foster father, Mr. Jackson, came home early from work. A minister at the church, no less."

I paused for a moment. Alex and Button hung on to my words.

"I heard his key turn in the lock on the front door, and I trembled. Knew who it was, and knew why he was there. Knew he would come. When I heard the front door slam, I jumped, and my heart began to pound."

I hadn't realized that tears were creeping down the side of my face, but I used the back of my hand to wipe them away. I continued.

"I could see the shadow from his shoes underneath my door. That's when I reached for my gun. It was tucked safely beneath my mattress. Aimed it straight for the door, my hands trembling the whole time, and tears streaming down my face. He slowly pushed my door open."

"Did you shoot him, Maxie?" Button wanted to know.

"He smiled. That same silly smile that was on his face the first time he had violated my body. I thought of those bloodstained sheets, and the stench from his funky, sweaty body on top of me the first time, and that's when I steadied my grip on the gun."

"Did you shoot him?" Alex asked.

I barely heard her, because I was trapped in a time of anger and fear; a time of ponytails, Jordache jeans, and canvas sneakers; a time when young girls should be cultivated and coming of age with delicacy.

"He looked me square in the eyes and said, 'I guess you gon' shoot me, huh?' and I didn't say anything. Just steadied the gun more, and then cocked it. When he heard the gun click, his smiled faded, and he became nervous and all jittery. His nervousness gave me the courage I needed. At that point, I was fearless and told him if he came any closer I'd blow him from here to kingdom come!"

"What did he say?" Button whispered.

"He said, 'You little bitch, if you shoot me, it'll be all over for you.' And I told him that I didn't have anything to lose. My mama was dead, and if I went to jail, I would at least be safe from perverts like him. Told him I would love to go to jail, because any place was better than here. And told him that when I got arrested, I'd make sure that everyone at that little holy-roly church of his knew what kind of man he really was. He was surprised by my words, and it was then that I pointed the gun right between his eyes. I got off on making him sweat. His fear gave me power."

"What did he do?"

"He turned around and walked out. Shut my door behind him," I said. "And I let out a long sigh of relief, my heart pounding so loud I could hear it. Soon I heard the front door slam, and I knew I had to get out of there. I packed my things and took off. Never looked back."

I could see the relief on Alex's and Button's faces: relief in knowing that I didn't use the gun.

"The gun was my savior. It gave me power in my most vulnerable state. And I swore from that day forward, I would never be without one. I carry a gun everywhere I go, and I ain't afraid to use it," I said. "Nobody will ever hurt me again."

"Wow," is all Button said, her face soaking wet from her tears.

We all sat in silence for a few minutes, each of us afraid to move.

Finally, Alex broke the silence as she blew her nose and said, "Here I was thinking that my problems with Nicholas were significant."

"They are significant," I said.

"Not like what you went through. I wish I had your courage, Maxie."

"Courage is not something you're born with. You have to build it," I told her.

"God gives it to you," Button said softly.

"And what is with your husband anyway, Alex?" I had to know. "Why does he treat you that way? Why doesn't he support the things that are important to you?"

"He's intimidated by her," Button answered for her. "He's afraid that she might be more successful than him if he allows her to use her brain."

"Is that true?" I asked Alex.

"I don't really know what his fears are. And I don't really know what I'm capable of achieving, because I've never had the opportunity to achieve anything," Alex admitted. "From the time I graduated from college, and Nicholas and I were married, my dreams went down the toilet. We immediately had the children, and Nicholas insisted that I stay home with them. And I agreed that it was best for the children."

"Yeah, but what about what was best for you?" I said. "What's best for Alex?"

"I've never really given it much thought, just have always gone along with his wishes," Alex said. "But I'm happy. Even though it might not seem that way. I really am happy."

"I'm not convinced," I said.

"I really am, Maxie," she said, trying to convince herself more than she was me.

"Well, if you're happy, I'm happy, Al," I said. "But when you get ready to make 'No More Drama' your theme song, you can borrow my CD. Okay?"

She laughed.

"Okay," she said, and we all stood in the middle of the floor and hugged each other.

Button started the song over, turning up the volume on the CD player, and the three of us began singing the words along with Mary J.

7

Dana

While standing in front of the bathroom mirror putting the finishing touches on my makeup, I listened to Alicia Keys wooing Mos Def in her video. Once my face was beautiful, I made my way to the living room, stopped, and stood in front of my thirty-two-inch color television just long enough to check out Mos Def in his Humphrey Bogart gear, wishing it were me wooing him instead.

"Ooh, it's something about that man," I mumbled and then slipped my stilettos onto my feet.

I heard the phone, but let it ring. I had to get to the studio, and no one of importance ever called my landline anyway. The people I really wanted to hear from knew to call me on my cell phone, so I continued to sing along with Alicia Keys. But the phone wouldn't give up, so I rushed into the living room and grabbed it off the hook.

"Hello."

The person on the other end was silent.

"Hel-*lo*," I repeated, and then gave my silent caller the dial tone.

I rushed into the kitchen, popped a bagel into the toaster, poured myself a half cup of decaf, and pulled the tub of margarine out of the refrigerator. My landline started ringing again, and I strolled into the living room to answer it.

"Hello."

The silent caller again.

"Are you planning on saying something, or you just gon' breathe in my ear like some psycho?" I asked.

No response.

I gave my silent caller the dial tone once again.

L.A. traffic was no joke, as usual, especially during rush hour. I sat in traffic, thinking of someone I could call to take the edge off. Dialed Rico.

"Yeah."

"Rico, it's me, Dana." He caught me off guard, as I was prepared to leave a message.

"What's up?"

"Have you given my proposal some thought?"

"What proposal?"

Now he was playing crazy.

"I told you I want to see Brianna."

He sighed, and was silent for a moment. I guessed he was considering, or perhaps I'd caught him at a bad time. I didn't care. I needed an answer. My relationship with my child was on the table, and I wasn't taking no for an answer.

"I'm planning on talking to Brianna about it. Let her make the choice."

"She's nine. And we're her parents. We have to make choices for her."

"She's nine, but she's not stupid. And *we're* not her parents. I'm her parent," he said. "Let me get two chicken, egg, and cheese biscuits."

I realized he was ordering food at the drive-through window of some fast food joint.

"Would you like to make it a combo?" the woman taking his order asked.

"Naw, just the sandwiches," he said, rudely forgetting that I was on the other end of his cell phone. "But gimme a large coffee, sweetheart."

"Will that complete your order, sir?"

Dag, was I on the other end of his phone or what?

"That's it," he told her.

"Pull up to the first window, please."

"Look, Rico. I did not call to get into it with you about this."

"Then why did you call, Dana?"

"I'm trying to get my life on track, and—"

He cut me off. "That's a first."

"I need to build a relationship with Brianna." Tears were forming in my eyes. Did he have to be so anal? "I'm trying to do what's right for a change. Okay? So can you cut me some slack?"

"Look, Dana." He sighed again. "Gimme a chance to talk to Brianna. I'll ask her how she feels about seeing you. She's a very bright little girl, and she'll know what she wants. If she wants to see you, I'll call."

"When?" I found myself yelling. "When can I expect you to call?"

"Soon." He hung up before I could say another word.

The tears flowed like the River Jordan. It hurt to be in

this place. A place where you knew you'd made the biggest mistake of your life, and it seemed almost impossible to correct it. It seemed as if forgiveness was not on the list of answers to the multiple-choice question. I think this is the place where you are supposed to cry out to God and ask Him for help. And I would have, but I didn't think I was worthy of even His forgiveness. So I just continued to cry as if there was no tomorrow.

I sat in traffic, which was at a complete standstill. And I hoped it would start moving again, because my gas dial was quickly approaching empty, and I didn't have any extra cash floating around anywhere. I needed to make it to the studio, do my thing there, and then make it to the other side of town to pick up my check from Mervyn's before the banks closed.

Boo-hooing, I reached into the glove compartment and grabbed a napkin from the stack I'd swiped from McDonald's, along with a stack of straws and packages of ketchup. You never know when you might need that stuff. I sat there in my Mercedes, the car payment on it already a month behind. I blew my nose and tried to get myself together.

My cell phone buzzed.

"Hello," I answered, even though the number was unknown.

Silence.

"Hello," I said again, before sniffing.

My silent caller had my cell phone number too.

I hung up, took a look at myself in the rearview mirror. My eyes were puffy and my makeup was ruined.

8

Rico

The smell of turkey bacon and fresh coffee brewing shook me out of my sleep. Pop was already up and cooking in my kitchen. I grabbed the remote and turned the television up a little. It was still on ESPN, as I'd left it on all night. I'd fallen asleep trying to catch what was left of the game the night before.

I sat up in bed, my back against a pillow, caught the latest sports news to get the score from last night's game. The stiffness from my manhood, which was about to bust through my sleep pants, let me know that a leak was needed. But I needed to find out the score first. After I realized my team had lost, I got up, aimed for the bull's-eye in the toilet, washed my face and hands, and took a long look at my shirtless reflection in the mirror. I ran my hand across the ruggedness of my five o'clock shadow, making a mental note to shave before I saw Maxie again. Didn't want her complaining. She was always making a fuss when I forgot to shave or keep my fingernails trimmed. She even threatened to take me to her favorite Asian spot for a manicure and pedicure if I didn't take better care of my hands and feet. I agreed that men shouldn't walk around with dirty fingernails and crusty feet, but walking into some Asian spot with a roomful of women looking at you as if you've fallen off the fairy truck was not my thing.

I spotted a gray hair right in the top of my head, and quickly yanked it out. Then I looked at it to see if my mind was playing tricks on me. It was a gray hair all right, and there were more just like that one, strategically placed around my head. I couldn't believe my eyes, but hey, gray hairs meant wisdom, to some folks. To others, it just meant you were gettin' old.

I threw a little mouthwash into my mouth, swished it around from side to side, and then spit it into the toilet. After checking out my physique in the mirror, I decided that a few push-ups wouldn't hurt, and hit the floor. Did fifty quick ones. I knew I needed to work out more, but just couldn't find much time to make it to the gym anymore.

I opened up the miniblinds to give my plants a little California sunshine, then turned on the radio to see what Steve Harvey and his crew was talkin' about.

Then I made my way to the kitchen.

"What you cookin' up in here, old man?"

"Morning, son. I knew you had to get to work, so I made breakfast."

"Since when do you cook?" I asked, taking the plastic container of orange juice from the refrigerator and turning it up to my lips.

"Hey, I can burn a little," he said. "Get a glass, boy! I know your mother taught you better."

I took Pop's suggestion, grabbed a glass from the shelf, and emptied the orange juice into it. I grabbed a piece of bacon and stuffed it into my mouth. "What's up with you, man? Why didn't you tell Ma about this Vietnamese woman and her son?" I cut right to the issue that'd been burning in my mind all night.

"Are you kidding me?" He looked at me as if I'd lost my mind. "You see how she was acting yesterday?"

"She only reacted that way because of the way she found out," I told him. "Why couldn't you just be honest? Not just with her, but with us?"

"I didn't want to disrupt your lives, son." He rubbed the rugged, graying stubble on his face. "Wanted to protect my family. I made a mistake, Rico. What can I say?"

"Tell me about her. What was she like?"

"Not much to tell. She was just someone to hold on to while I was away from home. She meant nothing."

"Come on, Pop. She meant nothing?" I sat at the kitchen table, and grabbed the sports page. "You would jeopardize your family for someone to hold on to, who meant nothing?"

"Look, son, you don't understand. You've never been away from home. Never fought in a war." He looked for the eggs in the refrigerator. "I was a million miles away from home. Lonely. Scared. Sitting in a bar getting drunk, grateful for the moment's peace. Vietnam was no place for a young, black, married…kid. I was a kid, Rico. Eighteen years old, and watching all my buddies being killed off like flies."

I'd heard Pop's stories about 'Nam a million times.

It was nothing for him to get lit on a Saturday night, make my brothers and me line up on the sofa in our living room, and give us a history of the war and tell us what role African-Americans played in it.

"I'm a Marine, you see." That's how his stories always began. "I was a Marine then, and I'm still a Marine."

Then he'd go into his wartime stories, me and Duane bored to death. Kenny's eyes would light up like a Christmas tree. He'd ask Pop questions, which made him go into more detail. And we'd give Kenny the eye and threaten that if he asked Pop one more thing, we'd kick his butt later.

Pop would be sitting in his easy chair, a glass of Jack and ice in his hand, his third or fourth drink by then. By the fourth drink, the stories would become livelier.

"We laughed and cried, drank rice wine and home-made banana rum, sang songs, and bonded like brothers. White men and black men alike. We were soldiers first. I lost brothers over there; some of them I don't even re-member their first names. We knew each other by our last names or nicknames, you see, but I remember their faces, and I will never forget them. I feared war, boys"— he'd hold his glass in the air, as if engaging in an imagi-nary toast, his speech becoming more slurred by the minute—"but you know what I feared most? Letting my brothers down. That's right. Yes sir-ree, that's what I feared most. And you better believe I let a bunch of 'em down too. 'Cause, look at me…I'm still here. And where they at? They dead."

He'd cry after telling us about the deaths. Then he'd cheer himself up by telling us about the day he found out that Duane was born. We listened in silence, hoping that he would skip over some of the details, but he rarely did.

"Still remember it like yesterday. It was a muggy

morning. The Red Cross had notified headquarters that my son had been born. Lieutenant Daniels ordered me to go call home. I called your mother. Reggi was the most beautiful woman I ever met in my life." He'd smile to himself, as if he was picturing his young wife. "Found out I had a baby boy. Told me his name was Duane. That was you, boy!"

He'd hit Duane in the chest so hard, causing him to almost cry.

"Suck it up, soldier!" he'd yell. "Don't you dare start crying like some little sissy!"

Duane would dry up the tears before they'd even have a chance to fall, his bottom lip trembling. Me and Kenny prayed that he wouldn't hit us.

"Nineteen sixty-seven . . ." He'd continue with his history lesson, his eyes rolling toward the ceiling as he contemplated whether or not he had his dates right. "Or was it nineteen sixty-eight?" He'd carry on a conversation with himself for a minute. "Naw, it was sixty-seven. I remember, 'cause Thurgood Marshall was sworn in as the first black U.S. Supreme Court Justice that year. At the same time, there were four hundred and seventy-five thousand troops in South Vietnam...."

My pop was a walking encyclopedia when he and Jack Daniel's got together.

"Dr. King was assassinated in 1968. And you know what he said about the Vietnam War, son?" He'd look straight at me when he said it.

I would shake my head no, and he'd look to Duane for an answer.

"I don't know, Pop," Duane would say, still angry about getting hit in the chest earlier.

"Said it was a white man's war, but a black man's

fight." Pop would answer his own question. "What you think he meant by that, boy?"

I shrugged. Duane was still pouting over his injured chest. Kenny would be looking at my father as if he were the smartest man alive.

"African-Americans represented almost one-fourth of the army's killed in action. In 1968 we made up only twelve percent of the army and marines put together, but made up the largest percentage of casualties." He'd laugh, take a drink of his Jack, and lean back in his easy chair. "Now what you think about that?"

"What's a 'casualty,' Pop?" Kenny would ask, and Duane and I would give him a look that said, "Shut up if you know what's good for you."

Kenny was stationed in Japan. I still believe it was those conversations with Pop that lured him into a military career of his own. He wanted to be the hero that he thought our father was.

"I'm glad you asked that question, son." Pop's speech would be slurred, and he'd start singing some Curtis Mayfield tune and forget all about the question at hand.

"Freddie, why you got these children in here listening to your foolishness?" Ma would eventually rescue us, but not soon enough. "Y'all come on in here and get some supper."

"After you eat, you boys come on back in here. We'll talk about the riots that took place in Watts. Right here in California in 1968." Pop would shake the ice around in his glass, lean back in his recliner. "And in Harlem too."

"Freddie, please," Ma would say.

We'd escape to the kitchen, not to return until Pop and Jack Daniel's found each other again the following Saturday night.

* * *

Pop pulled the carton of eggs out of my refrigerator.

"There will come a time, son, when you'll be faced with choices that will change your life too."

"Yeah? Well, I just hope I have the good sense to make the right ones."

"Yeah, me too," Pop said. "Now, how you want these eggs?"

"Scrambled," I said. "And put some cheese in them, old man."

I watched my father pretend that he could cook, cracking a few eggs into a bowl and scrambling them.

Traffic was bad as usual, as I made my way down Sepulveda to a construction site in Manhattan Beach. My Puerto Rican buddy, Jesus, knew I was looking for work and sent me to a job site where some new high-rises were being built. He said it was a temporary job, but with the potential of being permanent once I showed them what I had.

I grabbed my lunch pail off the backseat, something I'd thrown together from leftovers Ma had sent home with me—baked chicken, collards, smothered potatoes. Then I put my hard hat under my arm and headed over to introduce myself to the foreman.

"How you doing, sir? I'm Rico." I held my hand out to shake his. "Jesus Hernandez sent me over. Said you could use an extra hand."

The skinny white man, with blond hair that brushed his shoulders, never took my hand.

"I told Jesus I didn't need an extra guy."

"What?"

"Got all the help I need," he said, turning his back to

me and giving instructions to one of his men, who was drilling.

"Look, man, I was counting on the work. I need the money."

"Can't help you, buddy. I got one too many men already," he said. "Check back in a week."

"In a week, my children will starve."

"Wish I could help you, but I can't." This time he looked me in the eyes. "My hands are tied."

"Yeah," I said and headed for my car.

"Check back in a week," he said again.

I was tired of this. I needed something steady and soon, because I was running out of options. I had bills mounting, and children that needed to eat. Not to mention I had a fiancée who needed more of a reason to marry me. But it's hard to expect a woman to put her trust in you when you can't even be trusted to find steady work.

9

Maxie

After dropping Brianna off at school, Miles and I headed over to Reggi's for breakfast. When I spoke to her on the phone, she sounded like she needed some company, not to mention she was always up for a visit with her newest grandchild.

"Oh my goodness, he looks as if he's grown so much since I saw him last," she exclaimed, and grabbed Miles from my arms before I could get in the door good.

"He is growing by the minute." I laughed and shut the door behind me. "He eats too much."

"How's my sweet baby?" she asked him, and he smiled as if he understood.

"How you doing, Reggi?" My lips brushed across her cheek.

"I'm doing much better, sweetheart." She smiled, but I wasn't convinced. Her eyes told me something different. "You hungry?"

"Yes, but I can cook something for myself. You sit down and rest."

"Honey, I've already cooked. I haven't stopped living." She chuckled. "Come on in the kitchen. I've got a breakfast quiche in the oven."

"Smells good too."

"Want coffee?" she asked, kissing Miles and placing his head against her shoulder. Balancing him, she pulled a coffee mug from the shelf.

"I'll have a cup," I said, and she pulled another mug down.

She poured two cups of coffee, and then spiced hers with a shot of Kahlua. I sweetened mine with three spoons of sugar and dumped in a ton of cream.

"I see you like a little coffee in your sugar," she teased. "The quiche should be done in a little bit. Let's sit down and catch up."

I sat across from Reggi at the country kitchen table. She was kissing Miles's fat cheeks and spoiling him rotten.

"Rico tells me that Dana wants to see Brianna." She took a swig of her spiked coffee.

"Yep, she sure does."

"How do you feel about that?"

"I told Rico that he should let Brianna get to know her. I think she should know who her mother is."

"I agree," Reggi said. "But how do you really feel about Rico's ex-wife, showing up here after all this time? Aren't you just a little shaken?"

"Of course not. I trust Rico," I said, not sure where she was going with this. And I hadn't felt uneasy about it until now. "Why do you ask?"

"It's just that she's come back after all this time. I just

wonder what she's really after. It's not Rico that I'm worried about. It's Dana."

"You think she might be after something more than building a relationship with Brianna?"

"Honey..." she said, and got up to check on the quiche. "Here, take the baby." She handed Miles to me, put two oven mitts on her hands, and pulled the quiche out of the oven. "You have to keep your eyes open. Dana's never been much of mothering material. She's just like her own mother, Alice. And the apple don't fall that far from the tree, you know."

"What are you saying, Reggi?"

"I just find it hard to believe that she's suddenly grown up, turned a new leaf, and now wants to be a mother. What changed?" she asked rhetorically, as she placed the quiche on top of the stove. "Don't get me wrong. I like Dana and all. And Lord knows I love my grandchild. And I want her to at least know her mother."

"I know what it's like to grow up without a mother, so I'm all for that too."

"I'm just telling you to keep your eyes open, baby. Don't be so trusting," she said. "Do you love my son, Maxie?"

"Yes, I do."

"But not enough to marry him?"

"Reggi, I love Rico. And I plan on marrying him. I just want it to be right. Don't want to rush into it just because we have a child together. Plus, I wanted to get settled in and all before we made such a huge step."

"That's understandable," she said, slicing the quiche and placing a plate of it in front of me.

"Thank you," I said. "Rico's been married before. I've never been down this road before, and when I do, I want it to be right. Don't want it ending up in divorce because we didn't plan it carefully enough or because we rushed into it."

"I second that, honey," she said. "You know, of all my children, Rico and I probably have the closest relationship. We understand each other."

"Yes, I know."

"Rico is one of the good guys," she continued. "I never had to worry about him, because I knew he'd turn out okay. It's the others I worried about."

"Rico is a wonderful man."

"Don't wait too long, Maxie," she said, and fixed herself a plate. "A good man he is, but he's still a man."

I was speechless.

"Now, tell me about this weekend with your sisters," she said cheerfully, changing the subject.

"We just ended up going to the mall, and then hanging out at the house later." I still felt uneasy about what she'd said about Dana and Rico. It was as if she was trying to tell me something, but I just dismissed it as too much Kahlua in her coffee and moved on. "How are things with you, Reggi? Rico told me what happened... about the letter from Vietnam."

"Fred Elkins is a liar," she said in a matter-of-fact sort of way. "After all these years, I find out that he's been unfaithful."

She was hurt. "He kept receiving these letters in the mail from Vietnam, and each time I asked him about it, he'd brush it off as nothing, and tell me it was just junk mail," she said. "What kind of fool does he take me for?"

"I'm so sorry, Reggi."

"I'm hurt because he lied to me, telling me the letters were nothing. And because he spent time with another woman during our marriage. While I was here trying to hold our household together and raise his children, he was off somewhere making babies with someone else. And he never told me about her. All this time I've trusted Freddie, and all these years we've lived a lie," she said, taking a drink of her coffee. "And there were probably others too."

"Other women?"

"Is that so hard to believe?" she asked, leaning forward, eyeballing me. "If he did it once, he probably did it a hundred times. Who knows?"

Miles started whimpering, and I knew he was hungry again.

"I need to feed him," I explained, setting my fork down and pulling my breast out to feed Miles.

"If I weren't so old, I'd divorce him."

"You don't mean that, Reggi."

"Yes, I do," she quickly snapped. "He don't deserve me. I ain't perfect, but I've been a good wife to Freddie. Raised his children. And I was never unfaithful to him a day in my life. And I had opportunities too."

"He made a mistake," I said. "I know he loves you. And you love him. And the fact that he never went back for her says that he wanted you, not her."

"Yeah, yeah. Whose side are you on anyway?"

"Reggi, I'm not on anybody's side. I love you both and I hate to see this happening to either one of you," I said, Miles sucking on my sore breast. "I hope you work it out. I really do."

"There won't be peace in this house until I meet this young man," she said, taking a bite of quiche. "I need to see him for myself. Want to see what he looks like. And I got some questions too."

"When is he coming?"

"Soon," she said, raising her mug to her lips. "He called here this morning, looking for Freddie."

"For real? You talked to him?"

"Sure did. Had a nice long talk with him," she said, taking a swallow from her coffee. "He'll be here next week. His wife can't make the trip because she's expectin', but he'll be here."

"Really?"

"Yes, ma'am," she said, as the front door slammed.

Rico was dressed in work pants and steel-toe boots, his dreads pulled back into a neat ponytail. His face was clean-shaven, and his cologne found me as he entered the kitchen. He kissed my lips, and I realized just how much I'd missed him over the past few days. We hadn't spent much time together since my sisters were over, and he'd been busy babysitting his father. He kissed Miles's forehead, his cheek brushing against my breast, as Miles continued to eat.

"Every time I see this boy, he's eating." Rico kissed his mother's cheek as he went to the cabinet for a coffee cup. "What's up with my two favorite women?"

Reggi and I shared a glance.

"Uh-oh. What's up?" he said. "I smell some male bashing going on in the room."

"Wrong," Reggi said. "What are you doing here, anyway? Shouldn't you be at work?"

"Baby, I thought you were starting that new job today," I said.

"I thought so too. No luck," he said. "Dude told me to come back next week."

He dropped his head in disappointment. Working construction was one of those occupations that too often

89

sent you on wild goose chases in search of work that may or may not exist. And if it did exist, there was no telling for how long. You just hoped it was a job that would take some time to complete, and you did a good enough job so that you'd be asked to help on the next one. Rico was growing tired of the rat race, I could tell.

"You'll find something, baby. Don't worry about it." I was his biggest cheerleader.

"It's easy to say don't worry about it, when I got bills knocking at my door, and two little mouths to feed."

"I just started a new assignment with that local magazine," I said. "We'll be okay."

"That's cool, Maxie. But your assignment ain't my assignment. Gotta fend for myself," he said. "What I look like, living off of my woman? I can't let you continue to bail me out every time I can't find work. I'm the man here."

"I know you're the man, Rico. But it's not about that," I said, almost in a whisper, thinking this was an inappropriate time to be having this conversation. "What's mine is yours. And I don't mind steppin' in where I'm needed."

"I know you don't mind, Maxie," he said, wrinkles now forming in the center of his forehead from frustration. "But I mind. It's about me being able to take care of my family. And right now I'm not doing it."

"How's your father?" Reggi changed the subject, not wasting any time asking about her husband.

"He's fine, Ma." Rico poured himself a cup of coffee. "He's at the house. Why don't you give him a call?"

"When hell freezes over!"

"He misses you," Rico said.

"I just bet he does," Reggi said, walking over to the

kitchen window and pulling the dead, yellow leaves from a plant that sat on the windowsill. "I talked to the Vietnamese boy today."

"What?"

"Yes," she said, checking the plant next to the sliding glass door for dead leaves as well. "He called here for your father this morning. So you make sure you tell him that, okay?"

"What did he say?"

"He's coming here," she said. "Next week."

"What was he like? How did his voice sound?" Rico's curiosity was piqued.

"Like any man's voice, Rico. He speaks English."

"And he just talked to you without hesitation."

"He ain't got nothing to hide! It's your father who has all the secrets."

"You sure you can handle meeting him, Ma?" Rico asked. "It might not be as easy as you think."

"I can handle it," she said, pouring herself another cup of coffee and spiking it.

"I think maybe we all need to just sit down and have a coming to Jesus meeting," Rico said, and then immediately regretted it.

"Yeah, your father's gonna need Jesus by the time this is all over!"

10

Dana

The fridge had been stocked with Popsicles, Jell-O, and those little containers of juice that kids like so much. I had no idea what her favorite things were, but thought I should at least have something to greet her with. Rico agreed he would drop Brianna off at six, after she'd gotten home from school, and he had time to get her fed. It was six-thirty, and I'd already left a message at six-fifteen. I'd changed clothes twice, gone to the grocery store, and was ready for her visit by five-thirty. He was late.

I paced the floor, and when my phone rang, I jumped. My heart sank. There must be something wrong. He'd changed his mind, I thought. I answered.

"Hello."

Silence.

My friggin' silent caller again.

"Why can't you just say something?" I yelled. "Either that or stop calling me!"

I hung up. But he or she wouldn't give up.

The phone rang again.

"Look, either say something or quit callin' here!"

"Bad time?" Rico's voice on the other end was not what I expected.

"I'm sorry, but someone keeps playing on my phone," I said. "Where are you?"

"Stuck in traffic." He sighed. "But should be there in about fifteen, maybe twenty minutes."

"Okay, I'll be here," I said. "You still have the directions I gave you?"

"Got 'em."

"You sure?"

"I got 'em."

"Okay, hurry up." I was becoming impatient.

When I saw her, I couldn't believe my eyes. She was so big, and such a young lady. She'd lost much of the baby fat that I'd remembered, and had grown up to be a very pretty little girl.

"Hello, Brianna."

"Hi." She smiled Rico's smile.

He stood at my door, his arms folded across his chest as if he was security at the club. He looked good too, even in his tattered jeans and steel-toe boots, his face smooth, his dreads falling nicely onto his shoulders. And his cologne almost had me in a trance.

"You don't have to stay, she'll be fine," I told him, but something inside of me wished he would stay.

"Brianna, you'll be okay?" he asked.

"Of course, she'll be okay. What's that supposed to mean?"

"I'm just making sure she's comfortable, Dana."

"I'll be okay, Daddy."

"I'll be back to pick you up in a little bit, okay?"

"Okay." She seemed fine with his leaving her, which made me very happy. She jumped into her father's arms, hugged his neck, her legs wrapped around his waist. The years of my absence had definitely bonded them.

"You be good."

"I will, Daddy."

I was nervous to be alone with her at first. Didn't really know where to begin.

"You have a pretty house, Miss Dana."

Miss Dana? We would definitely have to come up with something better than that.

"You can just call me Dana."

"Okay, Dana."

"You do know I'm your mother, right?"

"Yes, I know." She looked around the place, her red-and-black plaid skirt twisted, her red tights gathered at the ankle, the tail of her white blouse not tucked into the waist of her skirt. She wore cornrows neatly braided to the back of her head, with red bows on the ends of them. She decided to make herself at home by grabbing the remote control and plopping down on my sofa. "Do you have the Cartoon Network? Because I usually watch *Power Puff Girls* at seven, after I finish my homework. I finished my homework early today, so I could come over here."

"You did?"

"Yes." She wasn't shy at all. "Daddy and I are spending the night with Maxie tonight."

"That's nice." And I sat on the sofa next to her.

"I like spending the night with Maxie," she said. "And I have my own room over there too."

94

"So you like Maxie?"

"Yes. She's going to be my mommy soon. Then I'll have two mommies."

"Is that so?" My heart began to race. I was jealous of this woman whom my daughter spoke so highly of.

"Yes. She's going to marry my daddy, and we're going to be a family."

The big-happy-family conversation was way too much for me, so I changed the subject. "I hear you have a new little brother."

"Yes, his name is Miles." She repeated what I was sure she'd heard some adult say. "He's getting so big. Do you have any Teddy Grahams?"

"I don't have any Teddy Grahams, but I've got some Jell-O."

"I don't like Jell-O."

"Popsicles?"

"Don't like those either," she said. "Do you have some Ben & Jerry's butter pecan ice cream?"

This kid was unbelievable. *Ben & Jerry's butter pecan ice cream?*

"No. I don't have any Ben & Jerry's, but come here, let me show you something."

She followed me to the kitchen. I pulled out four slices of bread and spread peanut butter across each slice, then peeled a banana and placed slices of it onto the bread. Peanut butter and banana sandwiches were her favorite when she was three. I wondered if they still were.

We sat at my kitchen table, eating and chatting.

"I love peanut butter and banana sandwiches," she said. "Maxie makes them for me all the time."

I'd already had my fill of Maxie. It seemed that everything I tried, Maxie had already beaten me to the punch.

This was going to be more difficult than I thought. Not only did I have to rebuild a relationship with Brianna, but I had to compete with another woman for my daughter's heart. And I could just forget about winning Rico's heart if he felt even a third of what Brianna felt for this Maxie.

Was she some sort of saint?

Nobody was that perfect. I had to win my daughter's heart somehow, and let this Maxie know where her place was. Even if I had fallen down on the job, I had to find redemption, had to reclaim what was mine. She was not Brianna's mother, I was. And moreover, she wasn't even Rico's wife. Yet.

And it was time I let her know.

11

—

Rico

I sat at the bar, sipping on a Budweiser. My phone buzzed, and when I checked the number, I realized it was Maxie. She'd called twice already, and normally if I was working, I'd call her back when I got a break. But I wasn't working, and wasn't man enough to pick it up. Didn't have the heart to tell her I couldn't find work again today, so I let it roll into voice mail.

"Can't be that bad, bro."

I looked up at the brother in the suit at the other end of the bar. He turned up a Heineken, and then held it up to me as if offering a toast. His thin fingers revealed nails that were perfectly manicured; his face was clean shaven.

"Can't be worse than my troubles," he said.

"What are your troubles?" I asked, not really interested in an answer. I had my own issues, and I really didn't need the added stress of hearing his. But I listened as he poured it all out.

"Wife's leaving me." He laughed a little. "After twenty-six years, she wants a divorce. Hell, she's fifty years old and has now decided that since our kids are all grown, there's nothing left for her to stick around for. That a trip or what?"

"Yeah, man. Sorry to hear that," I said, and really meant it. "Twenty-six years is a long time."

"Twenty-six to the date, as a matter of fact," he said, twisting his gold wedding band around on his finger. "Today's our anniversary."

"Happy anniversary."

"Thanks, but it's not all that happy." He stretched his hand out to me. "I'm Harold Majors."

"Rico Elkins," I said, taking his hand in a firm shake.

"Glad to meet you, Rico."

"You think it's another dude?" I asked, then regretted bringing the subject back up.

"Nah," he said with confidence. Then his eyes grew sad. "It's me. I'm a son-of-a-gun to be married to. When our kids were small, I was never there. Too busy building my business and making my millions to see that I was destroying my family. I expected her to pick up my slack and she did it. For many years, she did it. Her desire was to finish school, and start her own business, but I wouldn't let her. Got pissed off every time she mentioned it. Thought she shouldn't even waste her time thinking about it. Needed her at home with the kids while I built my empire…"

I listened while he talked. His blank stare told me that he'd gone back to the days that he wished he could change.

"…when the kids grew up, they didn't even know me. Just knew I was Dad. You know, the guy who paid for the food and the huge mansion they lived in, and footed the bill for all their extracurricular activities. And now I'm just the guy who writes the check for the tuition at the Ivy League colleges they attend. But they don't really know me, and neither does she for that matter." He turned his Heineken up again. "I was never there."

"I don't know, man. Maybe you could change her mind. Win your family back."

"You ever tried to change the mind of a woman when she's got it made it up?"

"Yeah, you're right about that," I said and took a sip of my Bud. "But twenty-six years has got to be worth fighting for, don't you think?"

"When a woman's heart grows cold toward you, man, it's all over. And especially when it's taken this long for her to figure it out," he said. "You married?"

"Not yet," I admitted. "Engaged."

"Think long and hard about what you're doing, bro," he said. "Don't end up like me, fifty-five years old, about to be divorced, don't know my kids. I've built a lucrative business, but no one to share the success of it with anymore. Writing out a seven-thousand-dollar alimony check each month and two others for college tuition is not my idea of sharing my success."

"Seven grand?"

"And that's not including her mortgage and other living expenses. That's what she's asking for as a part of the divorce." He laughed. "She's keeping the house and two of my cars."

I could only shake my head.

"Don't let me bore you with my troubles," he said. "What are your troubles?"

"Can't find work, man. It's hard out here, even when you got skills."

"What do you do?"

"I work construction," I said. "But my desire is to start my own construction company. Build some houses. I got the education and the licenses. Matter of fact, I used to work with a developer a couple of years ago, helping him build homes here in Los Angeles. But he moved his business to the East Coast, and I wasn't ready for the change. But I learned a lot from him. I always said I would start my own business, but you gotta have start-up funds. And funds I don't have. It's hard to even get a bank to look at you for a small business loan when you don't have a steady paycheck and you've never had a business loan."

"You got a business plan?"

"Absolutely."

"I'm planning on having a house built on the beach in Orange County."

"Let me know if you need a builder." I laughed, halfway serious, halfway joking.

"You want the job?"

I looked at him, trying to figure out if he was joking. "You serious?"

"Yes, I'm serious," he said. "I'll give you a chance. Someone gave me one."

"You are serious."

"Here's my card." He pulled a business card out of the inside pocket of his jacket, and handed it to me. "Call my secretary and set up a dinner meeting with me for next week sometime. When you come, you need to have your business plan, and a plan for what you'll need financially to launch your business. If I like the plan, I'll make the investment to get you started. I know some guys...some other investors who might also want a piece of this action as well. I'll invite them to have dinner with us."

I couldn't believe what I was hearing.

"Once you get the financial backing, then I'll hire you to build my house as your first job. That will get your name out there. I have many associates and friends who might be in need of similar work. Word of mouth is going to be your best advertisement," he said. "That sound like a plan?"

"What's the catch, man? What do I have to do?"

"Make your business a success. Help somebody else once you're successful."

"Just like that, huh?"

"It's a win-win situation." He held his hand out. "You make money, I make money. I say we have a deal. What do you say?"

"We have a deal." I shook this stranger's hand, God's angel disguised in an Armani business suit.

"Good," he said, throwing a fifty-dollar bill on the bar, covering my tab and his. "Look forward to doing business with you, Rico."

"You don't know what this means to me," I said.

"I think I do."

12

Maxie

Reggi was so excited to be able to spend the entire day with her grandson. I knew when I dropped him off that he'd be spoiled by the time I got back. But it was all right. Grandparents are allowed to spoil their grandchildren every once in a while. Not to mention, she and Fred were Miles's only grandparents. So, in reality, they were filling in for my parents, the absentee grandparents.

I made the two-hour trip to San Diego to Button's shop. We had an entire day of pampering planned, but she insisted that I let her hook up my dreads first. And I needed my eyebrows arched something terrible. Then later we were meeting Alex, heading over to the spa, getting full-body massages, manicures, and pedicures, having some lunch, and making a day of it.

"Hey, girl, have a seat," Button said when I walked into the shop, the cool breeze blowing the wind chimes above the door.

I took a look around. The walls were sponged in a

beautiful forest green. African art filled the walls. Huge mirrors, trimmed in gold, were positioned on the wall above every station. Plants were all over the shop and growing out of control. The shop was nice and warmth filled the place. It made me proud to know that my baby sister was the owner of such a beautiful spot.

She was busy pulling yellow, pink, and green rollers out of the hair of the woman who sat in her chair.

"Everybody, this is my sister Maxie," she introduced me.

"Hey, Maxie," said the heavy sister with red braids using a flatiron to curl her client's hair. "I'm Lena."

"Heard a lot about you." The short sister, who was shampooing a woman, looked up and offered me a smile. "I'm Darlene."

I waved and then had a seat in the waiting area.

"And I'm Dre." The very nice-looking, very flaming brother with gold hair waved at me, as he relaxed someone's shoulder-length mane. "Where's the baby?"

"Oh, Miles?" I asked, surprised that he knew about my child. "He's with his grandmother."

"Girl, we were looking forward to seeing him. We've heard so much about him." He smiled, and his dimples were very beautiful. "I can't believe you're really Button's sister. Y'all got the same mama? Or the same daddy?"

"Both." I looked at Button, and wondered where she'd managed to find Dre. She simply smiled.

"Girl, you are gorgeous!" he continued. He was already working my nerves with his over-the-top personality, and a voice too high pitched for a man of his build. "And that skin of yours is flawless. What do you use?"

What a waste of a handsome man, I thought.

"Nothing."

"Nothing? Aw, come on, girl. Do share," Dre insisted. He walked over toward me, and I braced myself. I wasn't used to people walking up on me like that. He didn't know that I kept my piece right inside the zipper in my purse, and although it had the safety on, it wouldn't take but a minute to get it ready.

Button must've sensed my uneasiness, because she offered me a look that said Dre was harmless.

"You see this face? I have to wear foundation just to cover up the blackheads and blemishes. I really need to know your secret," he said, waving a flaming-hot flatiron in the air.

"There's no secret," I insisted. "I just eat healthy and drink lots of water."

"I eat healthy and drink lots of water, but my skin does not look like that." He laughed, and then went back to doing hair. "Since you don't wanna tell me how you keep your skin flawless, tell me how you snagged that gorgeous man of yours. Umm-hmmm, that's what you can do."

My glance shot across the room toward Button. Puzzled again.

"I showed him you and Rico's picture."

"He is fine." Dre grinned, and everyone laughed.

"Get out of her business, Dre," Lena said. "You always up in somebody's business."

"Oh don't get me started on you, Miss Lena. I was trying to be nice since we got company," he said. "But we won't even discuss that sorry man of yours."

"Dre, behave," Button said.

"She started it, Beatrice." Dre said her name in such a feminine manner. He poked his lip out. "I was not even talking to her. I was talking to Maxie. This was an A-and-B conversation, and she just saw her way in."

"You are such a little punk, Dre," Lena said.

"Can y'all chill? This is my sister's first time in my shop. I'm trying to make a good impression, and here y'all are acting a fool."

"We just keepin' it real. Button, you know this is what we do every single day," Dre said. "Don't mind us, Maxie. We fight like this all the time. And this is mild compared to later on in the day, when we really get all the way live."

"He ain't lying about that," Lena agreed.

"Hey, just be yourselves," I said, and grabbed an *Essence* magazine from the coffee table and began flipping through the pages. "Pretend I'm not even here."

Button turned up the radio, and Jill Scott was singing about living her life like it's golden.

"Pump that up a little bit more, girl. That is my song," Dre said, and sang each word right along with Jill. His voice was high pitched and sounded like Jill's; sounded as if he sang in somebody's church choir. He moved his hips to the music.

The chimes above the door jingled every time someone entered the shop. A short, dark gentleman entered, carrying a briefcase.

"We ain't got no money today, Benny," Dre said, in between singing.

"How's everybody doing?" Benny asked, dressed in a suit like a Muslim selling bean pies on the street corner. He opened his briefcase anyway. "I got sterling silver earrings, necklaces, and bracelets."

"I'm broke today, Benny," Lena said.

"You broke every day," Dre said to Lena.

"Shut up, Dre," Lena said, but took a look at the loot Benny had in his briefcase anyway.

"Can you come back at the end of the week?" Button asked.

"You mean the end of the month," Dre said. "Or the end of the year. Matter of fact, don't even come back this way, little boy. When you walk past Beatrice's House of Beauty, just keep on walking, honey."

"Button, you need to get a leash for him," Benny said.

"Oh no, you didn't." Dre pretended to be offended.

"You don't even wanna look at the earrings I have, Button?" he asked, and pulled out a pair despite Dre's carrying on.

"They're nice," Lena told Button.

"Let me show you." He walked toward Button's station, held them up to her ears. "I know you like these."

"Yeah, they are nice." Button sighed, observing her reflection in the mirror. "How much, Benny?"

"Normally, I sell them for thirty-five. But for you, twenty-five," Benny said.

"Excuse me for a second, Miss Glover," Button said to the woman in her chair, and then reached into the pocket of her jeans. "All I got is fifteen."

"This is a fifty-dollar pair of earrings, Button."

"Fifteen is all I got," Button insisted, and I almost offered to give her the other ten, but realized she was engaging in the art of negotiation. "Guess I'll have to pass until next time, Benny. Come back at the end of the week."

"Gimme the fifteen." Benny snatched the bills before Button could change her mind, and handed her the earrings. "You messin' with my money, girl."

"Thank you, Benny. Come and see me next week and I'll get the bracelet too."

"I will," he said.

"Now get on up out of here, Hustle Man," Dre said, and Benny ignored him.

He packed up his briefcase, and when leaving, held the door for a short sister wearing her hair almost bald and carrying a couple of greasy paper bags from a take-out joint.

"Okay, who had the two-piece chicken and biscuit basket?" she asked.

"That was me," Dre said. "Please tell me you remembered the hot sauce this time."

"Yes, I remembered the hot sauce, Dre," she said.

"I had the wings," Lena said. "Button, you want some of these wings?"

"No thanks. Maxie and I are going out for lunch after I do her hair," Button said, as she finished up with Miss Glover. "I'm ready for you, Maxie."

I walked over to her chair, the smell of chicken wings pleasing my nostrils, causing my stomach to growl.

Miss Glover handed Button four twenties.

"You need some change, Miss Glover?"

"No, baby," Miss Glover said. "I'll see you in a couple of weeks."

"I got you down for ten o'clock. You take care."

"All right." Miss Glover threw her purse onto her shoulder and walked out, strutting with her new hairdo.

I climbed into Button's chair and she draped a cape around me, securing it around my neck.

"How was your drive down?"

"It was a nice drive," I said. "I just rolled my window down, and pumped up some Miles Davis."

"You and Miles Davis. I can't get with him."

"It's an acquired taste." I laughed.

"I guess," she said. "What did you decide about Rico's birthday?"

"I want to throw him a party."

"Really?"

"Yep. Maybe I'll have it at his parents' house. They have this huge house, with a pool. I'll invite his brothers and sisters, and maybe a few of his friends."

"I'll help you."

"Good. It's a plan then," I told her. "I'm planning on ordering his cake when I get back to L.A."

"And I know someone who can cater the party for you, for the low-low."

"Cool," I told her. "Guess what else?"

"What?"

"I'm going to propose to Rico on his birthday."

"Okay. But he's already asked you to marry him."

"Right. And I said no, because I wasn't ready. But I'm ready now. So, to make his birthday extra special, I'm going to ask him to marry me, right there in front of his whole family and all of his friends."

"That is so sweet." Dre worked his way into our conversation, placing his hand over his heart, still holding that flatiron.

"I think so too," Button said, pulling on my hair. "I'm glad you finally came to your senses and realized that Rico is a good man. You're practically married anyway."

"I know, I know," I told her. "That's why I'm trying to make things right. He deserves better than what I've been giving him lately."

"Speaking of Brianna's mother…" she said.

"Were we talking about Brianna's mother?"

"She just came to mind. What's going on with her and Brianna?"

"They've had one visit together so far."

"How did that go?"

"Okay, as far as I know," I said. "I hope it works out. I think she should be a part of Brianna's life. It's important."

"You inviting her to the party?"

"I said she should be a part of Brianna's life, not mine and Rico's." I laughed. "I'm not crazy."

"Whew. I'm glad about that," she said. "You had me worried."

When Frankie Beverly came on the radio, everyone shouted "Hey" in unison.

"Can you please turn that up, Button?" Lena asked.

Button did, and we all sang the words to "Joy and Pain," as if we were at a Maze concert.

13

—

Rico

Heading toward Santa Monica, I hopped on the 10. The Lobster was an upscale restaurant where I would meet my future business partners. My truck was valet parked, and I bounced inside with fifteen minutes to kill before Harold Majors and his colleagues were scheduled to show up. I admired the all-glass building, which overlooked the Pacific Ocean and the Santa Monica Pier. The place was lively as I sat at the bar, which opened out onto an open-air patio. I took a quick glance at the menu and had already decided that at these prices, I would just be having a salad. I ordered a Coke, as I didn't want to appear to be an alcoholic who had to have a drink in the middle of the day.

Wanted to keep my head clear.

"Just a Coke?" Harold Majors had walked up behind me, and I hadn't even noticed. He extended his hand to me, and I shook it. "Give this man a real drink, would you, Larry?" he asked the bartender. "And give me a black Russian."

"I'll just have the Coke," I told the bartender.

Majors looked crisp and polished in a tailored gray pin-striped suit.

"Rico Elkins, meet Jeff Donaldson and Mark Williams." He introduced me to the two brothers who accompanied him. I shook both their hands. "We have a table over here."

I sat facing the window, wanting to take in the view of the ocean. I usually never sat with my back to the door. It was just one of those things I never did. Just in case something jumped off, I wanted to be prepared. But the ocean was so beautiful, I wanted to take it all in.

"Did you bring your proposal?" Majors asked.

"Sure did."

I handed him my business plan, which was neatly arranged in a brown folder. I'd gone to Kinko's and made a few extra copies so that everyone could have one. I passed the other two across the table.

Mark Williams studied his copy carefully.

"My beautiful fiancée, who is also an English major and a professional writer, was very instrumental in helping me write the plan," I said. Maxie had made my business plan look like a million bucks, and I could tell right off that these dudes thought it was impressive.

Jeff Donaldson glanced up at me with skeptical eyes, as he flipped to the second page. "What experience do you have?" he asked.

"I worked with a developer for a few years, learned the trade well. I have a bachelor's in business management, and I have a contractor's license."

"Umm-hmm." Jeff nodded, still giving the plan a thorough look over.

"This looks good," Mark Williams said, finishing a shot of Jack Daniel's as the waitress immediately placed another in front of him.

"Are you ready to order?" she asked, and no one had looked over the menu.

"Give us a minute, sweetheart," Jeff told our waitress and she disappeared.

"You've come highly recommended," Mark said. "Majors here has a great deal of confidence in you. He thinks you're worth the investment."

"No doubt," Majors said. "I can tell he's serious about what he wants."

"Who will you hire to do the work? You got employees lined up?" Jeff asked.

"Got several young brothers who are looking for work, and willing to work. Have the experience," I said confidently, but prayed my boys from the hood would come through for me. They were always complaining that they needed work, had mouths to feed. I was willing to give them a chance, bring them along.

"What about subcontractors and suppliers?"

"Got them lined up as well."

When the waitress returned, Majors said, "We'll just have our usual, Sarah. Lunch is on me today." He then ordered for everyone else. "Give Jeff here the lobster and avocado salad. He's supposed to be on a diet."

Jeff was a heavy guy, who could use a diet, and a round on the weights at the gym, but I wasn't one to talk. I hadn't set foot in the gym for at least three months.

"Mark's gonna have the angus burger, as usual." He smiled at Sarah, and she smiled back as if they knew each other outside of the beautiful beachfront restaurant. "But I'm sure he doesn't care that some poor cow had to suffer for it."

"You're right," Mark said. "I don't care."

"Don't tell me, you're having the ahi carpaccio." Sarah flirted with Majors.

"You know me too well." Majors flirted with the beautiful sister with nice round hips and shoulder-length brown hair. She giggled and very comfortably placed her hand on his shoulder. "Rico, you should try the scallops. They're wonderful."

I wasn't usually down with people making decisions for me, particularly when I was trying to impress somebody. But since I'd never eaten at the place, I took Majors's advice and ordered the scallops.

As the waitress disappeared, Mark continued to study my business plan.

"I've seen enough," he said, and I bit my bottom lip, suddenly wishing I had written it myself, in my own words. *He hates it,* I thought, as I attempted to do something with my hands other than clasp them tightly together.

"Tell me what it is you want to do, Rico," Jeff said.

Majors must've noticed that I was a bit uncomfortable.

"Just tell them what you told me the other day," he said.

"I work construction," I began. "But my desire is to start my own company. Build some houses. I've got some development experience. I used to work with a developer here in Los Angeles, and he trained me well. I'm looking for the financial backing for my business, but it's hard to get a bank to look at you for a small business loan when you've never had a business loan."

"I told him that if I liked his plan, I would be willing

to give him the financial backing for his business," Majors said. "And after looking over his plan, I think it's a worthwhile investment."

"I like the plan," Mark said. "It's very well written."

"I like it too, Mr. Elkins," Jeff said. "And whatever Majors is investing in your business, I'll match it. I trust Majors. The three of us started out in business together many years ago, and we were a lot like you. Had skills and experience, but broke."

"As a joke," Majors said.

"Broke wasn't even the word." Mark laughed.

"The point is, someone took a chance on us," Majors said. "We were twenty-four years old, fresh out of college, when we started our first company. An old man, a friend of my father's, took a chance on us. And all he asked in return is that we help someone else along the way."

"And we've more than done that," Jeff said. "I've lost count of the number of young men and women like you whose businesses we've invested our money and time in."

"Successful businesses too," Mark said.

"A couple of them failed, but overall the investments have been worthwhile. It's all a matter of intuition," Majors interjected. "And I've got a good feeling about you, Rico. If I didn't believe in you, we wouldn't even be here right now. But from the moment I met you, I knew you had what it takes to succeed."

"And he's got a keen eye," Jeff said.

"I'm impressed," Mark said, and extended his hand to me. "We have a deal or what?"

"We sure do." I smiled and shook his hand.

"Rico, I'll have my secretary draft up an agreement.

You can come by my office next week and we'll get your signature."

"Sounds good," I said and resisted the urge to pull out my cellular and call Maxie.

14

—

Maxie

After Button finished tightening up my locks, she and I met Alex at a little Mexican spot at San Diego's Pacific Beach for lunch. And after one too many margaritas, the three of us headed to the spa for manicures, pedicures, and massages that made us feel as if we were having an out-of-body experience. Dante, Button's Adonis-looking masseuse, rubbed my shoulders with precision, his fingertips massaging the tight spots in my back and relieving every inch of it from the stress that had taken up residence there. I moaned with pleasure as therapeutic candles burned around the room, and the scent of sweet almond massage oil floated through the air. The speakers in the corners of the ceiling pumped out stress-relieving music that took me to a place of serenity, and I closed my eyes. I became lost in the warmth and gentleness of Dante's hands.

"I might have to take you home with me," I told him.

He laughed. I was serious.

"I do make house calls."

"To L.A.?"

"Now that might be a problem," he said. "But we might be able to work something out."

"I'm just kidding, bro," I said. "But I will have to come visit you every now and then."

"You do that, Maxie," he said. We'd become old friends. "Now, if you'll just turn over on your back."

I did as Dante asked.

"How's it going over there, Maxie?" Button asked, as another masseuse, Angelo, worked the knots from her lower back.

"I'm trying to talk Dante here into going back to L.A. with me." I laughed. "But he ain't trying to hear it."

"I needed this so badly," Alex said, and closed her eyes while Toby massaged her neck and shoulders.

"Does Nick know where you are?" Button started.

"Of course he does." She laughed. "At the spa."

"I mean does he know you drove your behind down here to San Diego?"

Once she'd rushed Ashley and Nicholas Jr. off to school and run some errands for her husband, Alex decided to drive the two hours to San Diego to meet Button and me for lunch.

"Not technically," she said. "But I did tell him I was meeting my sisters for lunch and a massage."

"That's what I thought." Button laughed.

"When can I see some of your art?" I asked her, still curious about this talent of hers.

"Maxie, it's not really art. It's just a hobby really."

"She's being modest," Button said. "What about the piece with the children from every race? That one was all that."

"I'm almost finished with it," she said. "But I've had

117

to put it on hold. Been so busy with this fund-raiser that's coming up in a couple of weeks. We're raising money to fund an organization that was developed to help find children permanent homes. Kids who are victims of child abuse and orphans."

"Tell me more," I said.

"The organization was established to help find homes for the kids who never find families because people are reluctant to adopt them. Like kids with illnesses or the handicapped."

"Or the ones who are too old for anybody to want?" I chimed in.

"Yes. The teenagers who end up spending their lives in foster care because adoptive parents don't want the hassle," Alex explained. "The organization believes that there are families out there who would take on these high-risk kids if they were given the extra dollars it takes to care for them."

"And that's where your snobbish organization comes into play, right?" Button asked as Dante and the other two masseuses finished our massages and left the room. Instead of getting dressed right away, we relaxed a bit.

"My organization raises thousands of dollars for the organizations that we target," Alex explained. "We had to choose from a couple of organizations to help. It was either this one or one that fights for animal rights. I fought for this one. Thought it was a more worthy cause. And since I'm on the board of directors, I had a little pull."

"Whew, you had me nervous there for a minute," I said. "I'm glad to hear that you fought for this cause. Homeless kids are way more important than animals."

"This cause hit home for me. I haven't forgotten what

we went through. What you went through." She leaned up on her elbow. "You have to know, I was devastated being separated from you too. You were my big sister. Was supposed to take care of Button and me, and suddenly you were gone. And I went through a very difficult time when our adoptive parents told us that you were dead. I wanted to die too."

"Why were you told that I was dead anyway?" I had to ask.

"I don't think our parents meant any harm. I think they were just trying to help."

"They didn't want us worrying about you," Button explained. "It was their way of helping us move forward. Make a fresh start."

"They didn't think that telling you that would devastate you more?"

"I guess not," Button said.

"I'll never understand." I just shook my head.

"You just have to know them. They're good people, Maxie."

"Yeah." I was cynical. "I can tell. First they reject me because I was too old for them to hassle with. Then they tell my two little sisters that I'm dead to keep them from missing me. You're right. They're good people."

"It was a very hurtful time for all of us."

"I'm sorry, I didn't mean to minimize what the two of you went through, but it's not a part of my life that I'm real proud of."

"I cried every night, Maxie." That was Button.

"She really did," Alex agreed. "Our parents took us both to see a therapist. We went through so much grief. First losing Mama, then Uncle Walter, then you."

"It was very helpful talking about it," Button said.

119

"I don't think we'll ever forget the devastation of it, but at least we got to deal with it in a healthy way," Alex said.

"Have you seen a therapist, Maxie? To help you deal with your grief?"

"Nah. I can't see sitting around telling somebody all my business, and thinking that they can actually help," I said. "I dealt with it on my own. Got a job and moved on with my life."

"You never talked about it with anyone? About how you felt?"

"Sure, I mentioned it to a few people. To my girl-friends, Charlotte and Reece in Atlanta. And I talked to the two of you about it," I said.

"I'm talking about a professional, Maxie. A thera-pist," Alex said.

"Never," I told her. "I don't need a shrink."

"Maxie, you should talk to someone."

"What?"

"You should see somebody," Alex insisted.

"I think she's right, Maxie," Button said. "And Lord knows I don't agree with Alex that often. But this time, I agree."

"You need to talk things out with someone. You've got some hidden anger and pain, I can tell. Your past has probably got something to do with your reluctance to marry Rico."

"What does Rico have to do with my not wanting to see a shrink? And what does me not marrying him right away have to do with my childhood?"

"Everything!" Alex said. "I think you're afraid that if you commit to him, he'll leave you like everyone else in your life did."

120

"That's crazy."

"And remember when you told us that you almost aborted Miles when you found out you were pregnant?"

"So?"

"So, you were just afraid of being a mother because you didn't want him to endure the same things you went through as a child."

"Or maybe you were just afraid of being a mother because our mother was such a lousy one."

"Our mother wasn't lousy! You hear me?" I snapped. "She was a good mother. She just had some issues that she needed to deal with."

"Like what, Maxie?" Alex's eyes became sad. "What could've been so bad that she wanted to kill herself?"

"She had trouble feeding us for one." I always felt as if it was my duty to defend our mother.

"Oh wow. She had trouble feeding us." Alex still had some anger. "That's a good reason to kill yourself and leave your three little girls without a mother. Who did she think was going to feed us then?"

"You don't understand."

"Well, explain it to me so that I can." She stared at me, really wanting an answer.

"It was hard for her," I said, remembering the many conversations that Mama and I had. She explained things to me that she hadn't shared with Alex and Button. "Did you know that Grandpa Ellis raped her?"

"What?" Alex raised herself up on her elbows again. "When?"

"She was fifteen years old, and he forced her to have sex with him," I told them. "And when she told Grandma Ellis about it, she didn't believe her. Instead, she sent her

121

and Uncle Walter away to live with their aunt. It was Mama's Aunt Francis who raised them."

"So, that's why we never spent any time with Grandma and Grandpa Ellis?" Button asked.

"And they were very wealthy, but never offered a dime to help Mama. Even though they knew she was struggling to raise three kids," I continued. "And when they died, they left all their money to Grandpa's niece."

"Mama told you this?" Alex asked.

"Yes."

"What else did she tell you?"

"Lots of little things that later I pieced together, and was able to make sense out of them," I said, but left it at that. "She felt trapped."

"Trapped how?" Alex asked.

"It's no secret she had a serious drug problem," I said. "Did you know that she had a significant amount of drugs in her system when she died?"

"What are you saying, Maxie? That she overdosed?"

"I'm saying that maybe she was so high, she didn't know what she was doing," I said. That was the story I was most comfortable with; the one that offered the possibility that the drugs had our mother in such a state that she didn't realize what she was doing. Not the story that suggested that she would intentionally leave the lives of her three little children to chance. "Maybe she was out of her mind."

"I don't know," Button said.

"She was the only parent we had," Alex said. "Why would she get so high that she'd risk our well-being?"

"It wasn't easy for her, being a parent."

"Nobody ever said that it was easy being a parent,"

Alex said. "But I would never kill myself because things get tough. Or do so many drugs that it would cause me to make irrational decisions."

"Don't ever say what you won't do," I said. "People don't choose to get strung out."

"I still blame her, Maxie," Alex said. "I'm not letting her off the hook that easily. We should've been worth more to her. Us, her children," Alex said. "It's my children who keep me going. They are the ones who give me the strength and courage to keep going."

"I second that," Button said.

"In fact, it's my children who keep me married to a self-centered, arrogant, anal bastard like Nicholas."

I couldn't believe my ears. Alex was actually saying something negative about her beloved Nicholas. She was always so defensive when Button spoke negatively about him.

"What? You're finally seeing that the zebra has spots?" Button added.

"Shut up, Button. I don't need your sarcasm," she said. "Of course I see his spots. I saw them long ago, but I just wanted my marriage to work. Wanted to be a good wife and mother."

"And now?" I asked.

"He's a lying, cheating bastard!"

Button and I stared in amazement. She continued. "I stopped by his office last week, to take him some dinner. He was working late. I rode the elevator up the twelve flights, got off. The door was cracked just a little....I peeped in. And there they were, on the leather love seat in his office."

"What did you do?" I asked.

"I turned and walked away."

"What, you didn't say anything? You didn't let him know you saw?"

"No," she said, tears beginning to fill her eyes. "He still doesn't know I know."

"Well, do you plan on telling him?"

"No need," she said. "It's not the first time."

"What do you mean it's not the first time?"

"He's cheated before. I've found phone numbers, lipstick on the collars, credit card bills with hotel charges. All of it."

"Why are you still there, sweetie?" My heart began to ache as I witnessed the pain on my sister's face.

"The children," she said. "And he provides a nice home for us. I have a nice life."

"But he's a sleaze." Button frowned and blew air from her mouth.

"And you're not even happy," I said. "Are you?"

She didn't answer, but I knew her answer.

"Isn't your happiness worth more?"

The tears were rolling down her cheeks.

"Do you even love him, Al?"

She was silent, only cried.

"Let's talk about something else," she said, wiping her eyes. "In fact, let's just go. I've had enough massaging for one day."

She got up, wrapped the thick white robe around her body, and stormed out of the room.

15

—

Rico

It's amazing what a bottle of merlot, dimmed lights, and a few blazing candles can do for a room. I warmed the place with some Will Downing and had prepared roasted chicken, the way Ma taught me, with the new potatoes and other vegetables on the side. It was the only dish I knew how to make to perfection. And this was a night that had perfection written all over it. My meeting with Harold Majors and his rich investor friends had gone much better than expected. And I needed to celebrate.

When I heard the uneven rumbling of the garage door going up, I could barely wait for Maxie to get in the house. I'd purposely saved my news, didn't want to tell her over the phone.

"What is going on in here?" Maxie asked as she walked in carrying Miles, his diaper bag flung across her shoulder. He was knocked out, resting his head on her shoulder.

"Here, you take this." I handed her a glass of wine.

"And I'll take him, and put him in bed. Kick your shoes off, sit down, and get comfortable. I'll be right back."

I kissed her lips and then tiptoed into Miles's nursery, praying he didn't wake up. I carefully placed him in his crib, pulled his shoes off. I left the door cracked a little and rushed back to the living room, where Maxie had kicked her shoes off and had collapsed in a chair.

"How was your day?" I asked, pulling my girl up from the chair in her living room, hugging her, and moving to the sounds of Will.

"Obviously not as good as yours," she said. "Your meeting must've gone well."

"They're not only going to give me the start-up cash I need for my business, but they're going to provide me with a company truck, and Harold owns a building in Orange County that he's practically giving me, to run my business from."

"Wow."

"And I already talked to Pete and some of the other guys. They're coming to work for me."

"I'm speechless."

"We start construction on our first house next week. I spent all afternoon lining up the subcontractors and the suppliers."

"I'm so proud of you, baby." Her kiss told me she was sincere.

"I cooked for you," I boasted, proud about the dish that I'd prepared.

"You cooked?" She placed the palm of her hand over my forehead and felt for a fever.

"Roasted chicken and new potatoes."

"Your mama cooked for me."

"No, baby. I cooked for you," I said. "Okay, Ma told me how to do it, but I cooked it myself, I swear."

"And you didn't burn it?"

"It's perfect." I smiled, feeling good about my feat. "Now, come on over here to the table, sit yourself down, and sip your wine."

"You dropped Brianna off at Dana's?"

"Yes," I said, and then went to the kitchen to fix our plates. "I'm going back to pick her up in a little bit. But not before we have a chance to celebrate."

"You had a very eventful day, huh?" she said.

"Yes, I did."

I placed a steaming hot plate of chicken and veggies in front of her. The aroma floating through the air made my own mouth begin to water. I sat down and waited for her to taste my cooking.

She tasted the vegetables first.

"Veggies aren't bad."

"I hope you don't mind me using your place," I told her. "Pop's still at my place, and I wanted to make sure we had some privacy."

"I don't mind." She cut into the chicken with a steak knife and I prayed it was tender.

I watched as she placed the first bite of it into her mouth. Waited.

"Well?"

"This is really good, Rico."

"For real?"

"For real," she said. "You sure you cooked this?"

"I swear." I cut into my chicken and was very surprised to find that it was as good as she proclaimed.

Will Downing was crooning, and once we finished eating, I pulled my sweetheart up from the table and led her to the living room, where we started to slow-dance. I nibbled on her ear, kissed her lips. My hands began to probe the small of her back, as I worked my way down to her shapely hips. My manhood began to have a mind of its own, but I didn't care. Maxie was feeling my vibe, and pulled in closer.

The phone interrupted my groove.

"Let it ring," I whispered.

"Baby, it might be important."

"They'll leave a message."

"I should get it. What if it's Dana calling about Brianna?"

"You're right." I released my grip, reluctantly.

She answered it.

"Hello."

"Who is it?" I whispered anxiously, as she held the cordless up to her ear.

"Hey, Reece," she said. "Baby, it's Reece."

"Tell her I said hello," I said, disappointed, as Miles's cry rang through the room. "I'll get him."

I went into Miles's room, grabbed him from his crib, and tried quieting him. I rocked him a little, but his eyes were bright. I realized he was not going back to sleep.

When I went back into the living room, Maxie was laughing and talking to her girlfriend Reece, who lived in Atlanta. She was oblivious to Miles's crying and to our ruined moment, all wrapped up in her conversation.

"When are you coming?" she asked Reece. "For real? Charlotte too?"

I rocked Miles, who was still whimpering.

"Baby, Reece and Charlotte are coming," she said. "In a couple of weeks. They'll be here for your birthday."

"That's nice, baby."

She was so excited, I didn't want to ruin her moment by expressing my disappointment. She missed her friends like crazy, and hadn't made any new ones since moving to California. I was happy for her, but wished Reece had chosen a better moment to share her news. I needed this to be my day, my special moment. I wanted Maxie to be as excited about my news as she was about her girl-friends coming to California.

When she got off the phone, I handed her Miles and bounced out the door.

16

Dana

Alice was her usually rude self, but I didn't care because I wanted her to meet Brianna. Wanted Brianna to know her grandmother, despite the fact that she was a miserable old woman.

"Alice, meet Brianna," I told my mother. "This is your granddaughter."

"Keep it down, child. I'm trying to watch *Jeopardy* here. And I can't hear for your chattering." She sat at the kitchen table and watched the small black-and-white television that rested on the kitchen counter.

"Alice, I'm trying to introduce you to your grand-daughter. You can't even say hello?"

"Hello, I'm Alice," she said, never looking away from the television set. "Glad to meet you, Brianna."

"Hi," Brianna said.

"Have a seat," I told her. "You hungry?"

"Just a little," Brianna said.

"Didn't you feed the child before you brought her over here?" Alice asked. "This ain't a food kitchen, you know."

"I was just going to make her a peanut butter and jelly sandwich," I said.

Alice looked up at me and rolled her eyes. I made Brianna a sandwich anyway, placed it on a saucer, and set it in front of her.

"I went to see Daddy yesterday," I told Alice. "He's not doing so well."

"It's his own fault," she said.

"What? Alice, how can you say that?"

"All the dirt he did in the past. You reap what you sow, you know."

"He's very sick, Alice. The Parkinson's disease is literally eating away at him," I said. "Every day, he's getting weaker and weaker."

"What is the French Revolution?" she yelled, answering one of the questions on *Jeopardy* and completely ignoring my last comment. She laughed when she realized her answer was correct. "I need to go on that show. Show 'em how it's done."

She was absorbed in the television set. She pulled a Salem Light out of its package, lit it, and took a drag.

"He asked about you. Said he wants to see you," I told her.

"Wants to see me? What does he want to see me for? I don't have nothing to say to Henry. Nothing at all."

"He said something about making peace with you."

"There will never be any peace between your daddy and me. Not as long as he's alive." She dumped ashes in an ashtray.

"He's dying, Alice," I explained. "Why can't you open up your heart for once in your life?"

131

"I don't have a heart," she said, looking me right in the eyes, her stare piercing.

"Why don't you tell me what happened to make you hate my daddy so much?"

"I don't have anything to say about it."

"No? That's just it. You always have all these mean things to say. You never talk to me unless you're criticizing me or belittling me. You've never even tried having a conversation with me unless it was about the money I owed you for rent or something. And you've never been much of a mother to me."

"Well, that's because you shut me out. You always thought your daddy could do no wrong. Thought he was a saint," she said. "Where did I fit into your life?"

"You could've been a part of my life if you really wanted to, Alice. But instead, you gave me up to go live with Daddy."

"I gave you up, huh?"

"That's right."

"You had Sophie. You didn't need me."

"I did need you!"

"You had everything you needed." She stood. "And it wasn't me."

She looked at Brianna as if she wanted to say something. I thought she might smile at her only grandchild or say that she'd been glad to meet her. But she just looked at her. Alice's caramel skin looked nothing like mine. I was my daddy's chocolate brown. I often wondered why I didn't resemble Alice at all.

"Clean up your mess when you're finished here, Dana. And make sure you lock the door behind you."

She left the room, leaving me behind just as she had so often in my life.

"She doesn't like me very much, does she?" Brianna asked softly.

"Oh baby, it's not you," I explained. "Alice is just set in her ways."

"Why is she so mean?"

"I don't think she means to be." I often wondered the same thing myself. "But it's not directed toward you. You haven't done anything wrong. Okay?"

"Okay," she said and finished her peanut butter and jelly sandwich.

17

Maxie

While waiting for my girls to show up, I stood outside in front of the automatic glass doors, watching intently. I hadn't seen them since the day I'd packed my U-Haul and driven it across the country from Atlanta to Los Angeles.

I remember that day like it was yesterday. Charlotte had given me a tight squeeze. And I remember being worried about leaving her, because since the breast cancer had spread throughout her body, there wasn't much to hold on to when we hugged. I remember thinking that I shouldn't leave as I straightened the wig on her head, and tried smiling through my tears. But the truth was, I was uneasy.

"Don't worry about me, girlfriend," she'd said. "I'll be just fine. When I need someone's nerves to get on, I still have Reece."

"She's right about that," Reece said, and hugged me too. "I'll be taking up the slack for the both of us. You owe me, big time!"

"Besides, I don't know if I can put up with your behind when you become fat and cranky with this pregnan-
cy," Charlotte said.

"I will never be fat and cranky," I said, and rubbed
my stomach where Miles was beginning to grow. "I am
going to miss y'all, though."

"Oh sweetie, we'll miss you too," Reece said, tears
streaming down her mocha-colored face. "But we'll keep
in touch. Don't worry; it'll be as if you never left."

"Will you visit?"

"Of course we will," Reece said. "We have to come
and see the new baby. Right, Charlotte?"

"Yep, we'll come and see that wrinkled-up little rug
rat once he's born."

"Or once she's born," Reece said. "I bet it's a girl."

"If it is, I hope she has better table manners than her
mother," Charlotte said. "Now let's stop with all this
mushy stuff. You're causing my makeup to run. And this
is not cheap makeup; I paid a pretty penny for it."

"Charlotte, be nice."

"The girl is just moving to California, not out of the
country, for crying out loud," Charlotte said. "Now get
your behind in the truck. That man of yours is waiting."

"Good-bye, Charlotte," I said, and smiled. "I know
you'll miss me, even though you're playing hard."

"Yeah, yeah, yeah, good-bye." She shooed me off.

I knew she was saddened by my leaving and found
out from Reece later that she cried after I pulled off. I
knew I would miss them too. They had been my best
friends and confidantes; I didn't make a move without
consulting with them first. They were my sisters before I
found my real sisters, Button and Alex. They had been
my family for the past six years, and here I was about to

walk away from them and begin a whole new life without them. I remembered how frightened I felt that day as Rico and I drove away in that U-Haul, my car hitched to the back of it. I rolled down my window, waved good-bye to my girls, and blew them kisses.

Although I talked to them nearly every day, that day was the last time I'd seen them. Until today. And I was so excited, I couldn't keep still.

I checked my watch, waited some more. Watched as people retrieved taxi cabs, throwing their bags into the trunks and speeding off from LAX. I glanced over at Rico, who was waiting in the car. He smiled, and I waved. He couldn't understand why I couldn't just sit in the car and wait for Charlotte and Reece. Why I just had to stand next to the door, in fear that I might miss them. He was still a bit perturbed because I hadn't shown as much enthusiasm about his business venture as I had about seeing Reece and Charlotte. In all honesty, I was thrilled for him, and was relieved that he could finally stop pounding the pavement for work and feel like the strong man that he is. However, he didn't understand the dynamics of my friendship with Reece and Charlotte, and because of it, he was a bit intimidated. Friendships between women run deeper than most men will ever understand.

"Wanna make sure they see me when they come out," I told him, but the truth was, I was so excited I couldn't sit still. The anticipation had me bouncing around.

I peeked inside the window at the baggage claim and checked my handwritten notes to make sure I had the right flight information.

"All I'm saying, Charlotte, is you could've just let it

go." I spotted Reece first, as she walked through the automatic doors of an entrance opposite of where I stood, arguing with Charlotte about something and shaking her head in frustration. And I knew that look on her face, because Charlotte had frustrated me many a day.

"Let it go? No, Reece! I wasn't about to let it go," Charlotte said. "She made a comment about my wig, and I did not appreciate it!"

"Charlotte, she didn't say the wig was ugly. She was simply inquiring about it."

"Well, she should've simply kept her mouth shut. I wasn't all up in her business like she was mine," Charlotte said. "Did you see me all up in her business, Reece?"

"Charlotte, please," Reece said, and then looked up and spotted me. "There's Maxie. Hey, girl!"

Reece rushed toward me, and hugged me tightly.

"What is Charlotte fussing about?" I had to ask, as I hugged her back.

"Some woman on the flight asked about her wig and she went off. Made it a bigger issue than it had to be," Reece said.

"No, Reece, she made it an issue when she asked her sarcastic questions about it," Charlotte corrected her, and then hugged me too.

This time when I hugged Charlotte, I smiled because she'd gained her weight back and she looked healthy again, the way she had looked before the cancer.

"Charlotte, you look good."

"Thank you, girl. I've decided not to let this cancer kick my butt," she said. "You don't look too bad yourself, Maxie. L.A. has been good to you."

"That's good living and a good man," Reece said. "Where is Rico anyway?"

"He's in the car, waiting at the curb for us," I said. "We need to hurry because he's double-parked."

Rico threw Charlotte's three Louis Vuitton bags and Reece's one bag on wheels into the back of his Explorer.

"Hi, Rico," Reece said, hugging him.

"How's it going?" he asked, situating their bags.

"Rico," Charlotte said, and hugged him too. "So nice to see you again."

"Good to see you too, Charlotte. You look good," he said, and he was right.

"Thanks," Charlotte said, handing him her garment bag. "Can we get something to eat when we leave here? I'm starved."

"Yep, and I have the perfect spot," I said.

"Not one of your greasy spoon ghetto spots, I hope, Maxie," Charlotte said. "You know the ones that you and Reece like to drag me to. I'm not up for all the lard today."

"You can choose the place, Charlotte," I said. "And then I thought we'd do something...uh...you know... spontaneous."

"Spontaneous? Like what, Maxie?" Charlotte was skeptical.

"You know I'm game for whatever," Reece said. "And I like the sound of spontaneous."

"I thought we'd go to Tijuana."

"Tijuana what?" Charlotte asked. "Mexico?"

"It's just across the border." I smiled and began doing a little dance right there in front of the airport. "There's lots of fun and shopping."

"I say we go home where I can kick these shoes off and get comfortable," Charlotte said. "My dogs are killing me."

"I say let's go to Mexico," Reece said.

"You say let's go to Mexico, huh, Reece?" Charlotte rolled her eyes. "We fly clear across the country to see this child, and now she wants to take us out of the country. You have serious issues, Maxie."

"Charlotte, step outside of your box," I said.

"Why can't we just do what ordinary people do when they vacation? Eat and relax."

"Because, my dear"—I wrapped my arm around Charlotte's waist—"we are not ordinary."

"Whatever, let's just go get this over with."

In Tijuana, we began our daylong expedition by taking a stroll along the famous *Avenida Revolución,* Tijuana's main strip, where you could find cheap blankets, cigarettes, pottery, and tequila. The minute we crossed the border, we were immediately rushed by shabbily dressed food vendors, and children trying to sell us their woven bracelets and chewing gum, begging for change or asking for a drink of our cold bottled water. In Tijuana's mild sixty-seven degrees and beautiful sunshine, we took in the ambiance, shopping for authentic handmade Mexican crafts and artworks. Shopkeepers enticed us into their establishments by entertaining us with musicians dressed in tight red serapes and huge sombreros.

"Let me show you something." The Mexican dude in a sombrero reached for my elbow and guided me into his shop.

You were often asked to step inside someone's shop, while others humored you by bluntly saying, "Give me a chance to rip you off." Natives peddled their items, while tourists haggled over the prices until a satisfactory price was agreed upon. Enticing smells of spices floated through the air from food that you dared not partake of for fear of getting sick. It was usually in the best interest of the tourists to pass up on the grub, although it literally made your mouth water at the smell of it.

"Man, that chicken is definitely smelling good," my vanilla sweetheart said, rubbing his stomach.

"Come try." The woman selling roasted chicken with chipotle glaze tried to entice Rico by offering him a free sample.

"No, thank you," he said, and kept moving. He turned to Reece and Charlotte. "Just so you know, we don't eat the food down here."

"Really? Why?" Charlotte asked.

"Because we just don't."

"But it smells so good." Reece's nose followed the chicken wing that was now on a plate, and being offered to her graciously. "One little chicken wing won't hurt."

"Keep walking, Reece," I told her, and began checking out some Mexican sombreros.

"Hola," I said to the woman who was peddling her handmade pieces. I asked her how much. *"El sombrero. Cuanto cuesta?"*

"Es barato," she responded, telling me that the sombrero was cheap, and then went on to tell me that she could offer me a good price.

She and I began haggling in Spanish over the price of a sombrero, until I finally got her down to a price that interested me.

"What do you need a sombrero for, Maxie?" Charlotte asked.

"Because I need to show you my version of the Mexican hat dance." I smiled at Charlotte.

"Ooh, I want a sombrero too," Reece said. "Can you negotiate a price on one for me too, Maxie?"

I talked the lady into giving me a two-for-one deal.

Reece and I placed our sombreros on our heads, walked the avenue arm in arm. Then I threw my hat on the ground and began doing my Mexican hat dance for Charlotte. She tried to resist a laugh, but couldn't resist for long.

"You are so silly, Maxie." She laughed.

"Let me show you how it's done, Charlotte," I said, dancing around my hat.

Reece had hers thrown on her head, her braids underneath brushing her shoulders. She popped her head into several little shops, collecting pottery and a few souvenirs, placing them in her woven bag until it was full. Charlotte bought a beautiful handmade blanket and a pack of cigarettes.

"What are the cigarettes for?" I had to ask my friend, who'd recently been diagnosed with cancer.

"I smoke when I get depressed," she said. "Not like I can get cancer or anything."

"Give me those." Reece snatched them from her.

"It was a joke, Reece," Charlotte said.

"Well, it's not funny." Reece rolled her eyes at Charlotte.

She could be downright tacky sometimes.

When the sun went down, and nighttime fell upon us, the traditional music that had been pumped from one of the street vendors was now being drowned out by a Mexican version of Michael Jackson's "Billie Jean." To Charlotte's dismay, Reece and I started singing it in English, and dancing while sporting our sombreros.

"I swear I can't take y'all nowhere," Charlotte said, and pretended not to know us.

"Oh come on, Charlotte." I laughed. "You know you know the words to 'Billie Jean'."

"I know the words, but I am not interested in singing it in the middle of Tijuana, in front of God and everybody else," she said. "And the two of you shouldn't sing it so loud. People are watching."

We sang "Billie Jean" and bounced down the avenue through the crowds of folks, who looked at us as if we'd lost our minds.

"Come on, Charlotte, you need a drink," Rico said, rescuing her from us. He locked arms with her. "Let's go see what they got in here."

Rico led Charlotte into a bar with a sign that read TWO-FOR-ONE MARGARITAS. PISTA DE BAILE.

"Now that's what I'm talking about," I said, following them inside. "They got a dance floor!"

Rico and Charlotte ordered the two-for-one margaritas, while Reece and I opted for shots of tequila. I placed salt between my thumb and forefinger, sucked on a lemon, sucked the salt from my hand, and downed my shot in one gulp.

"Baby, do you think you should be doing the tequila shots again?" Rico asked. And then he tried to whisper, "You know what happened last time we were down here."

"What happened the last time?" Reece asked, placing salt on her hand, tasting her lemon and salt, and then turning up her shot glass.

"I had to carry her to the car, and she was passed out all the way from San Diego to L.A."

"Dag, for real?" Charlotte asked.

"No more tequila shots for you then, girlfriend," Reece said.

"Just one more, and that's it," I said, tossing the last one down my throat after the bartender obliged with another.

Reece dragged Rico out onto the dance floor, and they started dancing to what sounded like the Mexican version of "Do the Hustle." Before long, everyone on the dance floor was following their lead and doing the Hustle.

Charlotte and I sat at the bar.

"So how have you been, Charlotte? I mean, really doing?" I asked once we were alone.

"Better than ever," she said, and she looked so healthy and happy that I actually believed her. Her head bounced to the music, as she took a sip of her margarita.

"You look good."

"I feel great. My cancer is in remission. I've gone back to work." She smiled. "And don't tell Reece, but I'm getting married too."

"What?"

"The guy, Herb, who I met before you moved away . . ." Her eyes searched mine. "Remember him?"

"The one you met at the blues club in Atlanta?" I remembered. "He lives in Dallas, right?"

"That's him. We've kept in close contact, and he's been flying to Atlanta from Dallas just about every other weekend to see me. He asked me to move to Dallas."

"Get out of here."

"I'm serious." She smiled again, and became giddy.

"What did you say?"

"I told him I wasn't moving to Dallas to shack up with him! So..." She hesitated and smiled.

"So what?"

"So, he asked me to marry him," she said. "I haven't told Reece yet, though. Don't want her to think that I'm abandoning her."

"She won't think that," I said. "She has Kevin, and they're still in the honeymoon stage. And her family is still there, right?"

"Yeah, but you don't know Reece like I do. She'll genuinely be happy, but inside she'll be in turmoil. Like when you left. It took her a while to get back to her old self again, even with Kevin there. The three of us had been tight for so long, and then suddenly you were gone. We missed you, girl."

"I missed you too," I admitted. "It took me a while to get used to L.A. and motherhood, and all that. It was all an adjustment. And I'm still trying to get it together."

"But you did it, girl. You moved clear across the country, not knowing what your life would become, and here you are looking as wonderful as ever," she said. "I'm proud of you, Maxie. I really am."

"Thanks, Charlotte. That means a lot coming from you."

"Now I'm ready to take my life to the next level."

"Then do it."

"I'm just afraid of leaving Reece," she said. "Look at her."

We both took a look at Rico and Reece, who were still doing the Hustle on the dance floor. I had to smile.

"She's a trip."

"She is that," Charlotte agreed. "Now let's talk about you. Maxie, when exactly do you plan on marrying Rico?"

"Since I haven't accepted any of his proposals for

marriage, I have a surprise for him on his birthday. I'm going to propose to him."

"At his birthday party?"

"Yep. Right there in front of his family, God, and everybody."

"Are you sure you want to do that? I think marriage proposals should be done in private."

"I disagree," I told her. "I think it's something that should be shared with the people you both love. Right out there in the open. In front of the whole world."

"You would think that." Charlotte sipped her drink. "I don't think you leave anything to be desired, Maxie."

"True that."

"What am I gon' to do with you?" she said. "Got me down here in Mexico, drinking margaritas and listening to disco-era songs in a Mexican bar. Only you."

"Tell me you're not having fun." I laughed and waited for Charlotte's response. "And we can leave right now!"

"I am having fun."

"Then come on, let's get out there and shake our booties."

I pulled Charlotte out onto the dance floor, and we danced like John Travolta did in *Saturday Night Fever* to the Bee Gees' retro eighties tune "Staying Alive."

18

Maxie

Thirty-seven is so close to forty.

But not quite. I had to convince Rico that it was a blessing to see another birthday. Not everyone is so lucky; he should be grateful for another year.

"It's easy for you to say, when it's not you who's pushing forty."

"I'm not that far behind," I said and gave my man a kiss he'd remember for the next thirty-seven years. "What you wanna do for your birthday?"

"Nothing." He moped around the bedroom, pulling on a pair of sweats and the oldest T-shirt he could find. "Going to shoot some hoops with Duane and some of the other guys. Think I need to exercise more, I'm getting thick around my midsection. Need to find my way back to the gym. And I need to start eating better too."

"I like your love handles." I rubbed his stomach and pinched him on his sides.

"Baby, nobody likes love handles," he said.

"Well, I do," I said and hugged him tightly around his waist.

"One of Duane's partners died of a heart attack last week. He was only thirty-nine years old," he said, and pulled away from my embrace.

He grabbed the remote control, flipped the channel to ESPN, and found a pair of tube socks in the bottom drawer of my dresser. He sat on the edge of the bed and pulled them on, his eyes steady on the television.

"What can I do to cheer you up, baby?" I asked. "Today's your birthday, and you seem so unhappy. You should be celebrating. Life is a celebration!"

"Right," he said dryly, pulling his sneakers on and lacing them up.

"I have plans for you tonight." I smiled and sat on his lap, pressing my nose against his. "I'm taking you to your favorite place for dinner. Then we're coming back here, and I'm gon' show you what a birthday celebration really is, if you know what I mean. Can you dig it?"

"Sounds good, baby." He stood, and I stumbled as I fell from his lap. "But what about Charlotte and Reece? I figured you might wanna hang with them. They came all the way out here to see you."

"They have plans. Charlotte's got some clients here in L.A., and they have some event going on. She's taking Reece with her."

"You don't wanna go with them?"

"I want to hang out with you, baby. Celebrate your birthday with you."

"That's sweet," he said. "But you know, if you change your mind and decide you want to hang with your friends, I'm okay with that."

"I need you here by five o'clock," I said, completely ignoring his comment. "I know how you and Duane can lose track of time when you get together."

"We're just going to shoot some hoops, maybe have a couple of brews."

"Then you shouldn't have any problem making it here on time."

"I'll meet you back here by four, I promise."

"Don't be late, Rico," I said. "You know how busy it can get at the Grand Lux on a Saturday night."

"I know, I know." He kissed my forehead. "I'll be here, baby, I promise."

He put his watch around his wrist and grabbed his keys from the nightstand.

"Have fun," I told him.

He left, but not soon enough.

I had already warned Duane to keep Rico busy all day, and not to show up at their parents' house for any reason. Reece, Charlotte, Reggi, and I had some major decorating and preparing to do for Rico's surprise birthday party. Reggi had already gotten started on the decorations, and when I'd spoken with her on the phone, she'd said that the pool guy was there cleaning the pool. The caterers were scheduled to show up by three, and Rico's sister Elise was making her famous rum punch.

I changed Miles and laid some clothes out for Brianna, who was spending the day with Dana. This would actually be her first sleepover with her mother, and she was excited about it. I was happy that Dana had turned out to be all right, and that she and Brianna were beginning to build a relationship. I helped her pull her Sponge-

148

Bob shirt over her head, then went to find out what the wonderful smells were coming from my kitchen.

Charlotte was wearing my apron, and cooking turkey bacon and scrambled eggs.

"Hope you're hungry," she said.

"It smells good, but you and I both know you can't cook to save your soul," I said, and grabbed the OJ from the refrigerator. Poured myself a glass.

"I'm a much better cook than I used to be, I'll have you know, Miss Thing. Now get a plate off the shelf and have a seat."

"Where's Reece?"

"Right here," Reece said, walking slowly into the kitchen, holding a wet cloth over her forehead.

"What's wrong with you?" I asked.

"Hangover," she said.

"That tequila kicking your butt?"

"I can't believe I was trying to keep up with your alcoholic behind last night."

"I can't believe it either." I laughed. "You know you can't hang with me."

"And you are not a spring chicken anymore, either, Reece," Charlotte added, and placed a load of scrambled eggs and overcooked turkey bacon onto my plate.

"I know she is not up in here trying to cook," Reece said, and had a seat at my kitchen table. "Who gave her that apron?"

"We won't even discuss who can't cook in this room," Charlotte said. "I don't think either one of you heifers has a Martha Stewart bone in your body."

"But we know our limitations," I said. "At least some of us do."

I felt sorry for Reece. I knew that a hangover was

never a welcome state, and particularly not when drinking Cuervo Gold tequila. She looked like death warmed over.

"It's too early for jokes," Reece said.

"Oh sweetie, let me hook you up with an elixir," I told her, and commenced to cracking a few raw eggs into a glass.

Before I could even finish mixing up my concoction, Reece was running to the guest bathroom, her head buried in the toilet. It was definitely going to be a long day.

At Reggi's, I loaded the CD player with some of Rico's old-school tunes. Button showed up with her caterer friend, carrying loads of chicken, shrimp, and little salmon and spinach appetizers. Charlotte helped Reggi hang streamers and blow up balloons. Rico's sister, Rachel, came through the door carrying Rico's butter pecan birthday cake, which she'd agreed to pick up from the bakery for me. Reece was passed out in the guest bedroom, trying to get herself together so that she wouldn't miss out on the festivities that were ahead.

When I played Aretha Franklin's "Respect," it must've struck a nerve with Reggi because she began singing along with Aretha.

"R-E-S-P-E-C-T!" she said. "That's what I'm talking about, Aretha! Turn that up, Maxie, would you please?"

I did as she asked, and she sang even louder as she hung blue-and-white streamers in her living room. Charlotte and I joined in on the lyrics.

"Y'all wouldn't know nothing about that," Reggi said. "Before your time, girls."

"I know a little something, Reggi," I insisted.

"Yeah, right. You still wet behind the ears." She

laughed. "Do either of you know how to play bid whist?"

"Not me," Charlotte said.

"I can get by," I told her. "But spades is more my game."

"Come on in here and let me show you how to play." She pulled a deck of cards out of a drawer in the living room. "When my sisters Margaret and Minnie get here, they're gonna try and whip your behinds in bid whist, and make fools out of you if you don't know the game."

Charlotte and I followed Reggi to the kitchen table, where she shuffled the cards and tapped the deck on the wooden table. She spent the next hour showing us how to play bid whist like professionals.

19

Dana

Hospitals always seemed cold, eerie, and depressing. I tapped on my father's door and then slowly pushed it open. He lay there in his bed, hospital gown on, eyes opened wide.

"Hi, Daddy," I whispered and he forced a smile.

Brianna stepped in after me, and his eyes lit up at the sight of her.

"Bri—" he said slowly, his speech slurred, and drool creeping down the side of his mouth. He twitched nervously, as the Parkinson's disease had destroyed his nervous system.

"Yes, sir." She smiled back at my father, and he tried unsuccessfully to lift his hand to reach out to her.

"He's trying to reach for your hand," I explained to her.

She grabbed his hand, and stood there nervously, looking back at me for approval.

"This is your grandfather," I told Brianna.

"Pa Pa," Daddy told her, struggling with each syllable, as he held on to her small hand. There were tubes in his nose and something taped across his chest underneath his gown.

"Hi, Pa Pa," she said.

A tear crept down his cheek as he forced a smile.

"Where's Sophie?" I asked, surprised that his wife wasn't at his side. She'd been there every day and night since Daddy had been hospitalized.

He struggled to tell me, but couldn't quite get it out.

"It's okay, Daddy. Don't try to talk."

It was hard seeing my strong father so weak, his nervous system nearly shut down.

"How are you feeling?" I asked.

He nodded his head to say he was feeling okay. My father lied, knowing that the Parkinson's disease was slowly eating him away.

He was in the latter stages of it, and each time I looked at him, I wanted to break down crying. It was hard seeing him this way, but I knew I had to be strong. He had been strong for me all of my life, and it was the least I could do to return the favor.

"The television series is going fine, Daddy. When you get better, I want you to come down to the studio and see me."

He smiled.

He was the only one who had believed in my dream of becoming an actress. Everyone else just criticized me and told me that I needed to find a real job. They said becoming an actress was just a fantasy of mine, and I needed to wake up and stop dreaming. He was always supportive, even when I didn't get the roles that I'd auditioned for. He kept the faith even when I'd given up, assuring me that if I kept trying, I'd eventually land a role in something.

When I was a little girl, he made sure I took dance lessons, piano lessons, whatever my heart desired. He was sure I'd make something of myself.

"Daddy, I'm going to be a star," I'd say.

"Yes, you are, baby girl," he'd say, and I believed him. In my eyes, my father had always been the strongest and smartest man alive.

"You should see me, Daddy." I smiled, trying to keep from crying at the sight of how vulnerable my father was right then. "I'm really a good actress."

He started coughing, and I picked up his plastic rose-colored pitcher and poured him a glass of water. I lifted the plastic cup to his mouth and he attempted to drink, water rolling down the front of his gown.

Brianna looked frightened, and I knew that I couldn't stay much longer.

"Al-lice," he whispered.

He'd been asking for my mother lately, wanted her to come and see him. For some reason, it was important that he see her. He had his reasons, and I tried talking to Alice, but she was reluctant to see him. She downright refused, claiming that his illness was just what he deserved.

"I told her you wanted to see her," I said. "But she's not interested in coming, Daddy. I'm sorry."

His face became saddened.

"It's time to check your vitals, Mr. Donaldson." The nurse was my salvation, as she walked into the room. "How are you today?"

Daddy said nothing.

"When will his doctor be by to see him?" I asked. "I'd like to talk to him."

"Oh he'll be by sometime tomorrow morning," the

heavy nurse said, placing a thermometer under Daddy's tongue. She checked his blood pressure too.

My father looked so weak, and I knew I had to get out of there before I broke down crying. I wasn't as strong as I pretended to be.

"Daddy, Brianna and I are gonna go," I said. "We'll come back tomorrow to check on you, okay?"

Tears formed in his eyes. He shook his head "no."

What did he mean, no?

"What's wrong, Daddy?" I asked, and still remained strong.

He shook his head "no" again, and attempted to reach for my hand. I grabbed my father's hand. Tears rolled down his dark brown cheeks.

"What is it, Daddy?" I asked, tears threatening to fill my eyes as well, but I held back for his sake.

"He's just tired," the nurse said, writing something down on his chart. "He should get some rest."

I kissed my daddy's cheek, grabbed my purse and Brianna's hand, and left the room. When I got into the hallway, I lost it. I cried harder than I'd ever cried before. Brianna watched, but didn't quite understand. At that moment, I was nine years old again, just like her.

My daddy was dying.

"Don't cry," Brianna whispered softly, and intertwined her fingers with mine. "He'll be okay."

I kissed her forehead, and wished her words were true.

"I would be sad too, if my daddy was sick. But I know that he would want me to be a big girl," she continued. "Sometimes it's hard being a big girl, though. Right, Dana?"

"Yes, it is." I almost laughed through my tears.

"But you just have to think of all the fun you have

155

with him, and that might make you feel better," she said. "And God will make him feel better too."

"Yes, he certainly will, Brianna," I said.

"When I say my prayers tonight, I'm going to ask God to make Pa Pa feel better."

"That would be really sweet. Thank you," I said, and the two of us strolled down the hallway, hand in hand, and past the nurses' station.

At my place, Brianna and I kicked our shoes off at the door. We'd picked up a couple of DVDs, popcorn, and a two-liter of grape soda.

"Can we watch *Shrek* first?" Brianna asked before we could get in the door.

"Yes, we can," I said. "But you have to go put on your pajamas first. I'll pop the popcorn and start the movie."

"Okay," she said and then bounced into the bedroom to get changed.

I pulled microwave popcorn out and placed it into the microwave. The phone rang, and I grabbed it off its base.

"Hello."

My silent caller again.

"Hel-*lo*," I said again, before hanging up.

I poured two glasses of grape soda and took them to the living room. As I started the DVD, Brianna raced to the sofa and jumped on it, looking colorful in her SpongeBob SquarePants pj's.

"Aren't you going to put on your pj's too?" Brianna asked. "You have to if we're going to have a slumber party."

"Yes, I think I will," I said, thinking it a great idea to have a slumber party with my daughter.

I went to the kitchen, poured the Orville Redden-bacher's into a large bowl, placed it on the coffee table, and then went into my bedroom to get changed. Once I was out of my clothes, the doorbell rang. I couldn't imagine who would be dropping by at this hour. Rico knew that I was keeping Brianna overnight, and he wouldn't have dropped by without calling first.

"I'll get it, Brianna," I yelled from the bedroom, grabbing my silk robe from the foot of my bed and wrapping it around me. Before I could get to the living room, Brianna was standing at the door with it wide open, talking to someone on the other side.

When I got to the door, I was horrified by the sight of my uninvited guest.

Tony. My psychotic, abusive ex was standing in my doorway, smiling as if it were perfectly normal for him to be there.

20

Maxie

A rainstorm had crept into the city while Rico and I were having dinner at the Grand Lux, an upscale version of the Cheesecake Factory with a Venetian feel. It had recently become one of Rico's favorite places, a place where he claimed the young, beautiful Hollywood people hung out. And since he was a new business owner, he insisted that we needed to be a part of the young and beautiful Hollywood crowd. I, on the other hand, was fine just being ordinary.

All I kept thinking about through dinner was how to get Rico to his parents' house, where his surprise birthday party awaited his arrival. His entire family and his friends were waiting for him to walk through the door so they could surprise him out of his mind. It wasn't going to be an easy task, because he was so intuitive, and it was next to impossible to surprise him, but I had to make it happen.

We talked over dinner about his new business and his ideas for making it a success. He'd already begun work on his first project, and I was so proud of him. He shared his fears about failing, and it was all I could do to keep him positive. He also shared his fears about getting older, and how it took him so long to get to a place where he could live his dream.

"I should be farther along by now," he said.

"Baby, you're still young. Some people never live their dreams, and here you are finally living yours."

"But look at what I had to go through to get here. And I'm almost forty."

"You're blessed. That's all I can say," I said, tasting my salmon to make sure it was cooked right. "Now cheer up. You don't have anything to complain about. Try and see the good in things."

"I'm happy to have you." He smiled. "You, Miles, and Brianna are my world."

"And you're ours."

"You were worth waiting almost forty years for."

"That's so sweet, baby." I leaned over and kissed him. Couldn't resist. "Now eat up. We have a long night ahead of us."

"What's the hurry?" He cut into his chicken and tasted his rice.

"No hurry," I lied. "I just don't wanna be here all night. I got plans for you."

"What kinda plans?"

"Making up for lost time." I smiled a seductive smile and held my fork at the tip of my tongue a minute longer than necessary.

"I can't wait."

"I just bet you can't."

In the car after dinner, I began to work my magic.

"I told your mama we would stop by for a minute,"

I told him. "She said something about a birthday present."

"What? Whatever Ma has can wait. I'd much rather go to the house and see what you got for me." He smiled a seductive smile.

"Baby, it can wait. Your mother wants to see you for a few minutes, and I promised her we would stop by. This is the day that she brought you into this world. The least you can do is stop by and say thanks."

"I can call her on the phone and tell her thanks for bringing me into the world." He was being difficult, and I suspected he'd caught wind of our attempts to surprise him. "I got my cell phone right here."

"Will you just drive to your mama's house and stop being difficult?" I yelled, and then calmed myself. "I promised her, baby."

"Okay, okay. Don't get all upset." He tried his best to keep from laughing, and drove to Reggi's as I had asked.

When we pulled up, the block was lined with cars.

"It sure is a lot of folks over here," he said, and pulled into the only open space on the street. "There's Duane's car, Rachel's car, and Elise is even here. Hmmm, that even looks like my buddy Craig's truck over there in Miss Lewis's driveway."

"Let's just go inside," I said, grabbing my umbrella off the backseat and getting out of the car.

I had to laugh myself, because I knew that my surprise was no longer a surprise. He was on to me.

An old George Clinton tune was being pumped as we reached the front door. I knocked loudly on the door instead of ringing the bell, an indication that it was us, and that they needed to prepare for our arrival. Someone turned down the volume on the music.

When Rico swung the door open, everyone in the house yelled, "Surprise!"

Reggi rushed over to her son, grabbed his face, and planted a kiss right on his lips.

"Were you surprised, honey?" she asked.

"Yep, sure was," Rico lied.

Fred gave his son a strong hug, and everyone else followed with hugs and kisses for the birthday boy. I lost Rico immediately to his family and friends, and began to search for my own friends in the midst of the crowd.

When I found Reece, she looked much better than she had earlier, and was learning to play bid whist with a couple of Rico's aunts in the kitchen. She looked as if she'd been forced to play, and her eyes begged for my rescue.

"Hey, Reece, you gon' be much longer? I need your help in the bedroom for a minute."

"If it's urgent, I'm sure Aunt Minnie and Auntie Margaret won't mind if I throw this hand in," she said, grateful for my attempt to rescue her from Rico's aunts and bid whist.

"Do you mind, Aunt Minnie and Auntie Margaret," I asked, "if I borrow Reece for a minute?"

I took in the sight of Rico's aunts. Aunt Minnie's curly red wig was thrown on her head crooked, and her huge bosom rested on the table as she studied her hand. She was a much older, much heavier version of Reggi, but had the same skin color. Auntie Margaret was a darker woman, but resembled Reggi quite a bit. She was younger and slimmer than Aunt Minnie, but looked older than Reggi. She wore black-rimmed reading glasses that rested on the tip of her nose.

In my attempt to rescue Reece, I'd been cornered by Rico's aunts, who spent the next thirty minutes sizing me up, and trying to determine if I was worthy of their nephew's hand in marriage.

"Aren't you Rico's fiancée?" one of them asked.

"Yes, ma'am," I said, and knew I had just walked into a hornets' nest.

Reece took the opportunity to escape to the pool area, where Charlotte was lounging in a lawn chair, sipping on a glass of rum punch, and having a conversation with Rico's sister, Elise.

"Come on over here and give your auntie some sugar," Auntie Margaret insisted, and I did as I was told.

"Sit down here, child. Let us get to know you," Aunt Minnie said.

"So this is Maxie, huh?" Auntie Margaret started running her fingers through my dreads. "I'm your Auntie Margaret."

"She wears those things on her head. What do you call them?" Aunt Minnie asked.

"They're called dreadlocks, Minnie," Auntie Margaret said, as if she was an expert on the matter.

"Dread what? I don't know about these new hairdos that the young folks are wearing these days," Aunt Minnie said. "But her skin is absolutely flawless. And she's cute enough."

"And she's a nice size too." Auntie Margaret smiled. "What are you? About a size four or five, child?"

"Seven."

"Size seven?" Aunt Minnie asked, shaking her head. "My goodness. I can't even remember when I was a size seven. Been too many years."

"And too many helpings of neck bones and potatoes."

"You don't know anything about that, do you, child?" Aunt Minnie asked. "Do you eat that sushi mess that my nephew eats?"

"And he tells me that he will only eat chicken and fish. No pork and beef," Auntie Margaret said, her black-rimmed glasses at the tip of her nose. "What kind of foolishness is that? I know he wasn't raised that way."

"You play bid whist, baby?" Auntie Minnie asked, scooping up the cards from the table, shuffling, and preparing to deal again.

Button came through the kitchen from outside, carrying Miles, his head resting against her shoulder. He was knocked out. She smiled and gave me a look that told me she'd already met Aunt Minnie and Auntie Margaret earlier. She winked and gave me a look of sympathy, but kept on moving to put Miles in bed.

Before long, I was listening to the Sugar Hill Gang, and Rachel and I were whipping Rico's aunts at a game of bid whist.

21

Dana

"Hello, Dana." Tony's smile was as wide as my doorway.

"What are you doing here?" I asked.

"Aren't you going to invite me in? Or were you planning to just leave me out here in the rain?"

"Tony, I don't want any trouble."

"I'm not here to bring you any. I just have a few questions for you, and then I'll be on my way," he said, and I couldn't remember what it was I ever loved about him. "So, can I come in or what?"

Reluctantly, I invited him inside, but knew he couldn't stay. He shut the door behind him, and my heart pounded. I could actually hear it pounding, as if it were no longer a part of my body. I was frightened and didn't know what to do, so I made sure I remained calm. His presence brought back memories of the abuse that I'd so diligently tried to forget. The last time I'd seen him, it was a rainy night just like this one. His gun was softly caressing my temple, the coldness of it causing me to tremble. When I left him, I never looked back. He'd threatened that if he ever found me, he'd kill me. And up until now, he'd never found me.

"Who's the kid?" he asked.

"My name is Brianna," she said, before I could answer him.

"Oh that's your little girl, huh? What, you got custody of her now?" he asked and reached his hand out to her. "Hello, Brianna, I'm your mommy's good friend, Tony."

I pushed Brianna behind me, leaving Tony holding his hand out.

"Brianna, why don't you go into the back bedroom and let me talk to Mr. Tony for a bit?" I told her. "And don't come out until I tell you to, okay?"

"Okay," she said, and did as I asked.

Once she was out of earshot, I pulled my robe tighter and looked directly at him. "Tony, what are you doing here?"

"I told you I would find you," he said. "That wherever you were, I would find you. Didn't I tell you that? I've been watching you for a while. Following you."

I trembled at the thought.

"So it's you who's been calling me, breathing on the phone?"

"Didn't know what to say," he said, undressing me with his eyes. "Congrats on your acting role, by the way. I knew you had it in you. When is the sitcom due to air?"

"Tony, let's cut to the chase," I said. "What is it that you want from me?"

"I want my money, Dana."

"What money?"

"The money you took from my bank account before you left Seattle. You cleaned me out," he said. "And I've come to collect."

"Tony, I don't want any trouble. It's taken me a while to get my life back on track, and I just want it to stay that way."

"Seven thousand dollars," he said. "What did you do with it?"

"The money from that bank account was long gone before I left. The money I took was mine."

"How can you say that any of it was yours?" he said. "You worked for me, and you only got paid when I paid you."

What I did for Tony, turning a few tricks, was temporary.

When I first ran away to Seattle to be with Tony, we were both struggling actors. He worked part-time at a local gas station, and I held down a job at the local supermarket. He introduced me to some of his friends, who were quite heavily into the drug scene and spent all of their free time partying. We began partying with them just about every night, snorting coke or doing whatever the drug of choice was for that day.

"Take what you want," they'd say, and as long as it was free, I was along for the ride. I just wanted to be near my man, and as long as he was doing drugs, that's what I thought I wanted to do.

By the time it wasn't free anymore, we were already too far gone to go without. My body yearned for it, I needed it so badly. My entire paycheck went toward getting not only me high, but Tony as well. He agreed to pay the household bills, while I paid for our habits, and that worked out fine, until I realized that not only had he lost his job, but hadn't been paying our rent.

"What are we going to do?" I asked him one afternoon, as he lay passed out on our rented sofa. Nothing in our apartment belonged to us, as "Rent-to-Own" had become our middle name. And "Give it to me on credit" was our motto. Problem is, credit is only given when you're credible, and we were slowly becoming untrustworthy. When you can't pay your bills, nobody is willing to take a chance on you. Dope man included.

It wasn't long before my reluctance to show up at work landed me in the unemployment line. And Tony changed jobs as frequently as he changed clothes, so his losing his job at the local gas station was nothing more than ordinary. It didn't take a brain surgeon to figure out that we were both on a downward slope toward the gutter, without hope of ever finding our way back.

That's when Tony suggested I start working the streets. It was a means for making ends meet.

"Just until we get on our feet, baby, I promise."

He promised, and I believed him.

I did it, but hated every minute of it. I talked Tony into letting me start a bank account in both our names, where we could save the money that I earned on the street, and use it for bills and to supply our drug habits. He agreed, but I had to bring him a weekly statement, in which he calculated down to the penny how much should be there. And if it was off by one dollar, he would beat me until my face turned blue. It was later that I realized that our account was short because he'd been withdrawing money without my knowledge.

I'd had enough of disgusting, funky men climbing on

top of me and handling their business for what I considered to be pennies. And I was tired of all the partying and getting high. It was taking its toll on my body and my emotions. Every time I talked to my father on the phone, I'd cry myself to sleep. He and I both knew that the Dana he was talking to was not who he'd raised me to be. I needed to get myself together.

In the laundry room of our deteriorated apartment building, I pulled clothes out of the dryer and began folding them. I overheard the woman who lived upstairs talking about her church and the revival that was going on over there. I'd never been much of a churchgoer in my adult life, although Daddy and Sophie had taken me to church occasionally. But I knew I needed help. I began to ask her the details about it.

"You can ride with me," she said, "but I don't need no trouble from that man of yours. I hear the fighting going on down there between you two."

"He's gone most nights," I assured her. "We'll be back before he even knows I'm gone."

"Good." She smiled. "We'll leave at seven. Service starts at seven-thirty."

She was a recovering addict herself and invited me to one of her support group meetings as well, and I went. I soon entered into a night program for drug- and alcohol-addicted men and women, and completed it. I got clean, and knew I needed to get away from the life I lived with Tony. I began to plan my escape.

I opened up a separate bank account and began placing money in it that I earned from my new job as a receptionist. Tony was blowing hundreds of dollars daily on his habit, and nothing was being replenished in the bank account. Since I had a legitimate job and all my money was going into the separate account, the account that we had together began to diminish.

"As soon as that bank opens in the morning, we're going over there, and you're going to explain where all my money went." That's when he held a gun to my head and threatened to pull the trigger.

I was halfway to California before the bank opened the next morning.

"I took what was rightfully mine."

"What was rightfully yours, huh?" he asked, touching the collar of my robe and running his fingertip down my chest, making a trail to my breasts. "What about what's rightfully mine?"

"Tony, please."

"What are you wearing underneath the robe?" he asked.

"Look, I think you should go."

"Not until you show me what you're wearing under the robe," he insisted, and began to undo the belt.

I allowed him to open my robe, just to keep his temper from flaring. My body began to tremble from fear and from the cool draft that suddenly brushed against me.

"Don't be afraid, baby." His words were gentle as he began to caress my breasts with his huge, rugged hands. For a minute I thought he was the same Tony whom I'd once fallen in love with.

He grabbed my waist and pulled me close to him.

"You should go now," I whispered.

His lips pressed against mine, his breath reeking of alcohol just as I remembered. I welcomed his kiss. I closed my eyes and pretended he was someone else: pretended he was Rico. I'd been fantasizing about Rico since the day I'd hit his car at the A.M./P.M. I wanted him back, and knew I'd have to work my way back into his heart. And the first step was to become a better mother to my daughter, and prove to him that I was stable. I'd worked hard to do just that, but now, with Tony here, all that I'd worked for was being threatened. He had to go.

"Please go, Tony."

"Not until you give me back my money."

"I don't have it."

"You don't have it," he said. "That's not the answer I was looking for. Where is it?"

"I used it to pay bills and to get on my feet."

"And how was I supposed to pay my bills?"

All I could do was shrug my shoulders.

"Well, I have a way that you can make it up to me." He pressed himself up against me. "You can make up for every cent of it. And for every hour and every day that you've been away from me. Starting now."

"Tony, the life we had together—it's over. I've moved on, and started a new life, and I'm happy," I said. "I'm afraid of you, and I can't live my life in fear like that."

"You left with saying good-bye." His whisper was wet against my ear.

"You put a gun to my head and threatened my life. You abused me physically and verbally."

"I didn't mean to hurt you."

"I've forgiven you, Tony," I told him.

"I don't want your damn forgiveness, Dana!" He grabbed my arm and pulled me across the room. "I want my money!"

"I don't have it." It was almost a whisper.

"Well, you'll just have to work it off." The same silver pistol rested against my cheek. "Now, go get some clothes on. We're going back to Seattle."

"Tony, please."

"Tell the kid to come out here until you get dressed," he demanded. "And don't try anything stupid."

I stood there, pleading for mercy with my eyes, but he was angry.

"Why are you still standing there looking at me? Go tell the kid to come out here!"

I rushed to my bedroom and told Brianna to go out into the living room, but to stay away from him. I pulled on a pair of jeans and a T-shirt as quickly as I could. I grabbed the cordless from its base on my nightstand and took it into my bathroom.

I sat on the toilet with the lid closed, shut the bathroom door, and locked it. My hands shook as I began dialing 9-1-1. I began whispering to the woman on the other end of the phone that I was in trouble and needed an officer out here right away.

Tony tried opening the bathroom door, but once he realized it was locked, he kicked it open.

"What are you doing, Dana?" he asked. "You calling the cops?"

"I, uh—"

"Gimme that phone." He snatched it and threw it up against the wall, the battery flying out as it hit the wall and then the floor.

He stormed out of the bedroom, grabbed Brianna, and ran out the front door.

"No!" I screamed. "Where are you taking her?"

"Shut up!" he yelled and kept moving.

"Bring her back!" I ran after him, pulling on the

171

sleeve of his tattered leather jacket, and then trying to pull Brianna out of his arms.

Brianna was screaming at the top of her lungs, but Tony kept going.

"Don't take her, take me!" I screamed.

I was right on his heels as he quickly made his way to his truck. I grabbed his sleeve again and he pushed me so hard, I fell down into the wet, muddy grass. He threw Brianna into his truck. Just as I tried getting up, I slipped and fell back down into the mud, rain mixing with the tears that were streaming down my face. By the time I made it to the truck, Tony was slamming his door and burning rubber out of the parking lot of my quiet little community.

"Bring her back!" I screamed, but to no avail. "I'll give you back the money!"

I ran back inside and grabbed my purse and the keys to my car. I ran back outside and jumped in my car, started it, and took off out of the quiet apartment complex, tears streaming down my face. My daughter had been kidnapped by my psychotic ex-boyfriend.

22

—

Maxie

Rico's father, Fred, was shaking what his mama gave him to the sounds of "Atomic Dog." It was hard for me to keep up, particularly when he started doing his version of the Robot.

"You haven't danced one time with Reggi tonight," I told him.

"She's not speaking to me, in case you haven't noticed."

"You have to try harder," I said. "She'll come around."

"You don't know Reggi. She's tough."

"She might be tough, but I know she still loves you. She just needs to digest all that's happened," I said. "You should go ask her to dance. No harm in dancing."

Reggi was dancing with one of Rico's cousins, a drink in her hand. She was having the time of her life.

My eyes searched the room for my vanilla prince. I wanted to make sure he was having a good time, particularly since he'd been struggling with this whole getting-older thing all day. Our eyes locked when a slow Boys to Men song was played. He found his way across the floor toward me and placed his arm around his father's shoulder.

"Sorry, Pop, but I need to cut in on this one," he said, and then grabbed me around my waist, holding me close as we began to slow-dance.

"Go find your wife," I mouthed to Fred, and he did just that.

He found Reggi, pulled her out onto the floor, and held on to her. She resisted at first, but he wouldn't let her go. Rico and I both smiled.

It was getting late, and I knew I needed to get to the highlight of the evening: my marriage proposal.

After the song was over, I went to the kitchen. Reggi was behind me.

"When are you going to...you know?" she asked.

"Right now," I said, taking a deep breath. "I'm ready."

"Good. I'll get everybody to gather around."

She began banging a fork against a glass in order to get everyone's attention.

"Everyone, can I have your attention please?" she said loudly. "Maxie has something she wants to say to my son Rico."

Charlotte, Reece, and Elise came in from the pool area. Aunt Minnie and Auntie Margaret found their way to the living room. Button stood in a corner, a huge smile on her face. All of Rico's family and friends gathered around in anticipation.

Rico's eyes found mine, a confused look on his face.

"What?" he mouthed to me from across the room.

"Come here," I mouthed back.

"Gather around, everyone!" Reggi yelled again, and it

was so quiet I became nervous. But I had to get to it. I'd put my man off long enough, and it was time I let him know just how special he was. That I'd be honored to marry him. Today would be the first day of the rest of our lives.

Rico made his way over to me.

The doorbell rang.

"Can you get that, Duane?" Reggi asked.

"Okay, but, Maxie, don't say anything until I come back," he said. "Hold that thought."

Duane rushed to the door, and we all awaited his return. He almost immediately came back into the room.

"Rico, Dana's at the door," he announced. "I think you need to come and see what she wants."

"Dana?" Reggi asked with attitude.

Whispers filled the room.

I followed Rico to the door, and so did just about everyone else. Reggi was right behind me.

"Dana, what's up?" Rico asked. "Where's Brianna?"

Dana's hair was all over her head, her clothes were muddy. My heart fell to the floor. I knew whatever it was she had to say couldn't be good.

"Brianna's gone."

"What the hell are you talking about?" Rico asked. "Where is she?"

It took her a minute to get herself together and to a point where she could speak though her tears.

"My ex—" She wiped tears away. Her eyes were puffy and looked as if she'd been crying all night. "My ex-boyfriend Tony, he came to the house… When I tried to call the police, he took Brianna."

"What do you mean he took Brianna?" Rico asked, taking the words right out of my mouth.

"Dana, what is this nonsense you're pulling?" Reggi asked, pushing her way to the door. "Where is my grandchild?"

"How did all this happen?" Rico was asking.

"Any idea where he could've gone, Dana?" Duane asked. He was the calm one in the bunch.

"No. I don't have a clue," Dana said. "I've been driving around looking for them for the past hour."

"She's been gone for an hour and you're just now telling me?" Rico screamed. "What's wrong with you? There's no telling where he could be!"

"I hoped to have her back, and wouldn't have to tell you."

"Did you call the police, Dana?" Fred asked.

"Yes."

"I gotta go find her myself." Rico dashed out the door, Duane behind him.

"Be careful, baby," I yelled to him, and my eyes locked with Dana's. Mine pleaded for an answer to this madness, but also were sizing her up. She was pretty, I could tell, even through her jacked-up appearance.

"I'm sorry," she whispered, not really to anyone in particular. Crying, she trembled as she walked off the porch.

23

Rico

"There's nothing you can do but let us do our job." The officer kept telling me that, but it had gone in one ear and out the other.

If they were expecting me to sit around and wait for something to turn up, it wasn't happening. For all I knew, she could've been halfway to Seattle by then. I needed to find her. Duane and I had probed the city for the blue Dodge pickup that Dana had described to the police. When we were finally convinced that driving around was a lost cause, we took the officer's advice and decided to let them do their jobs. I had Duane drop me off at Dana's place. I wanted to be there in case the cops called, or in case Crazy decided to show back up with my daughter. I figured if anything went down, it would be at Dana's place.

I was angry and began to pace the floor. Knew I would kill this guy with my bare hands, if I was given half a chance. Wanted to choke Dana for allowing this to happen, but knew that it wasn't really her fault, so I decided to cut her some slack. But I needed some answers, and although it was already one o'clock in the morning, I needed her to give them to me.

"Tell me again why you let him in."

"Well, I was in the bedroom changing clothes when the doorbell rang. Before I knew it, Brianna had opened the door and was talking to him," she explained.

"I've told her a million times about running to the door like that, and especially talking to people she don't know. She knows better."

"I don't even know how he found me, Rico. You have to believe me. I was very careful."

"What did he want?"

"Money," she said. "He claims I stole his money before I left Seattle."

"Did you?"

"It was mine," she said. "My money."

"If you knew he wasn't safe, why did you let him in?"

"I don't know, Rico." She began to cry.

"What do you mean you don't know? You put our child in danger when you knew what this dude was capable of!"

She was silent.

"I'm sorry...for all of this," she said, and began crying harder. "This is all my fault."

"Look, Dana. Stop crying," I said, not up for all the boo-hooing. "I'm not blaming you. I just want to find my baby, that's all."

I ran to the window when I heard a car pull up. Headlights shone brightly in my eyes. The driver turned off the lights, shut off the engine, and got out. It was Dana's neighbor. He went into his place and shut the door.

"I want to find her too. Rico, despite what you think, I love Brianna," she said. "I've changed. I'm not the same irresponsible Dana that you remember."

I paced the floor some more, then found myself at her picture window again, running my fingers through my dreads. The rain had eased up. I was frustrated. Felt like my hands were tied. Felt helpless thinking about my little girl out there with some crazy dude, and there wasn't a thing I could do about it. A father is supposed to protect his daughter, and here I was doing just the opposite. I'd failed her, and fallen down on the job.

"Maybe if I'd just been more cooperative with him," Dana said.

"Then he'd have the both of you. You did the right thing by calling the cops," I said. "Don't beat yourself up about it. Let's just try and remain calm. Do you know where he might have gone?"

"I didn't even know he was in L.A. until tonight when he showed up on my doorstep."

"Does he have any people here?"

"No. His family is in Seattle."

I sat on her sofa, my face buried in my hands. I felt frustrated. Scared. Angry enough to hurt somebody.

Dana started crying uncontrollably and I made my way over to her. I held her in my arms. Her head fell onto my chest, her arms held me tightly around my waist.

"It's okay. Stop crying," I whispered. "Why don't you go get cleaned up and try and get some sleep?"

She was still wearing the muddy clothes she had on earlier.

"Okay," she said, and went to her bedroom. When I heard the shower, I pulled my cell phone out to call Maxie. The battery was dead. I took Dana's cordless phone off its base and dialed Maxie's home phone. It rang and rang. No answer. I tried her cell, but couldn't reach her, so I left a message explaining where I was, and that I was waiting for something to turn up. Called Ma's, but when the line was busy, I decided to stretch my worn body across Dana's sofa and shut my eyes.

When the phone rang, I jumped to my feet. Dana had picked it up in her bedroom, and was talking to someone. Maybe it was Crazy calling to give her an ultimatum, and at least give a clue of where he was with Brianna. I paced the floor, waiting to hear who was on the phone. Her door opened.

"It was the cops," she said, and my heart raced. "They found her."

I exhaled, then breathed deeply. Relieved.

"She's okay?"

"She's fine," Dana said. "She's at the station."

"Thank God." I sighed.

"I'll get my keys." She smiled.

When we arrived at the police station, Brianna was seated atop the desk of the chief of police, giggling, and sipping on a cup of hot chocolate.

"Daddy!" She set her hot cup down, jumped down from the desk, and raced into my arms when she saw me.

"Hey, baby," I said. "I'm so glad to see you."

"Me too," she said. "Smith taught me a card trick."

"Smith?"

"That's me." The white, blond officer held his hand out to me. "I'm Officer Charles Smith. But everyone calls me 'Smith.'"

"Glad to meet you."

"Let me show you, Daddy!" Brianna said, and

grabbed the deck of cards from Smith's desk. "Pick a card, any card."

"Bri, it's really late. Aren't you ready to go home?"

"Yes, but can you pick a card first?"

I pulled a card from the deck.

"Now, don't let me see it."

She spread the cards out across the desk into four smaller decks.

"Now, put your card on any one of the decks, Daddy," she said. "And I'll close my eyes."

I did as she asked, and then she put all four decks together into one. Then she pulled a card from the middle.

"Is this your card?"

"Nope," I said, observing the four of diamonds, when I had had the ace of clubs.

"What about this one?" she asked, holding up the six of hearts.

"Nope, that's not it, Bri," I said. "Can we go now?"

"I did something wrong, Smith," she said. "Now we have to start all over."

"No, we're not starting over, Brianna. We're goin' home." I looked at Smith. "Can she go home now?"

"She sure can," he said. "We just need to finish up a little bit of paperwork here. I'd like to ask Miss Elkins a few questions."

"Where did you find them?" I asked.

"We spotted his truck at the motel where he'd been staying for the past month or so."

"He's been stalking me for a month?" Dana squealed.

"Yep," Smith continued. "He's locked up, and being extradited back to Seattle to face charges there. Police there have a warrant for his arrest."

"Come here, baby," I said and hugged my daughter. "You okay?"

"Yes, Daddy."

"It doesn't appear that he hurt her," Smith said.

"Probably not physically," I said. "But it's the mental scars that stick."

On the way home, I called Ma. She said that Maxie, Reece, and Charlotte had just left. I told her that Brianna was safe and that we were headed home. She was relieved. I tried Maxie's cell again. No answer. I left her another message.

Dana drove us home. Brianna fell asleep in the backseat of the car, and when we got home, I carried her inside to her bedroom. Dana followed, wanting to help me tuck her in.

"Good night, baby," I said to Brianna, who could barely hold her eyes open.

"Good night, Daddy," she sang. "Good night, Dana."

"Good night, Bri," Dana said, and kissed her forehead. "We still have some movies to watch, you know."

"I know," she said, and closed her eyes.

I turned off the light in Bri's room, and Dana and I tiptoed out, leaving the door cracked open a little.

"I'm so relieved," she said.

"You don't know the half of it."

She stuck her hands into the pockets of her jeans. "Rico, you think I can just crash here?"

"I guess it'll be all right. I have an extra bedroom, and it appears that Pop won't be coming home tonight."

"What do you mean, 'coming home'?"

"Ma kicked him out," I explained. "It's a long story. I'll explain it to you later."

I showed her to the guest bedroom.

"Let me get you some clean sheets and stuff," I told her, and went down the hall for fresh linens.

I grabbed a couple of sheets from the hall closet. Together, we changed the old sheets and put the clean ones on the bed. I found one of my shirts for Dana to sleep in.

"Rico, I'm sorry about all of this."

"Don't worry about it," I said. "She's home safe now and that's all that matters."

Before I could say another word, she'd snuggled into my arms. I was too tired to push her away, and held her. Her lips touched mine, and I didn't fight it. I allowed her to kiss me. I was aroused, and knew I should quit while I was ahead, but it was difficult.

"Dana, look…"

"Rico, I've missed you."

Her lips found mine again.

"We can't do this. I'm practically a married man," I whispered.

"Practically married and married are two different things," she said. "Have you two even set a date?"

"That's beside the point, Dana…I…"

"What is the point, Rico?" she said, rubbing her hands softly against my chest, arousing me all the more. "You know you miss me too."

Her tongue probed the inside of my mouth, as she pulled my shirt over my head.

"Don't fight it, Rico," she whispered. "You know you're feeling me."

"I admit, I am," I whispered back. "Which is why we can't…we shouldn't…I shouldn't even put myself in this position.…"

"I've been thinking a lot about you lately…fantasizing about us...." Her voice was filled with lust. "You're so tense. You should relax. You remember those nice massages I used to give you?"

"Yes, I remember."

"Let me give you one."

"Just a massage, right?" I asked, my eyebrows rising, knowing I *could* use a good rubdown.

"Just a massage." She smiled. "Now lie across the bed."

I stretched out across the bed, lying on my stomach. Dana straddled my behind, her behind warm against mine. Her hands began to work out the knots from my neck and shoulders. I felt as if I'd gone to another place, the motion of her hands relaxing me with every stroke. The softness of her fingertips was like magic. Before long, I'd drifted off into another world. I gave in to my weary body and my heavy eyelids.

I fell asleep right there in the guest bedroom.

24

Maxie

I drove to my place, my windshield wipers playing a tune as they wiped away the rain with every stroke. Charlotte and Miles had fallen asleep in the backseat, while Reece was softly singing the words to an old Whitney Houston song on the radio. I was worried sick about Brianna, wanting to know if she was safe or not. My nerves were on edge and I couldn't get to sleep. I'd tried Rico's cell phone all night, and never received an answer. I figured he and Duane were still pounding the pavement in search of Bri, or perhaps he'd crashed at Duane's and called it a night. But what I couldn't understand was why he wouldn't answer his phone. Surely he knew I'd be worried.

I pulled into the garage, and when the car stopped moving, Charlotte opened her eyes, and so did Miles.

"You okay, Maxie?" she asked.

"I'm fine."

* * *

After I put Miles to bed, I headed for the kitchen and poured myself a glass of milk, warming it in the microwave. Reece was still up.

"Maybe you should try and get some sleep, sweetie," she said, sitting at the kitchen table nursing a cup of tea.

"I haven't heard from Rico all night. And I'm worried sick," I told her. "I can't sleep."

"He hasn't called at all?"

"Nope. And he's not answering his cell phone."

"You think he's still out looking for Brianna?"

"I don't know." I pulled my glass of milk out of the microwave. "I know it's late, but I'm calling Reggi to see if she's heard anything."

I dialed the number. It rang twice.

"Hello."

"Hi, Reggi, it's Maxie."

"Maxie, what's wrong, honey?"

"Have you heard from Rico and Duane? I'm worried sick over here not knowing if they found Brianna."

"Oh yes, honey, Rico called earlier tonight. Right after you left. You probably hadn't been gone five minutes. Said the police had found Brianna and he was headed over to the station to pick her up. He said he'd tried you on your cell phone all night, honey, and couldn't reach you," she said. "They should be home by now."

"Oh okay," I said. "I'm sorry I woke you up, Reggi."

"Don't worry about it, baby," she said. "I'm just glad the child is safe. Now try and get some rest. Okay?"

"Good night, I'll talk to you tomorrow." I hung up.

"Well?" Reece asked.

"She's safe," I told her, and exhaled.

"Oh thank God."

"I'm going over there."

"It's late, sweetie. You sure you don't want to wait until tomorrow?"

"I never got the chance to give my baby his birthday gift." I smiled. "Maybe he's still up."

"I got you," Reece said. "Go handle your business."

"Will you listen for Miles?"

"I got you covered."

"If he wakes up, he has bottles in the refrigerator," I explained. "And if you have to change him, make sure you use his diaper rash stuff."

"I got you covered, Maxie. He'll be fine," she said. "Now go be with your man."

I ran to my bedroom, threw on a pair of sweats and a faded T-shirt, grabbed my keys, and searched my purse for my cell phone. I couldn't find it.

Nevertheless, I headed out the door.

When I pulled up in front of Rico's, Dana's car was parked in the driveway. That was more of a surprise than I was prepared for. I couldn't imagine what her purpose was for being at my man's house at this hour. But before I started tripping, I decided to find out what was going on before I lost it. Instead of knocking, I decided to use my key. I pushed the door open and went inside. The house was dark, and I turned on the lamp in the living room next to the door. Then I went to the kitchen and set my purse down on the breakfast nook table.

I strolled down the hallway to Brianna's room, my sneakers making a swooshing noise on the carpet. I peeked in on her. Her eyes popped open when she heard the door creak.

"Hi, Maxie," she whispered.

"Hi, baby," I whispered back. "How are you?"

"I'm fine."

"I was so worried about you." I tiptoed over to her bed, leaned over, and kissed her. "But I'm glad you're home."

"I was really scared," she said.

"I know you were, but you're safe now."

"I love you, Maxie."

"I love you too, sweetie," I said. "Now go back to sleep, and I'll talk to you in the morning."

"Okay."

I left her door cracked open a little, the way she liked it. She liked to be able to find her way to the bathroom in the dark. And she wanted to be able to see the bogeyman if he decided to pay her a visit. I made my way to Rico's bedroom. His bed had been left untouched, the covers still nice and neatly tucked. I checked the family room, thinking that perhaps he'd fallen asleep on the sofa, remote in hand, ESPN watching him instead of him watching it. When he wasn't in his bedroom, or in the family room, my heart sank. Where could he be? And where was Dana?

I slowly made my way to the guest bedroom. I didn't want to think about what I might find behind that door. I knew that Fred wasn't there. He was still at Reggi's, passed out on the sofa. I braced myself. Wanted to believe that what I shared with Rico, he wouldn't discount for a quickie with his ex-wife. Had to believe that he respected me more. But life had taught me not to put my trust in people, because they almost always disappointed you.

I tapped lightly on the door, and waited for someone

to respond. What I received was silence. I pushed the door open.

My heart skipped a few beats.

There was my man lying in bed, shirtless, asleep, his face buried in the pillow. Dana was wearing his Los Angeles Lakers T-shirt, lying next to him, her arm thrown across his back. I cleared my throat and her eyes popped open. She stared at me for a moment.

"Oh Maxie, hi," she said, as if it were perfectly normal for her to be in bed with the man that I called my vanilla sweetheart.

Rico woke up, searched the room, distraught for a moment. His eyes found mine. It took him a minute to understand fully what his future now held.

"Maxie?"

"Rico, what are you doing?"

He sat up in bed, trying to get himself together.

"Baby, what's up?"

"I should be asking you that."

He looked over at Dana, as if she had the answer. "Baby, it's not what you think."

"Well, what is it then?"

The silence in the room bounced against the walls, and rang loudly in my ears.

I stood there, still waiting for an answer. Even a lie would've been better than the silence.

I shut the door, made my way down the hallway—the hallway seeming longer than it ever had before—grabbed my purse and keys from the nook in the kitchen, and took off out the front door.

I could hear footsteps behind me, but never turned around.

"Maxie!" Rico yelled for me, and ran outside behind me, wearing nothing more than a pair of slacks, his chest and feet bare. "Maxie, it's not what you think."

"Well, what is it then, Rico?" I stopped long enough for him to explain. "I'm listening."

Again, silence. That dreadful silence.

"It's not what you think."

"You're no better than your father," I said, and ran to my car at a pace much faster than a leisurely stroll.

I fought back the tears as I pulled off, but the tugging in my heart was much more than I could handle.

I cried a river.

25

Rico

Hectic morning.

I couldn't focus on the plans that had been staring at me from my desk for most of the morning. Everything that could go wrong had gone wrong, and all before ten o'clock this morning. The supplies never showed up, although I was told I would have them first thing Monday morning. What was worse was there was work to be done, but nobody to do it. I'd made the mistake of hiring a few of my brothers from the block, but they were too trifling to show up. I should've known they'd leave me hanging. They always had. They were the type of brothers that you couldn't reach when you needed a hand, but they always had their hand held out needing to borrow a few bucks.

"I get paid next week, man," they'd say. "I just need a little something to get me over until then."

"I need to see you on payday," I'd say, knowing that I'd never see my money again. What they didn't know is that I never loaned money with the intent of getting it back. So the minute it changed hands from mine to theirs, I'd already written it off.

"I got you covered," they would tell me straight to my face, sealed with a handshake, and I wouldn't see them again for months. They'd avoid all the places they thought I might show up, and when I did see them, they wouldn't remember that they owed me, or they'd just play me off.

Funny how, when I started my business, I went straight to the hood, in search of some of the same brothers who never paid back loans, were undependable, and lied with a straight face. I felt an allegiance to them for some reason. I needed to see them do better than what they were doing, and kept hope alive that they would someday get it together. But they never did. They remained the same undependable brothers they'd always been, never promising me anything different, and delivering the same irresponsible behavior time and time again.

"I don't know why you keep fooling with Vinny and Bobby and the rest of them," Ma would always say. "You know they ain't gon' do right."

"They're my partners, Ma," I always defended them. "We grew up together."

"At some point you have to separate yourself from your childhood friends, honey," she said. "I'm not saying don't love them, or to walk around acting like you better than they are. But you have to realize that they don't want anything out of life, Rico. Not like you. And one of these days, you'll figure that out."

I was confident that one day I would do just as Ma said, and figure it out. Matter of fact, today was probably that day.

Joe Cook was my saving grace. He was my one buddy who had set himself apart from the rest. He was a brother who had money to loan sometimes, and didn't always have his hand out. He gave it to you straight, even when you didn't want to hear it, and was dependable. If Joe told you he was coming, he'd be there, willing to work, and showing up on time. When the knuckleheads that I considered to be friends left me short-handed, he jumped in his pickup and headed down to Home Depot in search of our Hispanic friends who were willing to work for half the day's pay that I'd offered to my irresponsible brothers. Cook had brought them back, and they were grateful for the work, and already asking if they could come back the next day. That's the type of commitment I was looking for, so I went with it.

I sat there staring out the window of my office, wondering where Maxie was and what she was doing. I wanted to see my son. It had been a week since I'd seen him, and at the rapid pace an infant grows, I'd already missed too much of his life. He'd probably grown five inches since I'd seen him last.

How do you convince a black woman who has just witnessed her man in bed with another woman that she didn't see what she thought she saw? It wasn't an easy task, especially when she refuses to answer your calls or to respond when you show up on her doorstep.

Maxie was hurt. Her eyes held a sadness that I'd never seen before. It was a look of betrayal, but moreover abandonment. She'd been abandoned so many times in her life, by so many people. She'd seen so much hurt and here I was hurting her again. Ultimately, I began to hurt, wishing I could change that night. But I couldn't. It was what it was.

She could've at least given me the benefit of the doubt. She had to know I would never betray her that way. But the truth was, for a moment, I'd considered it. I can't lie. When Dana pressed up against me and her lips touched mine, I almost lost it, almost gave up the struggle. But I held out. I should've been given credit for that alone.

Even though I'd promised Maxie that I wouldn't pressure her, I was growing tired of her resistance to marriage. I was the one who should've been upset. After all, it was me who'd been rejected by her more times than I could count. And if I *had* given in to Dana's advances, I would've been justified. Wouldn't I? After all, if Maxie loved me, she would sacrifice her principles and prove it. She would meet me at the altar.

I sat there thinking that she could at least let me see my son. She owed me that. And that's what I would've told her had she answered the phone. This was my sixth phone call to her house this morning. I knew she was there. The local magazine she worked for allowed her the luxury of working from home and e-mailing her articles to the company. She was there, probably listening to the phone ring. Still wasn't picking up.

I left my sixth message. "Maxie, it's me again. Rico. That's R-I-C-O. Miles's father. Remember me?" I said. "I would like to see my son if you don't mind. If you're not going to talk to me, at least let me see Miles."

26

Maxie

"If Rico calls here one more time, I'm going to scream."

"Why don't you just talk to him?" Charlotte asked, placing the last item in her suitcase and zipping it up. "Or tell him you don't want to talk to him. Something. Just pick up the phone. I'm sick of hearing it ring."

"Sweetie, you have to talk to him at some point," Reece said. "At least give him a chance to say his piece."

"I gave him a chance to say his piece. He said nothing," I said. "Now, I don't want to talk about it anymore."

Still in my pj's, I rushed to my bedroom and started the shower. I stood in front of the mirror, observing the bags under my eyes. I was done crying. There weren't any tears left, and crying was so exhausting. And for what? A man who doesn't even respect me? I should've seen it coming too. Even Reggi saw it coming, and had tried to warn me. She knew what Dana was about, and I was so oblivious to it. Walking around acting like Rico was some sort of a saint. Like he was different from every other man out there. He was no different, and I felt foolish for even thinking so.

I pulled my dreads back into a ponytail and removed my pajama shirt. I checked out my stomach—the little pouch that remained from Miles's birth—in the mirror. It was still there, and I'd done nothing to get rid of it. Should've been more proactive in doing some crunches to get my abs in shape. I used to care more about my body. I used to take better care of myself, but somewhere I'd fallen short. It's funny how you get careless when there's a man in your life. We take better care of ourselves when we're on the prowl, rather than showing him the same beauty it took to get him. I guess that's why he strayed.

I still had my membership at the gym and what better way was there to start feeling better about myself than to start using it? Get in shape. Stop moping around this house like a zombie and get my life back. Rico was living his life. Why shouldn't I?

I jumped in the shower, closing my eyes. The water was warm against my skin, as my mind drifted to the first time I laid eyes on Rico.

While vacationing with my girls, Charlotte and Reece, in Nassau, I took off for L.A. after Reece's detective friend had located my sisters. I cut my vacation short, and booked a ticket. There was a short layover in Miami, where I spotted Rico in a corner bookstore at the airport, flipping through magazines. It took all I had to keep from staring at his beautiful face, as he flirted with his eyes. His smile told me that he wanted to have a conversation, but I had a connection to make and I needed to get to my gate. I knew I should've stopped, wanted to, but didn't know what I'd say. A face like that would've had me speechless, so I kept moving.

Once comfortable in my window seat on the plane, I snapped my seat belt on. I pulled my book out of my backpack and flipped to the chapter where I'd left off on the first leg of the trip between Nassau and Miami. A tall, red-haired gentleman took his seat next to me. Across the aisle, the handsome brother from the bookstore forced his carry-on underneath the seat in front of him. He must've felt me stealing a glance, because his eyes met mine and then he started cheesing. I blushed. He got up, stepped over to Redhead, who was seated next to me.

"Excuse me, sir, are you traveling alone?"

"Yes," Redhead responded.

"Would you mind switching seats with me so that I can sit next to my wife here?" he said. "The airline over-booked the flight and unfortunately they weren't able to seat us together."

"Oh I'm sorry," the gentleman said. "I had no idea you two were together."

"Yes, it's a shame how airlines inconvenience us the way they do. If it's not a terrible inconvenience, I'd like to take this seat and have you take mine right across the aisle there."

"Of course. No problem at all." Redhead was very accommodating as he retrieved his things and gave Rico his seat.

"Thank you so much," Rico said, shaking his hand. "You will be blessed beyond measure."

It took all I had not to crack up. After stuffing his bag underneath the seat, he snapped on his seat belt and turned to me. "Since we're married, I guess I should find out your name."

"Maxie," I said, shaking my makeshift husband's hand.

"Maxie, you are beautiful." He was close enough for me to smell the breath mint in his mouth. "Has anyone ever told you that?"

"I tell myself that every morning when I wake up."

"Wow, beautiful and confident."

"Don't forget intelligent."

"Intelligent too?" he asked. "You're married then?"

"Happily single," I said. "But open for conversation."

"I like you already, Maxie," he said. "Why are you flying to L.A.?"

"To find my sisters who I was separated from as a child. Long story," I said, although he seemed interested. "Why are you flying to L.A.?"

"I live there. In Inglewood, actually," he said. "I'm a single parent with a beautiful eight-year-old daughter."

Now that was not what I was expecting to hear. He didn't fit the description of a single father, raising a daughter no less.

"I'm surprised."

"Why? I don't look like I could father a child?"

"Of course. Any man can father a child, in the sense of impregnating a woman. But to be a single father, with the sole responsibility of taking care of your child…I give you mad love, my brother. You're holding it down for all the deadbeat dads out there. I commend you."

"You mean that?"

"I mean that."

"You have children, Maxie?"

"No." I didn't bother going into detail about how I was raped by at least two of my foster fathers and I was convinced that I couldn't have children because of it. I didn't know him like that to be telling all my business. So I left it at "no."

"Who's your favorite musician?" He changed the subject, sensing my discomfort.

"Miles Davis." I said it without hesitation. "What about you?"

"Tyrone Davis," he said, laughing. "Naw, I'm just kidding. I can get with Miles or Coltrane, though."

"Tyrone Davis is cool if you're in the mood for the blues."

"Or some Z. Z. Hill."

"Or B. B. King."

"Martin Luther King or Malcolm X?" he asked.

"Definitely Malcolm."

"George Bush or Bill Clinton?"

"That's a no-brainer." I laughed. "The black dude, Bill, for sure."

"Even after he lied under oath?"

"Men lie all the time, what's new?"

"Maxie, that's cold," he said. "How can you say that men lie all the time?"

"How'd you end up in the seat you're sitting in right now?" I smiled.

"You got me on that one." He laughed hard this time, only to be drowned out by the flight attendant giving us instructions to fasten our seat belts and ensure that our seats and tray tables were in the upright position.

Rico and I spent the entire flight discussing music, politics, and everything else under the sun. We had so much in common, it was scary.

* * *

I loved him, I thought. But as the water from the shower streamed down on my face, I knew that it didn't matter anymore. Loving Rico Elkins had been a waste of my time.

On the way to the airport, my girls gave me words of wisdom.

"I'm not trying to get in your business, sweetie," Reece started. "But I really think you should give Rico the benefit of the doubt. I have a feeling that he's a pretty good man, despite the little incident the other night."

The little incident.

"I think so too," Charlotte said. "And I wouldn't just lie down and let that heifer get her paws on him. Fight for your man, girl."

"Charlotte's right. I have a feeling there's a little more to the story than what you know," Reece continued. "Give him a chance to explain."

"I gave him a chance to explain, and you know what he said? Nothing. He was silent, as if he was just busted and didn't know what to say."

I was tired of talking about it. They weren't there. They didn't see what I saw. It was a scene that I had to fight hard to get out of my head, one that I didn't want to re-visit. I just wanted to pull myself out of the dumps, and get back amongst the living. I needed that so desperately, which is why I drove a little faster to LAX. I loved Reece and Charlotte and hated to see them go, but I needed to be alone. I needed to think things through, and I couldn't do that with them constantly singing Rico's praises.

I pulled toward the curb, and popped the trunk.

"Here we are," I said, and almost let out a sigh of relief.

"Is she trying to get rid of us?" Charlotte asked. "Driving like she's lost her mind."

"Come on, Charlotte," Reece said. "Get the bags out of the trunk while I get someone to help us."

A tall, slender brother appeared out of nowhere, and started unloading luggage from my trunk.

"Call the minute y'all get to Atlanta," I told them.

"We will, sweetie." Reece gave me a strong hug, which lasted longer than I expected. "I love you, and remember what I said."

"Love you too."

"Good-bye, Maxie. Thanks for the hospitality," Charlotte said, hugging me.

"When you gon' tell her?" I whispered in Charlotte's ear.

"Tell her what?"

"You know. About getting married."

"When the time is right," Charlotte said.

"I'm happy for you."

"Me too," she said.

"What y'all over there whispering about?" Reece asked.

"Nothing," I said quickly. "Have a safe flight, my sisters."

"Maxie, take care of you," Reece said. "Take care of you, because I worry."

"I worry too," Charlotte said.

"Don't worry about me. I'll be just fine." I plastered a fake smile across my face, trying not to cry, because I didn't want my friends changing their flight arrangements. I had to be strong, at least until they were gone.

* * *

It was all temporary.

The minute they disappeared into the airport and I pulled away from the curb, I cried. I thought I didn't have any more tears, but I was so wrong. So, so wrong.

27

Rico

Pop's Asian son couldn't have been more nervous. He was the center of attention as he walked through the door, bearing gifts for Ma and my sisters. And Pop couldn't have denied him if he tried, because he was the spitting image of him and Duane.

"I'm Reggina Elkins," Ma introduced herself first. "Every-body calls me Reggi."

"Pleased to meet you, Mrs. Elkins," he said and did a halfway bow. He held her hand in his. "I am Bao Hoang."

"This is my daughter Rachel," Ma introduced my sister.

He grabbed Rachel's hand and greeted her just as he had Ma, by bowing his head and holding on to her hand.

"And this is Elise."

Elise waved from across the room, but wasn't up for the handshaking and head bowing. She was not the big-happy-family type. Just cut to the chase with her.

"Hello," she said, almost as chilled as a California night.

"This is my oldest son, Duane," Ma continued with the introductions.

"What's up, bro?" Duane asked, and handed our Asian brother a strong handshake.

"And finally, this is my son Rico."

"How's it going, man?" I asked.

"Glad to meet you."

He was tall for an Asian dude. Stereotypically, I thought all Asians were short, but he was far from it. And he looked almost black. His dominant genes were definitely from an African- American. Obviously Pop's genes were pretty strong. I know that had to cause Ma to tremble, because it made me just a little uneasy. His resemblance to my middle-aged father was disturbing.

"How was your trip here?" Ma asked, trying hard to be a trooper in all of this.

"It was a very good flight," he said. "I travel a lot with my job, so I'm used to it."

"And what type of work do you do?" Ma asked.

"I work for a computer software company," he explained.

I started to wonder why Pop hadn't arrived yet.

"Can I get you something to drink, man?" I asked, as Ma had completely forgotten. She was so busy trying to quiz the brother, just as she said she would.

"Some water if you don't mind," he said, and made himself at home on the sofa. It seemed that Ma had forgotten to offer him a seat as well.

"I'm sorry," Ma apologized. "Rico, can you get Bao some water, please?"

"Got it covered, Ma." I went into the kitchen.

I stood with the fridge open, looking for the bottled water.

"Rico," Pop whispered, standing in the corner of the kitchen, sweat beading all over his forehead.

"Pop. What are you doing in here?"

"What's he like?"

"He's cool, old man," I told him. "Why you hiding out in the kitchen?"

"Nervous," he whispered. "I don't know what to say to him."

"What do you mean, you don't know what to say?"

"I just don't know what to say, Rico." He swallowed hard. "Many, many years have passed. I'm sure he hates me."

"Probably so," I told him, keeping it real. "But you can't hide out in the kitchen all night. Don't be a coward, Pop."

"Yeah, you're right." He dabbed his forehead with a paper towel.

I grabbed my Asian brother a bottle of Dasani from the refrigerator, grabbed a glass off the shelf, and headed back toward the living room where he was being interrogated by my mother.

"Rico," Pop called.

"Yeah, Pop?"

"Do you think I'm a bad father?" he asked. Serious too.

"No."

"Have you lost respect for me?"

"I still love you, Pop, if that's what you wanna know."

"That's good enough for me," he said.

"Coming?" I asked.

"I just need a minute," he said, and sat down at the kitchen table.

* * *

I handed Bao his bottled water and a glass.

"Thanks," he said. "Rico, right?"

"Right."

We all sat there, staring at each other, looking for words.

"Fred should be here soon," Ma said. "I know you're anxious to see him."

"It was my mother's desire that I come here. She wanted me to make myself known to him," Bao said. "I resent having to come here, but I promised my mother that I would find him. She spoke highly of him. Said he was a good man. But I asked her, before she died, if he was such a good man, why didn't he come back for us? Why did she live as poor as dirt for all those years, when my father lived like this...like a king, in this huge house, with a pool, and all the luxuries that she and I were never accustomed to?"

I wondered what my father had to say about it. He was trapped in the kitchen, trapped in a web that he'd woven for himself. The truth always seemed to find you, no matter how long it took.

"I grew up in a time and in a country that treated me like an outsider. Children like me, who many referred to as 'children of the enemy,' were treated badly. That's what they called children who were born with an American soldier as their father, and a Vietnamese woman as their mother. We suffered so much discrimination and poverty. Most Amerasians were taunted by classmates and peers with names such as 'My Lai' or 'Con Lai,' and 'My Den.' 'My Den' is what I was called and is the worst name of all three, used to taunt black Amerasian children. My mother named me Bao, because it means 'protection.'" He laughed sarcastically. "Many children like me tried to hide their true identity to avoid discrimination. It is worse in Vietnam for a child to be a black Amerasian."

"So you resent being black?"

"I resent being fathered by a coward."

There was silence. I had to defend my father.

"Hey, my pop might be a lot of things, but a coward he's not." I hoped he was listening in the kitchen, and knew that it was his cue to come out and not make me a liar. "My pop was a soldier, who defended his country in a time when African- American soldiers were being killed off by the boatloads."

"He made my mother pregnant and then abandoned her."

"That he did," Duane said, and stood. He walked out onto the porch for some air.

"I've heard enough," Elise said, and grabbed her purse. "Where is Daddy, anyway? He's not even man enough to show up and face his son."

"How did you end up in the States, Bao?" Rachel asked, trying to change the mood in the room. She was a peacemaker like me.

"I took a course in English at the Philippines Refugee Processing Center, which is a program that was organized to prepare U.S.–bound refugees for life in America. They helped me come to America when I was a teenager."

"Why didn't you search for your father then?" she asked.

"It was advised that we not begin searching for our fathers right away because we should adjust to American life, look for jobs, and settle in. Many of my peers had very little information about their fathers, and others who found their fathers were rejected by them. I did not want to be rejected. Though, I've always known where to find him. He sent money to my mother when I was an infant," he said. "But unlike most Amerasians, I did not want to know my father. It was my mother who insisted that I make myself known to him. Now I have carried out my mother's dying wish. And I came here to let him know that I turned out okay, despite his absence in my life. I have a beautiful wife, a daughter, and a child on the way."

"How old is your little girl?" Rachel asked.

"She's two."

"That's sweet." She smiled.

There was silence again.

"I bet it was hard for you, moving to another country like that at such a young age. I bet it was really a culture shock," Ma said. "How did you manage to overcome?"

"Most Amerasians faced identity crises and were self-destructive. They found it very difficult to adapt to life in the United States, became depressed, and many committed suicide. I was much stronger and used my father's abandonment as a reason to move forward."

When my cell phone buzzed, I didn't want to miss what was going on, but excused myself to the kitchen where I answered Dana's call.

"What's up?"

"When you pick Brianna up, can you stay for dinner?" she asked. "We cooked fried chicken."

"That should be cool," I told her, thinking there was no harm in having dinner with my daughter and her mother. It wasn't as if I had dinner waiting at home. Since Maxie wasn't returning my calls, what did it matter who I had dinner with? "I'll be there shortly."

I hung up and my eyes found my father, still in the kitchen, pacing the floor.

"You listenin' to this, old man?"

"I heard."

"He called you a coward."

"I am, Rico," Pop said. "I had a lot of respect for his mother. She wasn't like the other women over there, the prostitutes who threw themselves at you. She was a respectable woman."

"You loved her or something?"

He was silent, but his silence was my answer.

"How could you fall in love that fast, man? And you had a family here in the States." I asked, "Did you love Ma?"

"Always have, always will," he said. "But I was there for a long time, and she was good to me."

"This is a lot to swallow right now, Pop."

"Was that Maxie on the phone?"

"Dana," I admitted. "Invited me over for dinner. She and Brianna cooked."

Pop shook his head.

"What? I know you ain't judging me. Your troubles are far worse than mine."

"What's going on with Maxie, son?"

"She won't speak to me," I said. "And I'm tired of trying."

"Did you...?"

"Did I what?"

"Sleep with Dana?"

"No."

"Then you should tell Maxie."

"I've tried. She ain't hearing me. So I'm moving on."

"With Dana? The woman who abandoned you and your daughter."

"People make mistakes, Pop."

"You got enough forgiveness in your heart for her?"

"I think so."

"You think your mother will ever forgive me?"

"Time will tell, Pop," I told him. "But you can't keep hiding out in here if you ever want to make restoration. It's not just Ma you need to face. You got a son in there, who is very angry. He thinks you're a coward."

"He's right."

"You're not a coward, Pop. You made a mistake and just need to make amends to some people that you hurt. That's all."

"When'd you get so smart?"

"Must be something in those African-American-soldier genes of mine," I said, and checked my watch. "I gotta run."

"Be careful, son. Don't do anything that will jeopardize your future. Think long and hard about what you want."

"I will, Pop," I said. "You going in there or what?"

"In a minute," he said.

"Well, I'm out. I got some fried chicken calling my name."

"Hey, Rico," Pop called. "What does my son look like?"

"You," I said and bounced out the back door.

I peeked back through the window and saw my father making his way into the living room to face his judge and jury.

When I got to my truck, I realized that I'd left my keys on the mantel in the living room. I headed back toward the house, and was glad I did. I decided that Pop's first encounter with his estranged son was an event I really didn't want to miss. I went back inside. As I stepped into the living room from the kitchen, Pop was offering Bao a strong handshake.

"I'm Fred Elkins," he said.

"Bao Hoang." The Vietnamese stood and looked Pop square in the eyes, his face like stone.

History was being made at the moment, when a father met his son for the first time.

Pop cleared his throat and said, "I'm very sorry to hear about your mother's death."

"It was painful to lose her, but I was pleased that she didn't have to suffer any longer."

"Was she sick?" Ma asked, observing Pop the whole time.

"She recently lost her battle with HIV/AIDS," he said, and his eyes revealed the sadness of a man who'd become motherless much too soon.

I looked at my mother, silently thankful that she was sitting there, alive and breathing. I couldn't imagine my life without her in it. Suddenly, I felt sorry for Bao. I'd had the priviledge of knowing my father all my life, and here he was meeting Pop for the very first time. My mother was alive and healthy, and here Bao had buried his just weeks before.

"HIV/AIDS is an epidemic in Vietnam," he said. "I watched her battle for many years, not only with the disease, but with the stigma of being labeled a drug user or prostitute, and being alienated by so many people including her family. My mother was neither a drug user nor a prostitute, but simply a victim of practicing unsafe sex with a man she trusted."

"I'm so sorry," Ma said, and I could tell that the maternal part of her wanted to reach out and give Bao a hug. But the aftertaste of my father's betrayal caused her to keep her distance.

"It seemed he was the second man she trusted, only to be disappointed yet again." The sarcastic comment was meant for my father.

"I never promised your mother anything," my father quickly said, glancing at Ma just to make sure that his statement had resonated with her. "She knew I was married and that I would be returning to the States to be with my family."

"Mother said that you promised to return for us."

"I never promised her that."

"Then you're calling my mother a liar?"

"I'm saying I never promised that," my father said. "Maybe she misunderstood."

Bao took his seat again, and thought for a moment. "Even if you never came back for her, you still had a child who needed you."

"I knew I had a child."

"Yet you never reached out to me."

"I didn't know how," my father admitted. "I sent money in the beginning, because I knew your mother was poor and needed to care for you. But soon I lost contact with her."

"You could've searched for us," he said.

"I didn't know how," my father admitted, and glanced at Ma. "I didn't even know how to tell my wife about you. I didn't know how to right my wrongs."

"So I was the wrong in your life."

"No, I'm not saying that."

"Then what are you saying, Mr. Elkins?"

"Fred. Call me Fred." My father raised his baseball cap and scratched his head. "I'm saying that I made a mistake by being with"—Pop let out a long sigh—"by being with your mother when I knew I had a wife and children at home." Pop faced my mother, his eyes pleading with her. "Reggi, you deserved better, and I'm sorry."

Ma looked away.

"My children deserved better." Pop glanced at me as if I represented all of his offspring.

I raised my hand in a gesture that said, "Don't even sweat it, Pop."

"And I'm saying that it was a mistake to run away like a coward once I realized your mother was pregnant with..." It pained Pop to say the words. "Once I realized she was pregnant with my child."

"I agree. You are a coward," Bao said.

"Now wait a minute!" I interjected on my father's behalf.

"Rico, please," Pop said and held his hand up to me. "I should've stood up and faced my responsibilities, but instead I hid. I hid in my safe life. I hid behind my wife and my children here in California. I hid behind the fact that I was a child fighting in a grown man's war. And I hid behind the fact that you were in Vietnam and not here. Because you were not here, I didn't have to face you or my responsibility as your father. But the truth always has a way of finding you."

"I only came here because my mother asked me to." Bao became defensive. "It was her idea, not mine. I could've gone my entire life not knowing you. It was she who said I should find you. Said you were a good man."

"She was a decent woman," Pop admitted, glancing at Ma again.

213

Monica McKayhan

Ma stood and made her way toward the kitchen. Pop grabbed her hand as she passed him, but she yanked it away. My sister Rachel followed her into the kitchen.

"But she was only good enough to sleep with and then leave behind."

"The war was over and I was sent home," Pop said. "To my family."

"What about the child you left behind?" Bao asked. "What about me?"

My father was silent. He found a seat in his recliner in the corner of the room, shut his eyes, and rested his head in the palms of his hands. This was a question that had obviously tormented him for many years. It wasn't a question that could easily be answered. It was possibly one that he'd never found an answer to. When he lifted his eyes to Bao, there were tears in them. I could count on one hand the times I'd seen my father cry.

"I'm sorry," he said in a near whisper.

"Yes, you are." There were tears in Bao's eyes too.

"I know that I can't change the past. And even if I could, I'm not even sure how to go about it. I can't promise that I wouldn't make the same mistakes again."

"You wish I was never born, don't you?" Now Bao was five years old, and his tone was softer.

"I wish I had been man enough to live up to my responsibilities," Pop said. "I'd like to do that now. If you let me, I'd like to—"

"Don't even say it." Bao stopped him. "Don't even say that you'd like to have a relationship with me now. Or you'd like to be a part of my life. It's a little late for that."

"It's never too late, son."

"This is not some fairy tale!" Bao said. "I came here for

214

closure, not new beginnings. Besides, if I hadn't contacted you, we wouldn't even be having this conversation."

"Not a day went by in my life that I didn't think of you."

"Right." Bao stood. "You expect me to believe that?"

"It's the truth." My father pulled his wallet out of his back pocket, opened it, and pulled out a worn photograph. He handed it to Bao. "Your mother sent me this when you were three. I've kept it, looked at it every day. Often wondered how you were doing. What you looked like after the years passed. I wondered what your life was like, and how you turned out. I stayed awake many nights, tormented by this whole thing."

"This means nothing to me." He handed Pop the photograph.

"I know that I have not been there for you in the past. But please"—my father chose his words carefully—"please think about it. I'd like to get to know you. At least begin to build on what we have now. All is not lost. We can't change the past, son, but we can certainly start over from here."

"I have to go," Bao said, checking his watch. "I have a flight to catch."

Bao handed me his empty water bottle and glass. "It was nice meeting you, Rico. Please give Reggi my best." He headed toward the door and placed his hand on the handle.

"Did you get closure, son?" my father asked.

Bao stood with his hand on the door handle, his back to my father. He stood there for a moment, as if contemplating Pop's question. Pop made his way over to him and rested his hand on Bao's shoulder. Bao didn't move away from my father's touch.

"I don't think you came here for closure, son. I think you came here because you need a father," Pop said softly. "Please think about what I said."

Bao never responded, just slowly opened the front door and left.

28

Dana

Fried chicken is definitely finger-licking good when you're sharing it with a handsome man who's enjoying every bite of it. It was nice having Rico in my home, at my dinner table, enjoying my cooking and conversation. I'd forgotten how nice it was to be a family, with my husband and little girl. And I was well on my way to having it back on a permanent basis if I played my cards right.

I felt a little bad about Maxie misinterpreting what went on with me and Rico. What she walked in on wasn't nearly what she thought it was, but if I know Rico, he explained that until he was blue in the face. If she chose not to believe it, then it was her loss. She had her opportunity to trust her man, and she chose not to. It wasn't my place to feel guilty for something that didn't happen. Not that I didn't want it to happen, because I did. I'd wanted to see just how dedicated he was to her, and to my dismay he rejected what I was offering. But she played herself, and now it was my turn to have a little happiness in my life. I'd been through so much, made some bad choices, hurt some people who didn't deserve it, but I was a changed woman, with a new direction. And I thanked God for second chances.

"Can I get you something else?" I smiled at Rico, and let him know that I meant more than chicken.

"Naw, I'm good," he said, patting his stomach and looking satisfied. "But let me help you clean up."

He was so thoughtful and such a gentleman, I couldn't believe I had let him slip away like I had. He was a good man, and I wished I'd only known it then.

"Don't worry about it. Why don't you see if you can pry the television away from your daughter over there?" I laughed. "I think the game is on."

Brianna was glued to the set and laughing at whatever animation was on the Cartoon Network. She watched too many cartoons, in my opinion, and not enough educational programs. I'd just barely finished high school, and wasn't as educated as Rico, who had his bachelor's in business. And I'd done my homework and found out that Maxie had a master's in journalism, yet they didn't seem to encourage my daughter to watch anything other than the Cartoon Network. And I never saw her with a book in her hand, or reciting what she'd learned in school. Next time I went out, I'd pick her up some books and some videos that would teach her more than she'd learn from SpongeBob SquarePants.

My shelves were filled with books that I'd read from cover to cover. I had a yearning for reading, and did it like a drug addict did drugs. It seemed that the more I read, the more I longed for it. It was my passion. When I was a little girl, Alice would often send me to my room and make me stay in there for hours. She'd make me read books, and I'd have to tell her what it was I'd learned from them. Her intent was to punish me, but little did she know she'd stimulated a new love in my heart that remained even to this day. It became a means of escape for me. Reading took me to faraway places where there was no Alice, no verbal abuse, and I could go anywhere I wanted to go, and be whoever I wanted to be. I could be a Snow White with my seven dwarfs, or Cinderella. I could be Shakespeare, or an African princess. I was Malcolm X, and I marched with Dr. King in the civil rights movement. I knew the names of every African-American who contributed something to my history. And my daughter needed to know it too.

I was happy to see Brianna freely give her daddy the remote to the television.

"Can you get my books out of the car, Daddy?" she asked, and it was like music to my ears.

She really did read.

When Rico came back in carrying a few of Brianna's books—Jada Pinkett Smith's *Girls Hold Up the World,* Mary Hoffman's *Amazing Grace,* and Louise Borden and Mary Kay Kroeger's *Fly High! The Story of Bessie Coleman*—my heart literally began to soar.

"Let me see what books you got there, Bri." I couldn't wait to snuggle up in my huge chair in the corner, a chair big enough for both of us to share, and have her read her books to me.

"This is a story about Bessie Coleman," she said. "She was the first African-American woman to fly a plane."

"Yep, and she learned how to speak French and went to France to learn how to fly."

"And it only took her seven months to learn how to be a pilot," Brianna added.

"How did you learn so much about Bessie Coleman?" I asked, and touched her little nose with my fingertip.

"Maxie taught me," she said, and I was sorry I asked. "She bought me this book and a bunch of other ones too. I have one about Ida B. Wells and one about Frederick Douglass. I have all sorts of books at home and at Maxie's house!"

Rico glanced over at us, briefly taking his eyes away from the game. I guess he wanted to get my reaction to Brianna's singing of Maxie's praises, or perhaps he wanted to sing her praises too. Either way, I needed to change the vibe in the room. Too much Maxie was filling my space, and there wasn't enough room for both of us. I ignored his glance and encouraged Brianna to read her book to me.

She did, and soon read herself to sleep.

I found my place on the sofa next to Rico, where he was yelling at the television.

"Yeah," he said, as Kobe dunked the ball and headed downcourt. "That's what I'm talkin' 'bout."

"Lakers winning?" I asked, and tried snuggling up close to him.

"Down by two points, but coming back." He moved to the edge of the sofa, abandoning my touch.

When Minnesota missed the next basket, he stood.

"Yeah!" he yelled again, and was engaged in his own personal party.

Brianna wiggled a little, and turned over in my oversized chair.

"Shhhh," I told Rico. "You'll wake Brianna."

"Sorry," he whispered, and sat back down on the edge of the sofa. The Lakers took a time-out, and Rico took a sip of his Heineken.

After the last basket was shot, a three-pointer that led the Lakers to victory, Rico danced around my living room.

"You still love the Lakers, huh?" I asked the obvious.

"Still and always will," he said, and collapsed on the sofa next to me.

I snuggled next to him again, and this time he didn't abandon my touch. I caressed his chest, and maneuvered my body so that I faced him, my legs tucked underneath my bottom. Then I just stepped out there, lifted my face to his, and found his lips. His lips invited my kiss, and I touched his face just to make sure it was real. His hands began to probe my body in areas that hadn't been touched in a very long time. I wasn't sure how to respond. Before long, I was lying down, and Rico was on top of me, his lips against mine, his fingertips running up and down my spine, his body strong against mine. When he began to nibble on my ear, and his lips made their way down to my neck, my heart began to soar.

I had accomplished so much in one evening. There was nothing like filling a man's stomach with a good meal, and making him feel good with some good loving. I had him just where I needed him to be, in my arms, vulnerable. It felt so good to feel his touch, the warmth of his breath on my skin. His tongue probed my earlobe, his fingertips caressed me with a loving gentleness that only Rico could give.

I was just about to suggest that we take this party to the bedroom, when he began whispering sweet nothings in my ear. The ruggedness of his voice was that of a hungry man, hungry for me...his wife. I struggled to hear his words, because they were muffled with passion.

"Oh baby," he said, moving his hands underneath my blouse.

"Yes," I whispered. "What is it, baby?"

"Oh Maxie, I love you."

What? Did he say Maxie?

"Please tell me you did not call me Maxie."

His stare was one of guilt as he sat straight up on the sofa and leaned his head back in frustration.

"Sorry," he said.

I got up, straightened my clothes, and struggled to understand what had just taken place. My entire evening had been ruined with one simple word. *Maxie.* She was all over my house again, and I hadn't even invited her in.

29

Maxie

*U*ncle Tom.

That was my first impression of my sister's husband, Nicholas. This brother was unbelievable, wearing a black tuxedo and bouncing around like he was God's gift to the world. What Alex saw in him wasn't visible to me. It had to be something he had on the inside. Something you couldn't see with a naked eye. Something other than the crap he was feeding me while sipping on Remy and Coke, and checking out every sister in the place as if he wasn't married, and particularly the one at the end of the bar.

"Maxie, it's time we stopped blaming the white man for our woes."

"We?"

"Black people." He continued, sounding just like Bill Cosby in the interview that alienated him from the black community, "We need to get off our lazy behinds and start changing our situations instead of sitting around complaining about it."

"What about those of us who aren't given the opportunity to change our situations?"

"Nope." He shook his head. "All of us are afforded the same opportunities; it's just that some of us don't bother to take advantage of them."

"You really believe that, don't you?"

"Yes. I do." He turned his glass up, emptying it with one last gulp, and motioning for the bartender to refresh his drink.

"So everybody who doesn't take advantage of their opportunities—of which we are all afforded equally— is lazy?"

"For the most part, yes," he said. "Now, granted there are some people who might be mentally or physically challenged, who might not be able to live up to their best abilities. But for the rest of us—"

"You a Republican?" I interrupted him. I had to ask.

"Born and bred," he said proudly. "How could you tell?"

"Lucky guess," I said, observing the sister at the other end of bar who had been cutting her eyes our way for the past twenty minutes. She was wearing a black, tight-fitting dress, and showing way too much cleavage. She was sipping a margarita on the rocks, and making small talk with a short bald man who seemed to be working her nerves. Her attention was obviously somewhere else. She was pretty, her honey-blond hair falling onto her shoulders, her skin the color of a shiny new penny.

"Alex tells me you live in Baldwin Hills," Nicholas said.

"Anything wrong with Baldwin Hills?"

"No," he said. "Not if you enjoy living in the hood."

"I do as a matter of fact," I said. "Helps to remind me of who I am, and where I'm from."

"I'm from South Central originally," he said. "But I don't need a constant reminder of where I'm from. I left there years ago and never looked back. Truth be told, more of us should do the same."

"Leave and never look back, right?"

"Absolutely," he said. "How can we ever expect to make any progress in life if we continue to live in the same environment that keeps us in bondage?"

"How can we help someone be progressive if we're constantly leaving our environment and never looking back?"

"I do my share," he said. "I give thousands of dollars to worthy organizations every year."

"How many hours of community service do you give, mentoring young men and showing them how to find the opportunities you say are out there for them?"

"It's not my place to raise someone else's child," he said. "That's the parents' job. I got my own kids to raise."

I'd had about enough of this brother, and was relieved when Alex came to my rescue before I set him straight. I couldn't help but wonder if she'd had this same conversation with her husband, and if so, if she was in agreement with his views. And if not, how she could've ever married someone who had such a warped way of thinking.

"What's going on over here?" Alex asked, smiling and looking beautiful in her sexy, peach, after-five gown with the back cut out, revealing more flesh than I ever imagined Nicholas would allow his woman to reveal. "You having a good time, Maxie?"

"About as good as it gets," I said, but wanted to say, "*I was about to set your ignorant man straight before you came to his rescue.*"

"So far we've raised a hundred and fifty thousand dollars." She beamed.

"You mean tonight?" I asked.

"In the past hour," she said nonchalantly. "I expect at least double that before the night is over."

"That's cool."

I smiled at the thought of thousands of dollars being raised for such a worthy cause, one that helped unwanted kids get placed in real homes. I wished there had been an organization out there like this one when I needed a home.

"And guess what else?" She smiled. "One of my paintings is being auctioned off tonight."

"For real?" I asked.

"Yes," she said. "Take a look at it when you get a chance. It's the one of the jazz player serenading the children."

"I saw that one," I said. "It's all that."

"Really?" she asked.

"Really," I assured her, and had no doubt that someone would scoop the painting up in a heartbeat. I was proud of her work. Button was right—Alex had skills.

"Baby, I wouldn't get my hopes up too high. Your painting is good, but you and I both know that this painting thing is just a hobby." Nicholas shot my sister a look that was meant to destroy every hope and dream she ever thought she wanted to have. "Don't be disappointed if it doesn't sell for that much."

"They're starting the bidding at ten thousand dollars."

Nicholas chuckled as if he'd just heard a joke. "Ten thousand dollars?"

"It's worth the price," Alex said, her feelings hurt, but she was used to it. She tried to clean up his comments for my sake. "You've had too much to drink, sweetie. No more Remy for you tonight."

"You're right, baby," he said, polishing off his drink. "I'm gonna call it a night. I feel a headache coming on, and I have an early morning. I'm gonna get a cab and go on to the house."

"You don't want me to drive you?"

"No. No, I'll be fine," he said.

"Okay, sweetie," she said. "Hope you feel better."

"I will once I get out of this tux and lie down." He gave her a peck on her forehead. "I'll see you later on at the house."

He stumbled toward the door.

"His comment about your painting cut deep, huh?"

"I'm used to it," she said. "Well, I'm going to go rub elbows with Janice Perkins. She has money to burn. And we need her to donate as much of it as she can stand to give."

Alex glided across the room, to mingle with her rich friends.

At the door, Nicholas stopped long enough to whisper something in the ear of the penny-colored woman who'd been sitting at the end of the bar. She sashayed out the door behind him.

"You just gon' sit here all night looking beautiful? Or do you intend on dancing?" The voice in my ear was sexy and soothing.

I turned and looked into the most beautiful green eyes I'd ever seen.

"Who wants to know?" I flirted with this sexy

stranger in a black tux, the night's required attire, but he didn't at all seem to fit in with this crowd.

"Phoenix." He held his hand out to me, his nails perfectly manicured. "John Phoenix."

"I'm Maxie," I said, and was glad I'd chosen the coral dress that made me look like a million bucks. It was definitely my color, and hugged my figure as no other dress ever had. And I was grateful for those crunches I'd been doing to lose the pouch that Miles had left me with. I'd actually found what resembled my abs in less than three weeks.

"The best thing going for this party is the music," Phoenix said, "and it would be a shame to let some good music like that go to waste. Can a brother get a dance?"

"Yes, you may," I said, and then followed him to the dance floor.

R. Kelly's "It Seems Like You're Ready" is one of those songs that forces you to get close, and I was close enough to feel Phoenix's heartbeat.

"So, who forced you to come here tonight?" Phoenix asked.

"Nobody forced me to come." I laughed. "My sister invited me."

"Your first time at one of these things?"

"One of these things?"

"Uppity sisters begging for money for what they claim is a worthy cause. Everybody gliding across the floor as if they think they're better than the next person, pretending to be something they're not."

"I take it you don't enjoy coming to these things," I said. "Who forced you to come?"

Phoenix was gorgeous, tall, dark, bald, and simply gorgeous. His teeth were perfectly white, his smile and charm lit up the room, although his green eyes did not match his dark skin. I wondered if they were contacts. His eyes could've been purple and he would've just been a beautiful man with purple eyes.

"I just show up for the food. Always some good grub to be had. Good music, and always the chance I'll run into a beautiful woman sitting at the bar alone." He smiled.

"So you come to these things to pick up women?"

"Only when they're as beautiful as you are."

"Are you flirting with me, Mr. Phoenix?"

"Absolutely."

I rested my head on his chest and got lost in the rhythm of the music.

The auction for Alex's painting had started at ten thousand dollars and bids quickly escalated to the fifteen-grand range and continued to increase. My only wish was that Nicholas had stuck around to see it. I would've loved the look on his face when her painting finally sold for seventeen thousand dollars. After the auction, Phoenix and I made a beeline for the dance floor again.

I felt his breath in my ear as he said, "What you doing when you leave here?"

His body was warm as he pulled me closer.

"What did you have in mind?" I asked, without even thinking.

"Wanna get out of here? Go somewhere and talk?"

"Cool," I said, not giving it a second thought.

When the song ended I made my way across the floor to the coat check, and picked up my wrap. I could feel Phoenix's eyes taking in the sexy view of my coral gown

229

hugging my hips. I pulled my wrap around my shoulders, then found Alex in the midst of the crowd, interrupting her conversation with a white-haired gentleman. I touched the curve of her back to get her attention.

"Excuse me, Alex," I said.

She turned to face me.

"I'm leaving," I whispered.

"So soon?" she asked, and then turned back toward the gentleman and shook his hand. "Ed, I'll give you a call in the morning and we can discuss this further."

"Do that, Alexandria." White-hair took her hand in his, and held on for longer than necessary. "I look forward to your call."

He disappeared into the crowd, and Alex turned back toward me.

"Who's the old dude?" I asked.

"Ed Mitchell. Very wealthy CEO of a pharmaceuticals company," she said. "Where are you going?"

"To get my groove back." I laughed. "Naw, I'm just kidding."

"You're not leaving with Mr. Phoenix?"

"You know him?"

"He's only the richest man in the house," she said. "He's donated at least a third of the money we've collected tonight."

"Rich and gorgeous, huh?" I asked, stealing a glance at Phoenix, who was sitting at the bar observing the interaction between Alex and me. I smiled, and he returned it with a wink and a gorgeous smile of his own.

"Maxie, I don't think it's a good idea, leaving with him. You hardly know him," she whispered. "And what about Rico?"

"I hardly think the man would harm me. Not to mention, I'm capable of holding my own. I carry my piece with me everywhere I go," I said, tapping lightly on my purse. "And what about Rico? Where is Rico anyway? Is he here? No, he's probably somewhere wrapped up in Dana's arms."

"I just think it's too soon to be..." She stopped midsentence. "Never mind. Go have a good time. Just be careful."

"I will, Mother."

"And call me when you get home."

"Okay," I hummed. "See you later."

My stomach churned as I made my way over to Phoenix. I wondered what the night held for me, hoping he really was harmless.

In his limo, we talked for hours about how he'd built his successful business on a shoestring budget and why he never married. We talked about politics and how Bill Clinton should've never been kicked out of the White House, discussed why brothers chose to be on the downlow rather than coming out of the closet, and why HIV was the number-one killer among African- American women.

When his driver pulled up in front of my house, he leaned over and kissed my cheek.

"I would love to come inside, finish this fascinating conversation. Would love to wake up beside you tomorrow morning, cook you an omelet that would make you slap your mama." He laughed. "But I don't want to complicate your life any more than it is."

I started to object, but he put his finger over my mouth.

"And despite what you say, I know you still love that

231

man. And even though he messed up, he deserves a second chance."

Who was he to tell me who deserved a second chance in my life?

"But"—his lips brushed against my neck—"a second chance is all he gets."

"Is that so?"

"That is so," he insisted. "You have my number. If he doesn't appreciate this opportunity I'm giving him to make things right, give me a call anytime."

He placed his hand on the door handle, opened the door, and stepped out. He grabbed my hand and helped me out of the car, the night's chill causing me to shiver. He grabbed me, wrap-ped me in his arms tightly, the warmth of his body making me feel safe. My heart was with Rico and I knew it. I wished it were his arms around me. The touch of this man made me miss Rico even more. He kissed my cheek and after a few minutes, he let go.

I walked to my door, turned to wish my new friend a good night, and could've sworn I saw Rico's Ford Explorer sitting in front of my neighbor's house down the block. But there were a million SUV's like his in L.A. I scratched that thought and waved to Phoenix as he climbed back into his limousine and drove away.

I went inside and kicked my shoes off at the door.

30

—

Rico

At first I thought my eyes were playing tricks on me, because I could've sworn I saw my woman step out of a limo with some other dude. And there I was, about to pull up in front of her house, park my car, go inside, and beg for her forgiveness, just like a little punk. I was about to lay my manhood on the line. I would've missed the whole scene if I'd pulled up a few minutes later.

My first thought was to roll up on the dude and ask him why he was with my woman in the first place. But the truth was, she looked as if she was enjoying his company, smiling all up in his face, giggling like he said something funny. Then she actually let this brother kiss her, on the cheek, of course, but a kiss is still a kiss.

Women are a trip! They make you believe that the world doesn't revolve unless you're in it, and then the minute you turn your back, another man is on the scene, just waiting to take your place. And there she was, stepping out of some cat's limo. I should've gone over there and let her know she wasn't slick, that I had her number, that I saw her with Dexter or whatever his name was. But I let it slide.

I had enough on my head with getting this business off the ground. Here it was, another Monday morning, and brothers still weren't showing up for work. So I made my way over to Home Depot, where my Hispanic brothers camped out waiting for contractors to offer them work. I needed the labor and they needed to feed their hungry children, so we made even exchanges. I transported as many as my truck would hold, and put them to work. In the morning, I would stop by a local Labor Ready joint and grab some help there too. All was not lost. At least the supplies had been delivered.

As long as I was working, I didn't think twice about Maxie. I discovered that the best thing to do was stay busy. An idle mind is definitely the devil's workshop. I didn't have time to be thinking of her and Dexter and what had taken place in that limo, or before he dropped her off at the curb. That would've messed my head up for sure. He didn't even have the decency to walk her to the door. But she claims she wants a man who treats her right. I would never have dropped her at the curb. If he was any kind of man, he would've walked her to her door and made sure she was safely inside before pulling off in his chauffer-driven limousine. I was afraid that soon he'd be singing lullabies to my infant son. Now that's where I'd have to draw the line. No man was about to be spending time with my son. That was out of the question.

By the time I got to the house, got Bri fed and in her pj's, it was late. The house was quiet since Monday night was Pop's bowling league night. He usually hung out until around ten with his middle-aged buddies at the bowling alley, talking junk and drinking pitchers of beer. Whoever won the pot for the night would spring for the beer.

I took advantage of the peace. I made myself a cup of green tea, and popped a chicken breast onto the George Foreman grill while I flipped through the mail. Bills were mounting and I needed to start netting some income from the business. I sautéed some veggies in butter and felt guilty about it for a moment. I was trying to watch my cholesterol and since I was pushing forty, that had become pretty important. But I couldn't resist.

I flipped on the television in the kitchen to catch the end of *The Best Damn Sports Show Period,* laughing at the antics of John Sally and Tom Arnold as they discussed what went on in sports for the day. The phone rang, and when I checked the caller ID, I realized it was Dana. I hadn't spoken to her since the night I called her Maxie. I left her place apologizing, but hadn't bothered calling. I felt awkward about it, and maybe she did too.

"What's up?" I said, picking up the receiver.

"You busy?"

"Just grabbing a bite to eat."

"Want some company?"

She'd caught me off guard, and to be honest I really wasn't feeling company at the moment. Just wanted to unwind after my hectic day, and have some time alone. Not to mention, I'd planned on trying to hook up with Maxie. I knew it was probably a lost cause, but I'd decided that Dexter wasn't about to steal my family away without a fight.

"Naw, maybe some other time, Dana."

"So you weren't feeling me at all the other night?"

"I don't really know what I was feeling," I told her. "Things were happening so fast."

"So you were caught up in the moment?"

"Something like that."

"You must still love Maxie."

"No doubt," I said. "I'm not trying to hurt you, though."

"It's okay. I realize that I blew my chance with you."

"I'm proud of you, though. It seems like you're getting yourself together. And that's a plus."

"That means a lot coming from you, Rico," she said. "I don't think Maxie knows how lucky she is."

"I think I'm the lucky one," I said, half into the conversation for trying to hear Tom Arnold cracking on the size of boxer James Toney's head.

"It seems like you're busy, so I'm gonna go." Her last couple of words were all I heard.

"All right, Dana. I'll holler at you," I said, anxious to get back to my show. "You picking Bri up from school tomorrow, right?"

"Yes," she said.

"Cool." I had my hand on the talk button, couldn't wait to push it. "Talk to you tomorrow."

Hoped she was done, because I hung up.

Later I dropped to the floor in the middle of my bedroom and did fifty push-ups. I grabbed a quick shower and then tuned my television to ESPN.

31

—

Dana

"I'm just here to pick up some things I left here."

"Good thing. I was about to put that mess on the curb next chance I got." Alice lit a Salem.

"It must be extremely hard being you, Alice," I said, and headed to the room that was once my bedroom. "You are one miserable old woman."

I grabbed a box of old things that Alice had so graciously packed in a cardboard box.

"How's that daddy of yours doing?" Alice asked when I came back into the kitchen, where she sat at the table, watching *Jeopardy.*

"He's not doing very well."

"Sorry," she mumbled, and I wasn't sure that I'd heard her.

"Did you say sorry?" I asked, Brianna and me both standing. I hadn't planned on making it a long visit. I was just there to pick up my things.

"I said sorry," she repeated.

"No I-hate-Henry speeches today?"

"I've hated him enough to last me a good while." She chuckled, took a draw from her cigarette, and yelled at the television set, "Who is Thomas Jefferson!"

"Alice, why do you hate my daddy so much?"

"Dana, get out of here with all that foolishness. I don't have time to discuss Henry with you," she said. "Why don't you ask him?"

"Because I'm asking you."

She completely ignored my question. "I see you've become quite chummy with your daughter here. I didn't think you could pull it off."

"Pull what off?"

"This whole charade of yours."

"This is not a charade, Alice," I told her. "I'm building a relationship with my daughter. Something you wouldn't know anything about."

"What about Rico? You building a relationship with him too?"

"Brianna, why don't you go into the living room and wait for me? I'll be ready to go in a minute." I didn't want Brianna to hear this conversation that Alice so untactfully brought up in front of her. "Why would you think I was trying to build a relationship with Rico?"

"Aren't you?"

"I would, but he's in love with someone else." I didn't even know why I was sharing intimate details with her.

"His fiancée?"

"How do you know about her?"

"I talk to Reggi from time to time," she said, and blew smoke into the air. "You had your chance with him, and now that he's trying to build a life with someone else, you wanna destroy that."

"I'm not trying to destroy anything, Alice."

"Then why don't you back off?"

I wanted to light into Alice. Tell her that it was none of her business, that she needed to get her old miserable nose out of my business. Wanted to tell her that I wanted to find happiness instead of growing old and being lonely like her. Wanted more for myself than she'd wanted for herself. Wanted to ask her why she'd run my daddy away, and never had a real relationship with her only daughter. Wanted to set her straight, but I didn't. I realized she was right.

"Do something right for once in your life," she told me. "Build a life with Brianna, but don't destroy that man's relationship. Give someone else a chance at happiness."

"What about my happiness?"

"When you do good things for other people, good things come back to you."

"How would you know, Alice?" I had to ask. "What good thing have you done for somebody?"

"I took care of you for twelve years of your life," she said, "and I let you come here when you had no place else to go."

"You took care of me for twelve years?" She was talking crazy, and I knew she had to be losing her mind. "You're my mother; you were supposed to take care of me! But instead you let me go live with Daddy. You never wanted me, did you?"

"You need to lower your voice in my house, child," she said, and turned up the volume on the television. "If you don't mind, I'm trying to watch *Jeopardy*. You know how I am when it's on."

"Yeah, I know how you are, Alice," I said. With the

cardboard box in my arms, I headed for the front door. "And I hope I never end up like you."

Brianna sat in the living room, patiently waiting for me as I had asked her to. Tears began to fall down my face.

"You ready to go, Bri?" I asked her.

"Yes," she said and followed me out the door.

I swore I would never set foot in that house again.

At my place, I lit a few candles and pumped up Alicia Keys. I fixed Brianna a peanut butter and banana sandwich. She looked sad as she took a bite from it.

"Why the long face, little girl?"

"Nothing," she said, taking another bite.

"Something," I said. "What's wrong, Brianna?"

"I miss Maxie. I haven't seen her in two whole weeks, and she hasn't even called to talk to me. She promised she would take me ice-skating if I got good grades on my report card, but she didn't even keep her promise."

"Baby, I'm sure she had a good reason for not calling you."

"Like what?" She looked up at me, a sadness filling her eyes. "And I miss my little brother."

My heart went out to my daughter. As tired as I was of hearing Maxie's name, I knew she was a very important part of not only Rico's life, but Brianna's too.

I placed a few dishes in the dishwasher, wiped down the countertop, and swept the kitchen floor. As I sang the words to Alicia Keys's "If I Ain't Got You," the phone rang.

I grabbed the cordless and plopped down on the sofa. Rarely did anyone call my landline.

"Hello."

"Dana, it's me. Sophie."

"Sophie, hey." She must've needed me to relieve her at the hospital. We'd been taking shifts at the hospital so that Daddy had at least one of us there at all times. "I was coming by later on. I know you need a break. You been there long?"

"Dana…" she said my name softly again. "You need to get over here."

"Why, what's up, Sophie?"

"Your daddy is dying. He won't last through the night, and he's asking for you."

I wasn't sure if I'd heard her right, so I asked her to repeat what she'd said.

"What did you say?"

"Your daddy won't make it through the night," she said. "Can you come quickly?"

"Yeah, yes…I can come…tell my daddy…" There was a lump in my throat. "Tell my daddy I'll be right there."

The tears didn't waste any time flowing.

I couldn't reach Rico. He wasn't answering his cell phone, and I couldn't reach Reggi either. I needed someone to take Brianna. I didn't want her tagging along on this trip.

I found myself pulling up in front of Maxie's house, and praying she was there. I was running short on time.

I stepped up to the door, rang the bell.

When she opened it, her jasmine incense met me at the entryway, and India Arie was crooning on her CD player. Maxie was singing along with India before she answered the door.

I was not who she expected; her look told me that.

241

"What do you want?" She was cold as ice, rocking her son, who was whimpering and sucking on a pacifier.

"I need your help."

"Excuse me?"

"I know I'm the last person you want to see on your doorstep right now, but—"

"Got that right."

"But I need to leave Brianna with you, because I—"

"You have Brianna?"

"She's in the car." I said. "I can't find Rico and—"

"So call Reggi."

"I can't reach Reggi, and I need to get to the hospital." I fought back the tears. This was not the place or time to be losing it, although my voice began to crack. "My father is dying and I need to get over to the hospital to see him as soon as possible. I don't want to take Brianna. It's no place for her. Don't want her seeing him like that. And don't wanna leave her in the hospital waiting room, either. Normally, I wouldn't have come here, but I need to leave her somewhere. With someone I trust."

She stood there for a moment, observing me.

"All right," she said, looking past me and at Brianna, who was in my car.

"Thank you."

Brianna was watching from the passenger side of my car, and when I motioned for her, she jumped out and ran up the steps.

"Maxie!" she yelled as she tripped a little and then caught her balance. "Hi, Maxie."

"Hi, baby." Maxie was just as glad to see her, even though she was resisting. There was definitely a bond there.

Brianna grabbed Maxie around her waist and hugged her tight.

"Thanks," I told her.

"It's okay," she said.

"Brianna, I'll try and reach your daddy and let him know where you are," I said. "I'll see you later, okay?"

"Okay," she said, still holding on to Maxie.

I began down the stairs.

"Hey, Dana," Maxie called, and I turned to receive the tongue-lashing I thought she was about to give. "I'm sorry about your father."

"Thanks."

I got in my car, and went to say good-bye to my daddy.

32

Maxie

Tuesday evening, I rebraided Brianna's hair. When Dana dropped her off, her cornrows desperately needed to be redone. She fell asleep on the floor in between my legs, and I struggled to keep her head from bobbing and weaving. I was glad to finally finish, and was glad that she and Miles decided to take a nap. It gave me the rest of the evening to get some things done—cleaning, dusting—I even had time to take me a nice long bubble bath, with candles and Will Downing telling me to wait for love. My mind drifted back to the time I'd seen him in concert at Chastain Park in Atlanta. I missed Atlanta. Life there was uncomplicated: no heartaches or lost loves. I wished I was still there, giving Charlotte hell and feeling the comfort of her and Reece's friendship. Feeling loved, and wanted. Not here feeling the sting of betrayal from someone I thought I trusted.

Will was singing the old Luther tune as if it were his own. Had he known that I'd already decided against love? Decided it was overrated, and wasn't worthy of another tear of mine? He must've known I was already contemplating not waiting for love, and his words were trying to convince me of the opposite. But my decision was made.

I shut my eyes, and let the music fill my soul, the scent from the jasmine candles filling my bathroom, the lights low. Only the flicker from the candles lit up the room. My body felt just as relaxed as the time when I received a massage from Dante, the Adonis from the spa. I remembered the softness of his fingertips massaging my neck and shoulders. I pretended he was rubbing them now.

When the doorbell rang, I became pissed. How often do you get a moment like this, where you're lost in a place where nothing else matters except the peace you're feeling right then? And now somebody was interrupting, intruding. I stood in the tub, grabbed my towel off the toilet seat, and wrapped it around me. I dried my body and threw on my silk robe. The bell rang again.

"I'm coming," I said, not caring if my uninvited guest heard or not.

When I peeked through the window on the side of the door, I realized it was Rico.

I wasn't ready for him to be standing on my doorstep. What happened to calling before you dropped by, dude? That way I would've had a chance to think about what I wanted to say. I wouldn't have been caught off guard. But here he was, standing at my front door, looking right at me. I slowly pulled the door open.

"Hello, Maxie," he said, all cheerful.

"Hi," I said to him, and that's all I could think of at the moment. So many times before I'd wanted to cuss him up one side and down the other. But this day, all I could think of was how much I'd missed him. Nothing else seemed as important.

"Dana told me that she dropped Brianna off here."

"Yes, she's here, but she's sleeping." I pulled the door open wider and allowed him to come inside. "Come on in, I'll wake her up."

"You can let her sleep," he said. "I really want to talk to you for a few minutes. I know you're not trying to hear what I have to say, but I need for you to hear me out."

I'd ignored him long enough, and realized I did need to hear what Rico had to say, to put some closure to this situation. To clear the air so we both could move on. I pulled my robe tighter and gave him a look that said, "I'm listening."

"Dana drove me home from the police station that night, and because it was so late, she asked if she could spend the night." He took a seat on the edge of my sofa and made himself at home. "I did not sleep with her."

"How did you end up in bed with her?"

"We weren't actually in bed together."

"Well, what would you call it?" I asked. "You were in the bed; she was in the same bed. Isn't that being in bed together?"

"But not like you think."

"What do I think, Rico?"

"You think that I slept with her."

"Didn't you?"

"No, I did not." His eyes pleaded for forgiveness. "I'm guilty of allowing her to massage my shoulders, which was probably not a good idea. I fell asleep in the middle of it. When I woke up, you were standing in the doorway. That's it."

"That's it, huh?" I said, and couldn't believe he

couldn't see how a simple massage from his ex-wife was inappropriate for a man in a committed relationship.

"Maxie, I'm sorry. I don't know what else to say."

"I'll go get Brianna." I wanted to leave the room before I fell apart. I thought I wanted to hear what went on, but it only proved that I should not take Will's advice, and I shouldn't wait for love.

I headed up the stairs to my guest bedroom where Brianna was asleep, light snores escaping from her little mouth. I whispered her name, and she looked up at me with those light brown eyes that were identical to her daddy's.

"Your daddy's here," I told her.

"Is he taking me home?"

"I imagine so."

"I want to stay here with you and Miles. Can I?"

My heart ached. I knew if she stayed, she'd be a constant reminder of what once was. And I couldn't handle that right now.

"I think your daddy probably wants to spend some time with you," I told her. "You can come back and see me whenever you want."

"Okay, Maxie." She sat up in the bed and began to put her shoes on.

When I walked past Miles's nursery, Rico was standing over his crib watching him sleep. I didn't interrupt. Instead, Brianna and I headed toward the kitchen. I filled a Baggie with Teddy Grahams and another with Gummy Bears.

"These are for the road," I told her, and handed her the Baggies full of goodies.

"Thank you, Maxie."

"You're welcome."

"Where are my goodies?" Rico asked Brianna, and she raced into his arms.

"Hi, Daddy."

"Hey, baby, you got all your things?" he asked, and I didn't remember Brianna having a bag or anything when Dana dropped her on my doorstep.

"She didn't bring a bag," I explained.

"Her things must still be at Dana's," he said.

"Must be," I said. "Give you a reason to rush right over there and get them."

That green-eyed monster began to raise its ugly head.

"What's that supposed to mean?"

"Nothing," I said, and wished I hadn't even gone there.

"Maxie, I don't know what else to say to you," he said. "I'm not interested in Dana. I love you."

I didn't respond, just walked toward the door and placed my hand on the handle. He got the idea that it was time for him to leave and followed my lead.

"Bye-bye, Maxie," Brianna sang, and I hugged her tightly.

"Bye, sweetie. I'll see you next time."

"What about me?" Rico asked.

"Take care, Rico."

My heart ached more as I watched my family drive away and leave me standing in the doorway.

33

Rico

"I don't know what else to say to her."

"Did you say you were sorry and beg for her forgiveness?"

"I explained what happened and told her I was sorry," I told Ma. "I ain't begging for her forgiveness. I've been asking Maxie for her hand in marriage ever since she moved here from Atlanta. All she keeps saying is 'I'm not ready.... Let's wait . . .' Well, I'm tired of waiting. I'm beginning to think that she doesn't really love me anyway."

"You ain't begging her forgiveness, huh?" Ma let me get it all out, and then began to set me straight. "I guess you think that you'll find happiness with Dana again. The woman who left you to raise your three-year-old daughter alone? Is that the woman you want to build a future with?"

She began placing dishes in the dishwasher, as I sat at the kitchen table. The kitchen table was where life-changing conversations had taken place all my life, where important decisions were made, bid whist was played, and fabulous meals were eaten.

"And for your information, I happen to know that Maxie loves you very much."

"I can't tell," I said. "And I caught her coming home with some dude the other night."

"What? Were you stalking her?"

"No. I was on my way over to talk to her," I said, "and she was hugging all up on the dude and she even let him kiss her."

"On the lips?"

"Naw, but…"

"Maxie loves you. She was going to propose to you that night at your party. That is before that tornado, called Dana, rushed through here and caused all that commotion."

"What are you talking about, Ma?"

"You mean to tell me you had no idea?"

"That Maxie was about to ask me to marry *her*? No, I didn't."

"That was your birthday present." Ma poured liquid detergent into the little compartment in the dishwasher. She shut the door and started the wash cycle. "Why do you think she had everybody gathered around, wanting to say something to you in front of all your friends and family? Did you think she wanted to tell you, 'Happy birthday'?"

"I didn't know what she wanted to say. And I didn't even give it a second thought after all that happened with Brianna."

"No, you were too busy receiving massages from Dana." Mothers always seemed to know things that they weren't supposed to know.

"How did you know about the massage?"

"I know things, Rico."

"Ma, I don't want Dana."

"I know you don't."

"But I don't know how to explain that to Maxie."

"She knows it too. She's just hurt," Ma said. "She'll come around. But you need to get rid of that cocky attitude of yours and quit saying that you ain't begging for her forgiveness. If that's the woman that you want, then you need to do everything you can to win her back."

She was right and I knew it.

"So she was about to propose to me?"

"She was so cute," Ma said, and started a pot of coffee. "Whipping your Aunt Minnie and your Auntie Margaret under the table in bid whist that night. Sent their behinds home complaining."

"Yeah, I'm sorry she had to run into the two of them alone." I laughed. "I should've rescued her."

"Don't you worry, she can hold her own." Ma laughed too. "She's tough. She doesn't run when the going gets tough. She sticks around. That's what I like about her. She'll make me a fine daughter-in-law."

I knew there was a message in that statement for me.

"What do I do now?"

"I thought you'd never ask," Ma said, and grabbed a coffee mug from the shelf. "You having coffee?"

"Yeah, I'll have some."

She grabbed another mug, and said, "What you do is you find a nice little romantic getaway. Go to Santa Barbara or somewhere. You woo her there, and you treat her like the woman you want to spend the rest of your life with."

"How do I woo her to a getaway when she won't even talk to me?"

"You leave that to me. I'll get her there, don't you worry. And I'll take the kids, so that you can spend some time alone with her."

The smell of coffee began to fill my mother's kitchen.

"Thanks, Ma," I said. "But what about you and Pop? How you gon' fix that?"

"I haven't figured that out yet, Rico," she said, and poured two cups of coffee. She dropped Kahlua in hers. "Gotta tackle one problem at a time."

"Pop loves you, and he wants to come home."

"You're just saying that because you're tired of him being at your place."

"Yep, I do need my space back, but that's not what I'm saying. He misses you, and he's sorry for what he did," I told her. "How can you expect Maxie to forgive me if you won't even forgive Pop?"

"This is different."

"How?"

"Just is."

"That was something that happened years ago. Pop was young and stupid. And he made a mistake. He disappointed you," I told her.

"Got that right."

"He disappointed me too, but he's not a perfect man, and I can't expect him to be. But I realize he was a good father, despite his flaws."

"I have to agree, he was a good father."

"And a good husband?" I asked, wanting her to dig into her heart a little deeper and cut my father some slack. "He never left you for that woman. He stuck around."

"Don't try to use my own words that I used on you."
We shared a laugh.

"You know you need to give him another chance, right?"

"I will. I'm just making him sweat a little," she said. "Besides, he's got to resolve the issues with his son first. That boy needs some answers. He needs some peace. He needs a father."

"Maybe you can help him resolve those issues."

"Hey, let's not move too fast. I'm not real comfortable with that whole thing just yet. Gonna take some time. But I will talk to Freddie, and try to work through this mess."

"That's my girl." I leaned over and kissed my mother's cheek. I pulled out my cell phone, anxious to call my father and let him know that she was at least willing to talk. I knew he'd be overjoyed just to hear that. Particularly since he'd practically begged me to talk to her, and convince her to go out on a date with him.

"A date, Pop?" I'd asked. "She's not even taking your calls. How am I supposed to get her to go out on a date with you?"

"You just get her on the phone," he'd said. "And I'll do the rest."

I had promised my father that I would at least try.

Things were finally coming full circle for Pop. Bao had made a second trip to L.A. It seemed he still had unanswered questions he needed to ask Pop. Turned out, that closure was not what Pop's Vietnamese son was looking for. He was looking for a father, just as Pop was looking to build a life with the son he'd abandoned. There weren't any fairy-tale-happily-ever-after endings yet, but at least they were talking, healing old wounds. Bao had even sent Pop photographs of his wife and children. He talked about his life growing up in Vietnam, a life of poverty, ridicule, and shame. He talked about how he watched his mother die and how he felt helpless because he couldn't save her from the virus that had held her captive. He told Pop about his fears, his anger, and all the things that had caused him to consider suicide when he was a teenager. When the conversation was near its end, Bao was in my father's arms, both men crying. They were making progress. I'd stood secretly watching my father become a man in that moment. Just when I thought I'd lost respect for him, I actually gained more than I had before. It takes a strong man to right his wrongs.

Now all Pop needed was forgiveness from his wife. And that's where I came in.

"Who you calling? Don't you dare call your daddy," Ma said. "I need some time."

"What kind of time are we talking about? The two of you aren't getting any younger, you know."

"Watch yourself, boy," she said. "You're not too old to get your behind beat."

"I'm just saying, Ma, the man is anxious to talk to you. It's all he talks about. I just want to let him know that you're in agreement."

"Okay, call him. I don't care."

I didn't waste another minute getting Pop on the phone.

"She said yes?" he asked before I could say a word. He had undoubtedly been waiting by the phone all morning.

"She said yes, Pop," I told him, Ma eyeballing me.

"Tell her I'm coming by tonight. And to put on that red dress that I like so much. The one I bought her for our twenty-fifth anniversary...."

I told Ma what he said.

"And tell her I'm taking her to that blues joint in Compton, the one with the live band that I used to take her to when y'all were little." He paused. "The one she likes so much...the one with the little corner booth where I asked her to marry me."

"Okay."

"Tell her what I said, boy."

I did as Pop asked and relayed the message to Ma.

"And tell her not to eat too much, because I'm taking her to that little Italian restaurant that has the best manicotti and the little cream-filled pasta things that she loves—"

"Pop?" I stopped him. "Can you leave something for the woman's imagination? Can't tell her everything you have planned for her."

Ma was blushing, as if I was hooking her up on a date for the first time.

"She's blushing, Pop."

"Stop telling all my business, Rico!" she exclaimed and threw a dish towel at me.

"She's blushing, son?" he asked, just to be sure.

"Yep, like a little young girl."

"That's all right," he said. "Tell her Daddy's gonna make her blush even more tonight."

"Naw, I'm not telling her that, old man," I said. "You can tell her that yourself."

"What did he say, Rico?" She was on the edge of her seat.

"Tell her what I said, son." Pop heard her asking, and begged me to repeat it.

"You tell her yourself," I said and handed Ma my cell phone.

I excused myself from the room, but had to smile.

34

—

Dana

The choir sang "Amazing Grace," which is like the national anthem for African-American funerals. And I prayed that God's grace had found him, before he was gone. I sat in the front row next to Sophie, her hand squeezing mine, tears streaming down both our faces. I stared at my daddy's casket, his forehead dull from all the makeup they had caked on his face. He hardly looked himself, and when I complained, Sophie simply said, "That's the way the funeral home likes to make dead folks look." So I left it alone. He was wearing his favorite blue suit, the one with the soft gray pinstripes, and a soft gray handkerchief stuck in the jacket pocket. He looked at peace, and although I would miss him desperately, I knew he was tired of suffering. So I was happy that he wasn't in pain anymore.

Knowing him, he wouldn't have wanted me crying and carrying on the way I was, but I couldn't help it. I started crying the week before in the hospital when he'd shut his eyes and stopped breathing. I'd cried all week, and tried to absorb my pain in my work, spending extra hours at the studio. But it didn't work, because once I'd finally make it home at night, the pain would hit me again like a freight train. I had come to the realization that I'd just have to endure it. There was no getting around it.

I dabbed my eyes with a Kleenex and sat up straight in my seat, crossed my legs, and tried to get myself together. The pastor at Daddy and Sophie's church said a few words about my father. Even though they didn't go to church that often, he seemed to know a little bit about the type of man my daddy was.

When Daddy's sister, Aunt Barbara, got up there, the entire atmosphere changed. The preacher spoke about going home, a celebration, that we should be happy to see my father move on to his next life. But Aunt Barbara spoke about pain, hurt, and questioned why God had to take him so soon. After that, she lost control of her legs, screamed, and fell out of the pulpit. She was definitely a drama queen.

"It don't take all that," Sophie whispered. "Barbara knows she need to quit."

A couple of deacons helped Aunt Barbara back to her feet, helped her over to the choir bench, where two sisters commenced to fan her.

"Oh, not my brother!" she'd yell every few minutes, and the sisters would fan her some more. "Not Henry."

"She never even came to visit him the whole time he was sick," Sophie whispered. "Now she's all up in the pulpit carrying on like that."

I just listened and observed. I was anxious to get on with the formalities, so that we could finally put my daddy to rest. When the congregation came up for the viewing of the body, that's when I realized that Rico was there. He looked at my father, then looked over at me and smiled. I smiled back, realizing how sweet a gesture it was for him to show up. Two people behind Rico stood Alice, awaiting her turn to say good-bye. I thought I would fall over in my seat at the sight of her showing up at my daddy's funeral. She glanced over at me and smiled. I smiled back, and she kept on moving. I don't know how long she'd been there, or how long she stayed. But I was grateful that she'd made her peace with Daddy.

In the church basement, fried chicken, mashed potatoes, green beans, and homemade rolls were piled onto paper plates that could barely hold the food. One of the sisters from the church made sure Sophie and I were fed first. I picked over my meal, because I wasn't much in the mood for eating. Aunt Barbara plopped right down beside me, her big behind taking up the entire seat, and I prayed she wouldn't go into one of her fits again. I didn't have the strength to deal with her.

"How you doing baby?" she asked.

"I'm fine, Aunt Barbara," I said. "Just glad my daddy doesn't have to suffer anymore."

"Ain't that the truth?" she said, her plate overflowing, and she didn't waste any time digging in. "How you doing, Sophie?"

"I'm doing just fine, Barbara. What about you?"

"Doin' fine, girl. This arthritis acting up every now and then, but it's all right." Aunt Barbara always complained of some ailment. You almost hated to ask her how she was doing. "Henry looked nice in his blue suit. Funeral home did a fine job with that makeup too."

I begged to differ, but kept my mouth shut.

"I saw Alice in there today," she continued. "I was

real surprised to see her. The way Henry did that woman, it's a wonder she didn't kill him when she had the chance. He'd have been dead long before now."

"What are you talking about, Aunt Barbara?" I asked.

"Barbara, I don't think this is the time or the place for this," Sophie said.

"What is she talking about, the way my daddy did Alice?" I had to ask. "And what's this about her trying to kill him?"

"You really don't know, do you, child?" Aunt Barbara's eyes searched mine.

"Barbara, this is not the time—" Sophie pleaded.

"Sophie, I really wanna hear what she got to say," I said, and Sophie gave in.

"You never did meet your mama before she died, did you?" Aunt Barbara asked, and threw me way off. "She was a stone trip, let me tell you."

"My mama?" I asked. "Alice is my mama."

"I'm talking about your real mama," Aunt Barbara said matter-of-factly, and stuffed a forkful of mashed potatoes into her mouth.

"Henry wanted to tell you, Dana," Sophie said softly. "He really did."

"Well, what stopped him?" Aunt Barbara asked, and I begged for the same answer.

"He just never found the right time. And then he got sick, and…"

"This child deserves to know the truth," Aunt Barbara said, and bit into her chicken breast like there wasn't a tomorrow. "And it ain't right that she didn't know that Alice ain't her mama. Henry should've told her by now."

"Start from the beginning, Aunt Barbara," I said.

"Tell me what you know, because it seems that no one else had intentions of telling me."

I glared at Sophie. Obviously, she and Daddy had kept something from me, and I needed to know what it was.

"Well, your daddy was a...let me see, how can I put this mildly?" She thought for a moment. "Oh hell, your daddy was a whore, plain and simple. Might as well just tell it like it is. Can't sugarcoat it. He's my brother and all, God rest his soul, but he wasn't worth a nickel when it came to women."

She wiped her mouth with a paper towel, and bit off half a roll. Chewed for a moment. "He was married to Alice a long time. About twenty- or thirty-some-odd years."

"Twenty-one years before they got divorced and he married Sophie," I said.

"Anyway, he stepped out on Alice, as he did quite often." Aunt Barbara chuckled. "Got this woman pregnant. That was your mama, and she was pregnant with you. Her name was... Bethlehem...Beverly...what was it?"

"Bethany," Sophie corrected her.

"That's right." Aunt Barbara snapped her fingers. "Bethany. Now what kind of name is that for a black woman straight from the projects in Chicago? Bethany?"

My heart began to race.

"Henry denied and denied that she was pregnant with his child. He tossed her aside, you see. But Bethany wasn't one to sit by and keep her mouth shut like all the rest of them had. She threatened to tell Alice." Aunt Barbara stuffed green beans into her mouth. "And she did just that."

"That's enough, Barbara," Sophie said.

"No, I need to know the rest." I was furious.

"You wanna know the rest, child?" Aunt Barbara asked.

"Yes, I do."

"Well, let me tell you. Bethany, your mama, went to Alice and told her everything. Told her all about how she was pregnant with Henry's child. Alice tried to kill your daddy, baby. The good Lord saved his soul that night."

"What else?"

"You were two months old when Bethany just about had enough of your daddy. He wouldn't send her any money, wouldn't help her take care of you. She drove right up to your daddy and Alice's front door, rang the bell, and handed you to Henry. Ran to her car and drove off. She never looked back."

I shot a glance at Sophie, who looked as guilty as sin.

"Alice raised you," Aunt Barbara said, and popped the remainder of her roll into her mouth. "She resented Henry for stepping out on her, but she raised you the best she could."

"No wonder she hated me."

"Oh she didn't hate you baby." Aunt Barbara rubbed my arm. "She was just angry. Do you know what it was like for her to have to look at you day in and day out? You were a constant reminder of Henry's infidelity."

"You okay, Dana?" Sophie asked.

"Is all of this true?" I asked Sophie.

"I'm afraid so," she said. "I wish you hadn't found out this way. Henry should've been the one to tell you."

"Yes, he should've."

"Excuse me." Sophie stood. "I'm going to the ladies' room."

"So did he cheat on Alice with Sophie too?" I asked Aunt Barbara once Sophie was gone.

"No, I think they were long over before Miss Thang came into the picture," she said.

"That's why I lived with my daddy after he divorced Alice," I said. "I never could understand why she allowed him to take me away."

"She did the best she could, baby," Aunt Barbara said and stood. "Now if you'll excuse me, I've got to go fix me another plate before the food is gone. You take care, okay?"

I sat there at the family table after my daddy's funeral, my plate of food now cold. I wanted to cry, but the tears wouldn't fall. Wanted to be angry, but with whom? I had questions for my daddy, but he was gone now. And I had a few for Alice. But mostly, I had a few for my dead mama. Like, why she abandoned me when I was two months old. Is that why I had abandoned my own child? Because I had the genes of a coward?

I felt somewhat relieved knowing that Alice had reason to treat me badly all these years, and she wasn't just the miserable person that I thought she was. Just like Aunt Barbara said, she did the best she could. I accepted that.

When I got home, I plopped down on my sofa, kicked my pumps off, and curled up in a fetal position, still wearing my gray suit. Too much information had been given to me today, and no time to absorb it all. I rested my head on the arm of the sofa and shut my eyes. No stereo, no television, just silence so that I could absorb everything. I thought of Bethany and wondered what she was like. What she looked like. What her life was like without me. That was a chapter in my life that I didn't even know existed before today, and it had already been closed. Daddy had gone to his grave without telling me the truth. And Alice never told me either. What was her reason for keeping Daddy's secret all these years?

I got up and put on Alicia Keys's *Diary*, deciding to make myself a ham sandwich since I hadn't eaten all day. I didn't finish my food at the church and knew I should put something in my stomach before I became sick. I spread mayo on wheat bread, slapped on a piece of cheese, some lettuce, tomato, and a couple of slices of ham. I took one bite, and was finished. My appetite was gone.

I knew I wouldn't be able to rest until I spoke with Alice. I picked up the phone and dialed her number, but the phone rang and rang. She wasn't home, or she wasn't answering. So I curled back up into the fetal position on the sofa and drifted off.

35

—

Maxie

Reggi had me all the way in Santa Barbara, trying to deliver a dinette set to a rich white woman who lived in a very beautiful cottage. She drove the delivery truck like a pro the whole way, Miles snapped into his car seat between us, and I stared out the window. I couldn't figure out why Reggi insisted on bringing the furniture herself, when she could've stopped being stubborn and let Fred drive the ninety-five miles to make the delivery. But since she'd put him out, and he'd moved in with Rico, she wouldn't let him set foot in the furniture store. Even though it was a business that they'd built together, she'd already staked her claim as the sole owner. And to keep the peace, he stayed away.

She hopped on the 101 freeway toward Santa Barbara, as I glanced out the window.

"What you thinking about?" she asked, noticing that my mind was a thousand miles away.

"Thinking that I should be at home finishing my article for the magazine. I have a deadline to meet," I told her, "but I understand that Fred couldn't make the trip and you needed somebody to ride up here with you."

"I appreciate it too, baby, you riding with me," she said. "You should've brought your laptop with you."

"It's okay. We won't be long, right?" I had to ask, because at the speed she was driving, we'd be traveling all day. "We're just dropping off this stuff and heading back, right?"

"That's the plan," Reggi said, and continued to creep up the 101.

Miles was asleep in his car seat, which was a blessing. I was grateful when we finally approached Santa Barbara. Reggi looked at her handwritten directions, her reading glasses placed on the tip of her nose.

"I think this is my exit right here."

She veered off the exit, turned a few corners, and ended up in a quaint little neighborhood in Solvang, a little town of windmills, quiet streets, horse-drawn carriages, and Danish-looking cottages. She pulled up in front of one, the lawn perfectly manicured, and the gardener planting what looked like mums in the front yard. It didn't look as if anybody was home, but they had better be, after we'd traveled all the way up here. We had furniture to deliver.

"Why don't you go and ring the bell for me, honey?" she asked, removing her reading glasses from her face and placing them into the side pocket of her purse. "I'll keep an eye on Miles."

I sighed, got out of the truck, and made my way to the door. I stepped up onto the porch and rang the bell.

No answer.

I turned to look at Reggi, who shrugged her shoulders. I rang again.

Knocked.

No answer.

Reggi stuck her head out the window. "Why don't you go on inside?" she said. "The woman who lives here doesn't hear very well. She probably can't hear the doorbell."

Was she crazy?

"Just walk in some people's house?" I mumbled, but Reggi obviously couldn't hear me.

Hesitantly, I pushed the door open. Took a step inside.

"Hello," I called, but no one responded.

Candles were burning all over the living room, and Miles Davis was blowing his horn on some stereo or CD player off in one of the other rooms. Roses were everywhere.

What is really going on? I had to ask myself.

I went to the kitchen in search of the elderly woman who supposedly lived here and couldn't hear that good, and wondered what she knew about Miles Davis, and why she had candles burning all over her place.

What I found was Rico wearing an apron and taking something wonderful smelling out of the oven in the kitchen.

"What's up?" He smiled.

I was surprised, but happy to see him. I missed him more than I wanted to admit, and realized at that moment just how much I loved this brother.

"You surprised?" he asked.

"That's an understatement." I had to laugh at Reggi and all she went through to get me here. "I've been set up."

When I went to the picture window to let her know that she was busted, she'd already pulled off. Probably

266

had burned rubber through the quiet little neighborhood and was halfway to the 101 by then. The gardener, who was tending to his mums, looked at me and smiled, as if to confirm that I'd been had.

"Don't be mad at Ma. I asked her to get you here."

"I'm not mad, Rico. But I can't stay. I have an article to write for the magazine, and my deadline is approaching fast. You need to drive me back to L.A," I said. "Where's your car anyway?"

"Pop dropped me off up here." He smiled, grabbed my hand, and led me to an office in the left wing of the house. "Come here."

My laptop was sitting on the mahogany desk, plugged in and ready to go.

"My laptop?" I looked at him. "How did you get my laptop?"

"I have a key to your place, remember? And I knew you never leave home without it," he said.

"You and your mama had this all planned out, huh?" I said. "And sounds like Fred was in on it too."

"I had to get you alone, to a place where I could talk to you, Maxie."

"So you strand me in this place that looks like we're in Holland somewhere?"

"Solvang is beautiful. Different. I thought you would appreciate its beauty."

"Yeah, it's nice. But we're stranded here, Rico."

"You wouldn't take my calls, and when I dropped by the other night, you just blew me off," he said. "This is the only way to ensure that we talk this through without either one of us running away."

"I really don't know what we have to talk about," I

said, plopping down in the plush chair in front of my laptop.

"We have to talk about us, and what you thought happened that night. We've danced around it, but we really haven't discussed it. You thought you saw something, and rushed off without even giving me a chance to explain."

"You wanna explain? Explain."

"Dana tried to seduce me, yes. But I can't place the blame all on her. I'm just as guilty. She asked if she could massage my shoulders, and I could've said no, but I didn't. I let her, knowing that I was playing with fire...."

I stood, not sure if I wanted to hear the rest. Rico stopped me from leaving the room, pulling me close, the warmth of his touch making me remember just how much I'd missed him. I shut my eyes for a moment. Then I opened them and my eyes met his.

"I have to admit, the massage felt so good, it put me to sleep." He pulled me into him, his nose practically touching mine. "That's all that happened, baby. I swear I didn't touch her."

"And the two of you just fell asleep in bed together?" I whispered.

"That's what happened."

"You didn't kiss her?"

He looked at me. He couldn't answer my question honestly, so he kept quiet. His silence suddenly began to pierce my heart. My heart began to ache at the thought of my man's lips touching Dana's. I couldn't breathe. I pushed past him and headed for the front door. He followed.

"You need to get me back to L.A," I said in a very unfriendly tone.

"Maxie, we can't just keep running away from this issue. We need to talk."

"You can't just kidnap me and bring me to some romantic cottage and think that I'm going to fall into your arms and forgive you, and we live happily ever after!"

"I know I messed up. But I didn't sleep with her! I could've slept with her, but I didn't. It was just a kiss. Didn't mean anything."

"How many times?"

"How many times what?"

"How many times you kiss her?"

There was that dreadful silence again. A silence that told me that it was more than just once. My heart ached again.

How did I get here? In this place where I felt trapped. I wanted to run, but there was nowhere to go. I opened the front door and stepped out into the California sunshine. I didn't know where I was going, but I needed some air. In the back of the house, I found a bench overlooking a little pond. I collapsed onto it, needing to think.

Rico gave me my space, and left me alone.

I wanted to cry, but I wasn't a crybaby. I had been through too much to let stuff get to me. It was rare that I shed tears. Since the day of my mama's funeral, I vowed to never let anything else cause as much pain. I knew when I opened my heart up to Rico that it was a mistake. But even though my heart ached at the moment, I knew I just needed to get him out of my system. Get back to my life before he came along. Get to a place where Rico wasn't.

36

Dana

It was difficult placing my father's life and everything he held dear into a cardboard box. But it was my only choice, especially since Sophie and her daughters were Ohio-bound. Ohio was her home before meeting and marrying Daddy, and now she was returning there to spend her elder years with her family.

"I'm sorry, Dana. That you didn't know about Alice."

I still wasn't quite right about that whole thing, but forgave Sophie after realizing it wasn't her fault. She was just obeying my father's wishes of not telling me the truth.

"It's not your fault, Sophie. I blame Daddy. And Alice, too, for that matter. One of them should've told me the truth."

"I agree, honey. But don't blame them too much. Your daddy loved you very much. And he felt like he was protecting you. Didn't want to upset your whole life," she said, folding one of Daddy's shirts and placing it in a box. "Don't blame Alice either. She did the best she could with what she had to work with."

"You're right," I said, piling Daddy's ties into another box, and sealing the one that held his shoes. "I'm hungry. You?"

"I ordered a pizza," Sophie said. "I have a few minutes before I need to get to the airport."

Sophie's suitcases had been packed, and were standing at the front door. Daddy's house had been willed to me, and I'd insisted that Sophie and her daughters stay there as long as they wanted. I had my little apartment, and wasn't sure what I would do with the house just yet. But she wanted to go home.

"I can't stay, baby. My home is in Ohio," she said. "But you should consider moving in here. The house is paid for, free and clear. And it's not a bad house. Needs a little work, but at least you wouldn't have to pay rent. If you get a roommate, you could probably handle the overhead pretty good."

"Or I could sell it."

"Or you could sell it. Yes, indeed," she said. "Or you could rent it out."

"But then I'd have to worry about keeping up repairs and collecting rent."

"They have management companies that could do that for you. They would screen the renters, collect the money each month. But I'd really like to see you live here," she said, as the doorbell rang. "Must be the pizza man. I'll get it."

She left the room to answer the door. My eyes observed the faded wallpaper and dull hardwoods, and I momentarily considered the possibility of making the old place my home.

"I might be able to work with this," I whispered to myself.

I stepped into the closet and grabbed the last of Daddy's suits that were still on hangers, suits I'd seen him in over the years. It was hard imagining that he would not ever wear them again. The thought brought tears to my eyes, and I stood there for a moment, and my mind went back to when I was a little girl. I'd be at one of my performances or a play at school, and look out into the audience, and there would be my daddy, cheesing and clapping. He was so proud of me, and supported everything I even thought I wanted to do. He was my hero. I wiped my eyes with the back of my hand.

"Wasn't the pizza guy," Sophie said, coming back into the room and finding me in Daddy's closet, tears streaming down my face. "You okay, baby?"

"Yes. I just had a moment," I admitted. "But I'm fine."

"Someone's here to see you."

My eyes met Alice's as I stepped out of the closet.

"Dana."

"Hello, Alice." I rubbed the tears away and cleared my throat. "What are you doing here?"

"I came here to talk to you."

"If you came to tell me that you're not my mother, I already know that."

"I'm sorry you had to find out the way you did, child. Barbara never could hold water," she said. "She told me that you knew."

"So, after all these years, I discover you are not my mother. I don't know whether to be relieved or saddened by it."

"Your father wasn't the saint you made him out to be. He was an awful husband. But I'm glad he was a much better father." She pulled a package of Salems out of her purse and pulled one out of its package. "Mind if I smoke?"

"Yes, I mind."

"Sorry," she said, placing it back into the pack.

We both stood in silence for a moment.

"I'm gonna go wait for the pizza," Sophie said, and excused herself from the room.

"I didn't know how to love you, Dana," Alice began. "You were a constant reminder of Henry's infidelity."

"Tell me about my mother."

"I don't know much. She just showed up on my door-step one day, handed you to Henry, and took off. I don't know where Bethany went after that. I always thought she was a terrible mother for doing that. And I thought she would come back for you, after realizing what she'd done. But she never did. It was an awkward situation." She shook her head. "I never could have children of my own."

"I'm sorry to hear that."

"Don't be," she said, matter-of-factly. "What's done is done. And the good Lord knew what he was doing."

"I turned out to be just like her," I said, "abandoning my own child."

"But at least you're trying to right your wrong. That's what makes you a better mother...a better person. That's what matters."

"I think that's the nicest thing you've ever said to me, Alice."

"Yeah?" She headed toward the door. "Well, I guess I've gotten a little soft in my old age."

"Within the last couple of days you mean." I actually chuckled a little.

"You gonna move into this old place?"

"Thinking about it."

"Henry always said that if anything happened to him, he wanted you to have this house. His father built this house, you know. Henry was born here; at least, that's what he told me. His mama gave birth to him right here in this room."

"Really?"

"He grew up here, and when his parents died, the house was left to him. And now he's leaving it to you. This is your family's home, and I wouldn't be so quick to get rid of it, if I were you."

"Thank you for telling me that, Alice."

"You grew up here too, you know," she said, her eyes becoming sad.

"I remember."

"I was a little hurt when Henry took you away from me. But what could I say or do? You were his child, not mine."

I didn't know what to say.

"Well, I'm gonna go," she said after a long, uncomfortable silence. "I wish you the best with Brianna. I hope things work out for you."

"Thank you, Alice," I said. "Can I come by and see you sometime?"

"I don't mind. Just as long as you're quiet while I watch *Jeopardy*."

"There are much better things to watch on television, Alice."

"Like what?"

"Like my new television series. The one I'm starring in."

"And when is it due to air?"

"Next month."

"I'll watch."

"Really?"

"Yes," she said, pulling her Salem back out of its package. "Will you bring Brianna when you come?"

"If you want me to."

"I do," she said, and left the room.

I began sealing the boxes with tape, grateful for the chance to start again.

37

Rico

When Maxie finally came inside, I was grateful. I tried giving her some space, but I needed her forgiveness.

"I'm sorry, Maxie," I told her. "I messed up."

"Did you think I would run into your arms and forget all about this whole Dana thing?"

"I didn't know what to expect. Just hoped."

I approached my woman, took her in my arms, and hoped she wouldn't resist. I hugged her with all my strength. "Baby, I'm sorry."

I found her lips and kissed them with intensity. She received the kiss and didn't pull away. Before long, she was against the door, both of us lost in a moment of passion.

"You forgive me?"

"Yes," she whispered. "But I won't ever forget."

"I deserve that."

"And it's going to take a minute for me to trust you again after all this."

"Okay."

"But I love you. And I've missed you. And as much as Dana might want you for herself, she can't have you. She had her chance."

"You're right."

"Now what's up with the food?" she asked, changing the subject.

"It's just about done. Why don't you go ahead and work on your article while I finish dinner?"

"You a trip," she said. "What else did you think of besides my laptop?"

"Let me see, I got the wine, the roses, the dinner, the candles." I stuck my hand into my pocket. "Oh, I forgot about this."

I pulled out the half-carat diamond ring with three stones set in platinum. It had set me back a couple of grand, but she was worth it. I held it between my fingertips, got down on one knee, and looked into her eyes.

"Look, I know I'm not out of the doghouse yet, but I'm hoping that you still love me. Even if it's just a little bit. And that I still have a chance at winning you back." I slid the ring onto her finger. "You don't have to answer right away, Maxie, but . . ."

"Yes." There, she'd said it. She knew exactly what she wanted, without hesitation.

"Yes, you'll marry me?"

"Yes, I'll marry you."

I exhaled, took her in my arms, and kissed her again.

The cottage I found in Solvang, a little town near Santa Barbara, was all that. It was equipped with a fireplace and Jacuzzi, both of which we'd planned on taking advantage of before the night was over. Although Solvang was definitely not a place that would normally appeal to Maxie, there was a certain romance about it that no woman could resist. It was a different world from what we knew in Baldwin Hills, but I hoped she would keep an open mind and know that her man had put a great deal of thought into making our time here special.

We laughed over dinner and talked about upbeat things, like my new business and the story she was writing for the magazine. We laughed about our trip to Tijuana and how my aunts had cornered her for a game of bid whist at my birthday party. The issue of Dana and that dreadful night that she'd found us together never came up. Neither of us mentioned it, and I was glad, because I was ready to put the whole thing behind us and start anew.

After dinner, we washed dishes and dried them together.

"I have a confession," I told her.

"Not another one," she said. "What is it?"

"I lied about Pop dropping me off. My truck is hidden in the neighbor's garage. I wanted you to think we were stranded here, so you wouldn't try and leave."

"You a trip."

"I know," I said, "but I got something I want to show you."

We jumped in my SUV and took a drive up the coast of Santa Barbara, toward Santa Ynez and the beautiful homes with acres of land, and past Michael Jackson's gated estate, where we waved to one of his bodyguards.

"You wanna drop by and see if Mike's at home?" I asked teasingly.

"Nah, we should probably call before we drop by,

don't you think?" she said. "You know Mike's a busy guy trying to keep up with all his animals and the teen-age boys he entertains from time to time. Let's keep moving."

"I agree." I had to laugh.

We strolled through the marketplace in downtown Solvang, purchasing one-of-a-kind handmade items. Later, I drove down the coast of Santa Barbara, and we got out and strolled along the beach, our fingers inter-twined, our hearts beating at a similar pace. Maxie took her shoes off and let the water rush between her toes.

We continued to make our way toward the Rideau Family Vineyard, where we stopped and bought a bottle of wine and, on the way back, discovered a beautiful sun-set. We sat there in my truck and took in the beauty of it, all plastered across the sky like something in a magazine.

Back at the cottage, I started a fire in the fireplace, put on a Marvin Gaye CD, poured two glasses of wine, and joined my woman on the floor in front of the fire, hand-ing her a glass. In each other's arms, we watched the fire and listened to the crackling of the wood.

"What type of wedding you wanna have?"

"Something small and quaint. Nothing too big," she said.

"Really? Because I want a huge wedding, like the ones on television," I said, "I guess you forgot how big my family is. I have four other brothers and sisters who would demand to be there. Not to mention Pop's sisters and brothers, and my other aunts and uncles from Ma's side of the family."

"Oh yeah, I forgot about Aunt Minnie and Auntie Margaret."

"Yeah, them." I laughed. "We don't have to invite them if you don't want to."

"You must be crazy. I wouldn't have a wedding without inviting them. We're old friends now."

"They weren't too happy with you whipping them in bid whist, you know," I said. "They consider themselves the bid whist queens. And here you come along and whip their behinds. That wasn't cool at all."

"Yeah, that was pretty jacked up. Maybe I'll let them win next time."

I tasted the wine on her lips as she kissed me.

"You want more kids?" I asked, knowing I wanted a big family just like my parents had.

"I don't know. I'm still trying to get used to Miles. It wasn't easy giving birth to him. And my breasts are sore all the time. And he cries all through the night sometimes; he's a handful. I don't know if I want to go through this again."

"This will pass, baby. He'll grow up soon."

"Yeah, but to have another one only means enduring this again."

"I want a big family. Maybe three or four more kids."

"I don't know about that, Rico. Maybe we can compromise or something."

"Okay, two more."

"How about one more, and a dog?" she said. "You forget that we're not wealthy. Barely feeding the ones we got."

"We will be better off once my business takes off. You wait and see, girl," I told her, no doubt in my mind that my business was on a slow incline toward heaven. "It's just a matter of time."

"Will we live in your house or mine?"

"Mine, of course."

"Why yours?"

"Because I'm the man."

"Please," she said. "What's that got to do with anything? And didn't you live there with Dana before she left?"

I was silent.

"I'm not living in that house where you and she lived together."

"Then I'll just have to build you a house," I said, moving away from the Dana comment before it put a damper on the mood. "What you think about that?"

"I think that's sweet," she said, kissing me again. "Can I design it myself?"

"With my help, yes."

"Thank you, baby." She wrapped her arms tightly around my neck and sat in my lap. "I love you."

"I love you more," I said, and kissed her, my tongue probing the inside of her mouth, tasting what the wine left behind.

I began to caress her breasts, hoping to relieve them from the pain they'd been enduring from Miles's greedy behind. I unbuttoned her shirt, lifted her bra, and gently placed her light brown nipples into my mouth. Her moans let me know that she was enjoying every minute of it. As Marvin Gaye serenaded us, my hands probed places that I'd missed touching, loving, and kissing for way too long.

I lifted my eyes to the fire that was raging, just as my hormones were. I had my love back. A love I had thought was gone forever.

38

—

Dana

The sound of a power drill is what greeted me when I opened the door. The hammering and the sound of an electric saw were just as loud. I made my way to the kitchen, where I found Malcolm hanging beautiful wallpaper on the walls, his chocolate muscles bulging through his wife beater. Sweat covered his chest and beaded on his forehead. He was a good-looking man, and I caught myself staring more than once. I'd found him in the yellow pages, and when he showed me some of his previous work, I'd taken the money Daddy left me and hired him to renovate the house.

"How's it going?" he asked, trying to be heard over the hammering that was going on upstairs in one of the bedrooms. His perfectly white teeth seemed to glisten when he smiled. "Sorry about all the noise. One of my guys is upstairs working on the bathroom."

"No problem. I just stopped by to see how things were coming."

"Just fine."

"Good," I said, observing his work. "The kitchen looks good."

He'd already restored the hardwoods, replaced the kitchen cabinets, and removed the dull wallpaper, giving my daddy's old house the contemporary feel it deserved.

I'd sublet my apartment, and decided to take Sophie's advice and move into the old place. My family history was here, and I wanted to be a part of that history, and pass it along to my own daughter. There was plenty of room for Brianna to run and play, a huge backyard where she could run around until she passed out. She'd have her own bedroom that would be decorated in a Little Mermaid scheme, and a playroom that would house all the dolls, books, and other toys I planned on purchasing. I needed her to feel at home, especially since Rico had decided to give me more than just an occasional weekend here and there with Brianna. Since we lived so close, I'd have her at least three nights each week, and we'd share in transporting her back and forth to school.

"I'm glad you like it." He smiled that beautiful smile again. "I'm just about finished here in the kitchen. But you should see what I have planned for your master bedroom."

Was he flirting? Because just the mention of my bedroom caused me to blush. He'd drawn a sketch of how he was going to build me a little sitting room right off my bedroom. He was going to take out Daddy's old bathtub and replace it with a jetted Jacuzzi tub, put in a double vanity, and build me a huge walk-in closet.

"And how much will all of this cost me?" I asked, as his cologne sent me to a place unknown. He was so close, I could feel his warm breath against my cheek, and could literally hear both our heartbeats.

"Won't cost you much at all."

"How much?"

"Have dinner with me, and we'll discuss it."

"I don't know about mixing business with pleasure."

"Well, we'll make it a business dinner."

"I guess if it's just business, it'll be all right." I smiled.

"You free on Friday night?"

"I think I am."

"Pick you up here at eight?"

"Oh wait," I said, remembering that Friday night was my night with Brianna. Rico had plans, and I'd already agreed to keep her. "I can't. I'll have my daughter that night."

"How old is she?" he asked, and seemed genuinely interested.

"Nine."

"Why don't you bring her along?"

"To dinner?"

"Yes. What could be better than having dinner with two beautiful women?"

"I would love to have dinner with you. But I don't think I'm ready to bring my daughter along just yet," I admitted. "Maybe we can just have dinner another time, like next Saturday night, if you're free."

"I am." He wiped his hands on the pant leg of his jeans, and pulled his wallet out of his pocket. "I know you have my card, but here's another one just in case. Call me when you're ready."

I took the card. "I will."

I made my way upstairs to what used to be my room, and would soon be Brianna's room. I had already picked out the canopy bed I'd place in there. Reggi and Fred had given me a deal that I couldn't refuse. I stood in the bay window overlooking the backyard and took in the garden that Daddy had planted years ago. Tomatoes, onions, okra, and green beans were still growing out there. I could see myself out there, pruning and pulling weeds. I'd probably have to read some books on how to do it right, because I'd never cared for a garden before.

I remembered running around out there in the backyard when I was a little girl, my pigtails flying in the wind. Soon, Brianna would be playing in the same backyard, making mud pies and drawing on the concrete in colored chalk. And I'd be out there with her, pushing her on the swing, jumping rope, and playing hopscotch. We'd pick flowers and chase lightning bugs all over the yard after the sun set. Then we'd come inside exhausted, get cleaned up, drink hot apple cider, and watch her favorite movies on DVD. The thought of it caused me to smile.

Just then, I thought about my mother, my biological mother, and wondered what she was like. Wondered if she had been beautiful or smart, or if she had a sense of humor. She'd left me just as I'd left Brianna, without a mother, and having to settle for a stand-in mom. The only difference between Brianna and me is *her* mother came to her senses and realized the importance of being a part of her life. She doesn't have to become thirty-six years old and wonder who or where her mother is. She'll know me. For that, I couldn't thank God enough. He'd given her and me a second chance. I had so much I needed to teach her, and today wasn't soon enough.

I wrapped my arms around myself and thought that I was one step closer to where I wanted to be.

39

Dana

The place had been finished and looked like a million bucks. I stood in my bedroom, with the little sitting room, the jetted Jacuzzi tub, and double vanity. I went to my walk-in closet and started hanging my things in it. It was huge enough to have a party up in there. And that's exactly what Brianna was doing. She'd placed her little table and chairs in my closet, pretending to be having a tea party, to which I was invited.

"Dana, sit down and have your tea."

I squeezed my behind into one of the little plastic chairs, prayed it didn't collapse from the extra weight, took my cup, and pretended to sip.

"You couldn't find anywhere else in the house to set up your tea party, little girl?"

"Your closet is so perfect," she said. "There's so much room in here."

She was right about that.

"You might be right, but we gon' have to move this party down the hall to your bedroom."

"Okay," she said reluctantly. "But can I sleep in here with you tonight?"

"Of course you can," I said. "What do you want to eat for dinner, pizza or tacos?"

"Tacos!" she sang, and clapped her hands. "Can we make them together?"

"Of course we can. I wouldn't have it any other way."

We made our way downstairs to the kitchen, and I pulled out a skillet from under the sink. I placed it on top of the stove and dropped ground turkey into it.

"Why don't you keep an eye on the meat while I chop up tomatoes and lettuce?"

Brianna dragged a stool over to the stove, stood on it as she stirred the meat around with a fork. She became impatient because it took time for it to brown.

"How long does it take for meat to brown?" she asked.

"Not long. Keep stirring," I said, and chopped tomatoes into little cubes. "It should be done in a minute."

"It's taking too long," she whined.

"Just keep stirring, Bri. It'll be done soon."

When the doorbell rang, Brianna jumped down from the stool and took off running toward the front door.

"I'll get it Brianna," I yelled. "Don't you dare open that door!"

She stopped in her tracks.

"I just wanted to see who it is," she said.

"I'll get it."

She followed me to the door as I peeked out and saw the most beautiful creature I'd ever seen standing on my doorstep. I opened the door.

"Hi." I smiled.

"Hi." He returned a more beautiful smile.

"Come on in."

Malcolm walked in carrying a bouquet of white roses, and a gift box wrapped in pink paper and a white ribbon. It seemed that every time he showed up on my doorstep, he was bearing gifts. After our first date—which was supposed to be a business dinner, but quickly turned into a quiet romantic one, followed by a stroll along Venice Beach sometime after midnight—we officially began dating. We were inseparable from the first night, and it didn't take long for me to discover what a wonderful man Malcolm was. I couldn't wait to introduce him to Brianna. And once I did, the two of them were just as inseparable.

"These are for you." He handed me the roses.

"Thank you, they're beautiful."

"And this is for you." He handed Brianna the pretty box.

"Wow! What is it?" she asked, shaking it.

"Open it and see," I told her.

She carefully opened the box, pulling out a beautiful musical jewelry box. When she opened the lid, a black ballerina danced in a circle as if she was dancing to the music.

"Ooh, that's so beautiful," I said.

"I can put my earrings and stuff in here," she said, and hugged his neck. "Thank you, Malcolm."

"You're very welcome."

We went to the kitchen, where I placed my roses into a vase filled with water. I placed the vase on the kitchen table, and watched the roses light up the room. Malcolm and Brianna had become old friends over the past few weeks. He was the only adult in the entire world who didn't mind watching hours of Cartoon Network with her without going out of his mind.

"You wanna help us cook, Malcolm?" She bounced up and down. "We're making tacos!"

"Are you hungry?" I asked him.

"Very," he said, tickling Brianna. "And I love tacos!"

When she giggled, he picked her up and tossed her in the air.

"I have an idea. Maybe you can brown the meat, Malcolm," she said, trying to catch her breath, and trying to get out of doing what I had asked her to do.

"Oh no, you don't, little girl. That's your task," I said, trying to teach her to follow through on things. "Sometimes we don't enjoy doing things, but we have to do them anyway."

"Okay," she said.

"Maybe I can help you, though, Bri," Malcolm said.

"Is it okay if Malcolm helps, Mommy?"

"What did you say?" I asked her.

"Is it okay if he helps?"

"What did you say after that?"

"Mommy?"

"Yes, that." It was nice to hear her call me something other than Dana.

"Is it all right if I call you mommy?"

"Of course it is." I smiled, tears almost filling my eyes. I had to blink them away. "I would like that very much."

I got lost in the moment.

"Well?" she asked.

"Well what?" I said.

"Can Malcolm help me brown the meat or not?"

"Brianna, come here."

She bounced over to me, and I gave her a kiss.

"What's that for?"

"Because I love you."

"I love you too," she said.

"Now, why don't you go on upstairs and get cleaned up for dinner? Malcolm and I will finish up here."

"Okay," she said, and took off upstairs.

I was happy to finally steal a moment alone with Malcolm. I wanted to devour him the minute he'd walked through the door, but I held back for Brianna's sake. My hormones were raging. But what I was learning in my life was patience. To let things happen naturally, and if they were meant to be, they would be. He pulled me into his arms, and it was a very natural thing for his lips to touch mine when they did. It was one month since we'd started dating and this was the first time he'd ever kissed me. And it had been well worth the wait.

"You don't mind if I kiss you, do you?"

"Not at all."

"Because you seem a little tense."

"Just savoring the moment. You've been spending a lot of time with me and Brianna. About a month now, and that's the first time you've touched me."

"Didn't wanna rush you. Make you think I was just after you physically," he said. "Wanted to get to know you and Brianna, so you'd know that I was for real."

"I appreciate that," I told him.

"You've been through a lot lately—just getting to know your daughter, the whole incident with your ex, your father's passing, finding out about your mother, and all," he said. "That's a lot to handle all at once."

"No doubt."

"I just want you to know that I'm here for you. If you need to talk, and you just need someone to listen, I'm here."

"That's sweet. Thank you."

Brianna interrupted our groove when she bounced back into the room.

"I'm all washed up."

She and Malcolm finished browning the ground turkey together, and I finished chopping tomatoes and lettuce. We ate tacos and watched a movie on the Disney channel. Brianna fell asleep on the movie, and Malcolm carried her to her room. I followed. We tucked her in under the covers, turned off her lamp, and left the door cracked open a little.

I headed toward the stairway, and he grabbed my hand, pulling me into my bedroom. He'd put his finishing touches on it free of charge. Shutting my door, he pulled me into his arms and nibbled on my neck. He found my lips and kissed them, and began to caress my breasts.

"I'm going to slip into something more comfortable," I said, wanting the first time to be special. I wanted to grab a shower and put on something sexy.

"I'll be right here," he said and climbed into my bed.

I went into my closet and found a sexy nightie that I'd picked up at Victoria's Secret, the tag still dangling from it.

"I'll be right back," I told him, and quickly went into the bathroom. I started the shower and waited for it to get hot. Then I stood in the shower, the water cascading over my body like a waterfall. I closed my eyes and got lost in the rhythm. I was singing Alicia Keys's "You Don't Know My Name," before I realized how loud I was singing.

I jumped out of the shower and rubbed lotion all over my body. Then I put on my sexy little outfit and dabbed a little cologne onto my neck. I opened the bathroom door, anxious to get back to Malcolm and show him what I was made of.

My eyes found him stretched across my bed, his back propped up on a couple of pillows, his legs crossed, remote in hand. He'd been watching ESPN, but now ESPN was watching him. He was asleep. He looked so sweet, like a little boy with light snores escaping from his beautiful lips. I grabbed the blanket from the foot of the bed and pulled it over him. I kissed his cheek, and knew that there would be other opportunities when the time was right.

Everything in my life was falling right into place.

40

—

Maxie

Before I knew it, my favorite dance partner was showing me up on the dance floor to Marvin Gaye's "Got to Give It Up," and was singing along too.

"Fred, you a trip," I said, trying to keep up with my father-in-law.

"Girl, you don't know the half of it," he said, holding on to a glass of Jack Daniel's. "Let me show you this right here. Hold my glass."

He did a James Brown move, and thought he'd done something. I moved my hips to the music, holding up the bottom of my off-white lace wedding gown so it wouldn't drag on the floor. It's amazing how no matter what you're wearing, whether it's conducive to dancing or not, when the music hits you, you have to move to it. Shake what your mama gave you, and show the world what you're made of.

Over two hundred people showed up for our wedding, which took place at the Baptist church where Rico grew up. They had to put chairs in the aisles in order to accommodate all of our guests, some of which weren't even invited. And double the people showed up for the reception, for the food no doubt. And there was plenty of it, as Button's caterer friend gave us a discount on tons of chicken wings, meatballs, and little quiches with spinach and cream cheese in the middle. There was enough champagne for everybody to take a bottle home. And the DJ was one of Rico's buddies from the neighborhood, and all he expected for his services was a six-pack of Colt 45.

I stole a glance at Rico dancing with his mama, looking fine in his white tux and lavender cummerbund that matched my bridesmaids' dresses. Charlotte's, Button's, and Alex's dresses were identical sexy, floor-length gowns with the backs cut out. Reece's dress was a little different since she was my matron of honor. She, by the way, was on the floor getting down with her husband, Kevin, who was giving her a run for her money. It made me smile. I remembered when they first met and danced together in the Bahamas, at the little café where we found good grub and good music one year on vacation. I knew then that she'd found the man of her dreams, and he definitely was that. He started doing Michael Jackson's moonwalk, and I knew he was feeling right at home.

Even Charlotte shook her booty with her new husband, Herb. He'd moved her to Dallas after their small wedding in the judge's chambers in downtown Atlanta. He was a handsome brother, and just what Charlotte needed: someone to keep her in check, someone who didn't mind telling her exactly what was on his mind. She had won her bout with cancer, which was still in remission, and she looked fabulous. She'd even started her own support group in Dallas, and had about five women who were fighting cancer and winning. Her hair had even grown back since she wasn't taking the chemo anymore. She had it in a cute funky style that was not at all what I expected her to wear, but she was wearing it.

Button, Alex, and I had come full circle. It was a long road to finding them, and now that I had, I was never letting them go. They were both dancing with Earl, Button's husband, as he struggled to keep up with both of them. Alex's husband, Nicholas, had no desire to come to my wedding since he thought it was me who'd convinced her to file for divorce. I didn't have a thing to do with her decision to leave his self-absorbed, trifling behind, but I couldn't lie and say I wasn't happy. I think without him she'd found that life was much more wonderful than she could have ever imagined. She'd decided to pursue her career in art, and was even talking about opening an art gallery.

"That's my girl!" I'd told her when she ran it by me. "Do something to make yourself happy for a change."

"I am happy," she said.

Looking at her now, out on the floor moving like she was lost in the rhythm, I could tell that she really was. The glow that was plastered all over her face looked genuine.

Brianna was dancing with her uncle Duane, moving like she actually knew what she was doing, wearing her pretty lavender dress with ruffles and a satin bow around the waist. She even had lavender ribbons in her hair to match. She was excited about being the flower girl and dropping rose petals on the drop cloth in the aisle at church. She was actually waving at the people she knew as she bounced down the aisle. Then she stopped and smiled for the camera just before she reached the front of the church. She and Dana were beginning to get pretty close, spending plenty of time together. I was happy about that. Every little girl needs a mother, and Brianna was blessed with two. With all that had gone on in Dana's life, she needed Brianna just as much as Brianna needed her. So for that, I thanked God.

Miles, who was sporting a tux identical to his daddy's, was receiving kisses from his aunt Minnie, who had him in the middle of the floor bouncing him around. It wasn't long before Auntie Margaret snatched him out of Aunt Minnie's arms and danced with him herself. They'd been fussing over Miles all evening. And he loved all the attention, as he giggled and tried to carry on a conversation of baby talk with his eccentric aunties.

Fred was all over the dance floor, and before long, the two of us ended up right next to Reggi and Rico. When Fred started doing the robot, a dance he obviously thought was okay to do in the twenty-first century, I knew I had to go. I inconspicuously danced my way over to my sweetheart, who was looking good in his tux, his face clean-shaven just the way I liked it. We both smiled as Reggi commenced to showing Fred some moves of her own. They were moving to a rhythm of their own, having found that love could be restored. They were even talking about renewing their vows. Fred grabbed his wife and held her close, his rugged beard rubbing up against her face. She pulled him closer and patted him on his behind. There was no doubt they belonged together.

I silently hoped that Rico and I would stay together as many years as they had, and have as much love for each other as they did. I rubbed my hands across his smooth face, and stole a kiss. This was the first day of the rest of our lives, and we promised to love each other from here to forever. It was a huge promise, but I was up for the challenge.

"You happy, Mrs. Elkins?" he whispered in my ear.

"Is that a trick question?"

"No."

"I've never been happier in my life," I said, and meant every word.

"You think we'll last as long as them?" he asked, pointing at his parents, who were both doing a dance that looked like The Swim.

"I hope so." I smiled. "What about you?"

"I'm here for the long haul, baby," he said. "You'll be bringing me my teeth in a jar and my reading glasses so I can read the newspaper."

"And we'll be sitting on the porch, rocking and talking about what used to be."

"And your wig will be on backwards, and I'll be too tired to tell you." He laughed and kissed my lips. "But I'll still love you."

"What you mean you'll still love me? You mean I'll still love *you* with your receding hairline and stomach hanging over your belt."

"It's all good. I'll still be able to put it on you, girl. I'll be seventy-five and still puttin' it on you. Chasing you around the house."

"You hope."

"I know," he said. "I'ma show you what I'm talking about later."

"You promise?"

"I promise."

* * *

When the DJ played Cameo's "Word Up," everyone in the room lined up on the dance floor, and started moving in unison. What's a party without the Electric Slide?